A UNIVERSE
DISRUPTED

A Universe Disrupted

Book 2 of Intersecting Worlds

Eric von Schrader

ABSOM Books

ISBN 979-8-9859304-3-6
Library of Congress Control Number: 2022905144

ABSOM Books
Carpinteria, CA

This book is dedicated to my dearest
Becky Brittain von Schrader.
Without her love and encouragement, HD would not
exist.

A Note on Terminology

In *A Universe Less Traveled,* Billy Boustany came up with a concise way of identifying the two slightly-intersecting worlds. *SD* (short for "Standard Definition") refers to the world he grew up in and (mostly) lives in—and where we, dear readers, also live. *HD* (short for "High Definition") refers to the other world that he stumbled into and where his adventure unfolded.

Billy's terms are much more elegant than the descriptions that others have used, such as "over there," "the other world," or "the other side." These are potentially confusing ("other" compared to what?).

So in this book, with all credit due to Billy, we will use SD and HD throughout, except when characters who don't know Billy's nomenclature are speaking.

CONTENTS

Eyes

THE SUN ROSE OVER THE CORNFIELDS of southern Illinois. Its light swept westward. A soaring hawk followed the light towards the glass pyramid of Cahokia, arriving with the first gleam at the top level of the massive structure. The hawk swooped in a graceful curve over the white buildings that surrounded the pyramid. He watched the early morning stirrings of the city—curtains opening, fires being lit on terraces, a woman praying for her absent son.

Flying low over the awakening neighborhoods, the hawk saw people in the streets on their way to the canal to board the hydrofoil ferry. The ferry sprang to life, lifted out of the water, and sped westward to the great city of St. Louis ahead. A plume of spray behind it sparkled in the fresh morning. With a few strokes of his powerful wings, the hawk ascended, then trailed the hydrofoil all the way to the Mississippi. He entered a forest of skyscrapers and studied the buildings and streets below. Cocking his head in one direction then another, he took note of the first workers on the sidewalks, the delivery vans, the smooth blue streetcars. No detail escaped the gaze of his crystal eyes.

The hawk flew on, in widening circles over the morning-caressed city. Spring was loosening the buds of ten thousand trees. Giant carved eagles on a building façade stared back at him as he sped past. On a street of elegant houses, an old man walked two corgis under blooming dogwoods. In a luxurious penthouse apartment, a man sat hunched over a desk, studying a small book, whose pages were filled with rows of numbers. As the hawk floated past the penthouse window, he studied the man's every movement. Even in this brief encounter, he could read the numbers in the book.

The hawk soared past the broad boulevards and tall monuments, over the river, and back east toward Cahokia. He landed on top of the ancient pyramid, built with a million basket loads of dirt, hauled by hand. The hawk looked out over the Grand Plaza at the immense image scraped into its packed earth: a sharp-beaked bird with outstretched wings and the legs of a man. It was his own image.

The hawk turned his head to look north, south, east, and west. Satisfied by all he had seen, he blinked. The world evaporated like a dewdrop in the sun.

Back to Normal?

On a Thursday afternoon in early March 2011, Billy Boustany had a big decision to make. The boneless chicken breasts were on sale, but the salmon looked pretty good too. Which would go best with the broccoli and pasta? As he pondered his choice, the familiar memories washed over him once again and threatened to crowd out everything else in his head.

He closed his eyes. He knew this was a bad habit and he was careful not to do it when he was driving. But other times, he surrendered to the images that put a smile on his face—egg-like cars gliding down a tree-lined boulevard, slender skyscrapers, iridescent like dragonfly wings in the afternoon sun, ribbons of light snaking through the trees of Tower Grove Park at dusk, an ecstatic mass of dancers under the spell of mad, impossible riffs from exotic instruments....

A wild shriek interrupted his reverie. A woman came around the corner from the breakfast food aisle pushing a shopping cart that carried a screaming toddler.

"Honey, we can't get that cereal. It's too sugary. It will make you sick and make mommy crazy."

The toddler's face turned red as he continued his tantrum. The embarrassed mother saw Billy and silently mouthed "I'm sorry." Billy smiled to her as she whisked her cart past him into the produce section. The annoyance didn't bother him. The memories were always there. He knew that shopping in a totally normal supermarket on an unremarkable weekday afternoon was his real life these days. And real life was a good thing—wasn't it? Every day, he did his best to act like a regular person, but it wasn't easy. He decided to go with the chicken breast, then moved on to look for the eggs, milk, and coffee that were the last unchecked items on his list.

He watched the other people in this suburban St. Louis supermarket going about their uncomplicated lives. They didn't know the big picture, that another world permeated this one and that other people were passing through them right now, leaving no trace. They couldn't know, and maybe they didn't want to know. Blissful ignorance.

But Billy knew. To say that the last year had turned his life upside down and twisted it inside out was the mother of all understatements. Now, everything was different and would always be different. The bell could not be unrung. What was he supposed to do with that? He couldn't talk about what had happened, about the magnificent city he had visited in the other world—which he called HD. Who would believe him? Also, people whom he didn't want to upset had made it abundantly clear that he better keep his mouth shut. Were they watching him now? Maybe or maybe not—he wasn't eager to find out. So he was expected to carry on like nothing had changed. No one had specifically told him to do that, but it followed logically from the prohibition on talking. Acting normal was a daily struggle. He couldn't forget about his secret, or the joys and regrets that went with it.

At the dairy case, another choice confronted him. 1% or 2% milk? Which one did Carol prefer? Brain fog was a constant hazard when images of another world which no one could see kept crowding in. He went for the 1%— she would probably want the healthier option. Then he decided to splurge on himself by picking up a small carton of half and half for coffee. Why the hell not?

Billy wondered if his memories of HD would ever become mere background noise, faint echoes from a time long ago that had nothing to do with his current life. Would he get to the point where he would be like everyone else at this supermarket, whose biggest decisions were between chicken or salmon and 1% or 2%?

In one sense, the completely amazing summer of HD had been just like the rest of Billy's life, but on fast forward. There were good times, serendipities, beautiful moments, and occasional insights. Also, he made some dumb decisions that created a mess for himself and the people he cared about. Then, somehow it all worked out.

Billy didn't want the memories of HD to fade. What he wanted was to go back there. Somehow, someday. And if he ever did manage to go back, he wasn't going to screw it up this time.

While standing in the checkout line, Billy scanned a rack of tabloids screaming about Brad and Angelina, Tom and Katie, and tragedies afflicting various celebrities he had never heard of. One headline caught his eye:

**Aliens Walk Among Us
Experts Say It Could Be True**

He pulled the paper out and looked more closely. A grainy photo showed a bug-eyed alien on a crowded sidewalk, surrounded by unsuspecting humans. Billy used to scoff at stuff like this, but now he didn't rule anything out. He tossed the paper onto the checkout belt, along with the items for that night's dinner. He looked up and saw the young mother wheeling her groceries out of the store. Her toddler was perched in her cart, clutching a box of Lucky Charms in his arms, like it was the greatest treasure in the world.

Billy's wife, Carol, and their college student daughter, Meredith, got a big laugh out of the *Aliens* article as they prepared the chicken and pasta.

"Hey, Diyami. You're in the newspaper!" Meredith said with glee. Diyami Red Hawk, tall and tattooed, came over to the kitchen island to look at the paper. He studied it intently, but didn't understand. Meredith explained the joke. "Nothing in these papers is true. They make up crazy stuff, and nobody really believes it. But here you are—an alien among us." Diyami had never seen a newspaper like this one. It was yet another strange aspect of this bizarre world he had committed to.

Diyami, a young engineer, was both a Native American and a native of HD. He had grown up in Cahokia, the thriving Native American metropolis across the river from HD St. Louis. He and Meredith had struck up a romance there when she visited HD the previous year. Diyami had taken on a mission: to build a new Cahokia in the SD world. It pained him to know that Native people in SD did not have the inspiration of Cahokia. He wanted to change that. The whispers of the spirits had led him to leave his parents and his life behind and go to SD with Meredith, Billy and Carol. Diyami was alone in SD, except for them.

Early on, the Boustanys and Diyami agreed to keep quiet about HD when anyone else was around. Billy made them all promise that they wouldn't say a word without consulting with the others first. Nothing good could come of a revelation. At a minimum, they would be branded as weirdos. Or they might attract unwanted attention from the sinister Knights of the Carnelian, the shadowy group that ran St. Louis in HD. When they departed HD for the last time, Martin Matsui, an elder statesman of the Knights who didn't care for their current intimidation tactics, made it crystal clear that the Knights' condition for allowing them to leave was strict silence—never say a word to anyone in SD about the existence of HD. Billy, Carol, and Meredith had seen what the Knights were capable of, so they took this warning seriously.

Billy fantasized constantly of telling other people about HD—once or twice he had come close to spilling his guts to a random stranger—but he knew better. The only consolation was that this pact of silence made him feel like a spy or a superhero with a secret identity.

Dinners at home gave Billy, Carol, Meredith, and Diyami the rare opportunity to relax and speak freely with no one else around. They were the only people in the SD world who knew that HD existed.

Or so they thought.

Anomaly

Silent and invisible, eighteen satellites in the secret NUCLEOSAT 2 system crisscrossed the planet several times each day. To maximize their gaze into seven continents, some were in polar orbits, others in inclined orbits. Their mission was to scan world regions that were considered risks for illicit nuclear activity, whether by rogue states or terrorist organizations. The capabilities of NUCLEOSAT 2, launched in 2009, represented a major, almost exponential, improvement over its predecessor, the original NUCLEOSAT. Finely-tuned sensors could detect faint whiffs of gamma rays and byproducts of radiation with pinpoint accuracy. Other onboard instruments picked up electromagnetic pulses and traveling ionospheric disturbances, which could be caused by weather phenomena or by underground nuclear detonations.

The National Reconnaissance Office operated NUCLEOSAT 2 and fed the data generated every day to its client in the U.S. intelligence community— the Department of Energy's National Nuclear Security Agency (NNSA). That data stream traveled through fiber optic cables to an unmarked NNSA facility outside

Washington, DC. There, it worked its way to the Office of Counterterrorism and Counterproliferation and settled on the shoulders of a lone analyst in a tiny cubicle in a large, windowless room. Lisa McDaniel peered at twin computer displays as she calibrated the new system's sensors and analytical algorithms to tune out the noise from benign radiation sources so that it would produce useful data when aimed at global hotspots.

During the calibration phase, the satellites' sensors were focused on the U.S., not because any threats were expected, but because many well-documented sources of radiation, like nuclear power plants and medical facilities, provided a baseline reference for training the software to ignore harmless radioactive signatures.

Plowing through all the glitches and noise in the signals from NUCLEOSAT 2 was tedious work, but solving puzzles was Lisa's greatest satisfaction. She had both an undergraduate math degree and a master's in computer science from Carnegie Mellon. In her short time at NNSA, she had earned a reputation as a careful, detail-oriented technical whiz.

Lisa was glad to have such important responsibility just three years out of graduate school and she threw herself into it. Over just a few months, she had diligently waded through most of the data NUCLEOSAT 2 had collected and had been commended by her supervisor for her elegant adjustments of the signal analysis algorithms to filter out noise. Now, in early 2011, there was one pesky anomaly left in the data that she couldn't figure out, no matter how hard she tried. Between June and October of the previous year, 2010, the satellites had picked up a series of short, weak radiation blips coming from, of all places, St. Louis, Missouri. The radiation signatures were odd, neither those of medical isotopes nor of heavy atoms, like uranium or thorium. So they were probably not signs of a nuclear terrorist or dirty bomb maker. They didn't correlate to any known sources, such as the research hospitals in St. Louis. Because they were so localized and time limited, they were also not likely to be natural phenomena. She set alerts in the system that would notify her if any additional, similar bursts popped up, but, so far, none had.

Lisa presented her problem at a team meeting.

"There's a recurring set of geographically isolated radiation signals that I haven't been able to account for. They appeared frequently for about four months, then stopped."

"Simple, obvious errors cause most problems. Have you asked one of the other analysts to review your code?" a senior analyst commented.

"I already did that," Lisa said. "My code is good." She bristled at his condescending tone.

"Maybe someone with more experience should take a look. I'm available if you need help."

The discussion continued as others around the table tossed out various potential causes, including interference from Chinese satellites trying to disable NUCLEOSAT 2. "Intel about the Chinese birds is Top Secret—code word: Farmers Market! Don't let it leave this room," the supervisor said. Lisa took notes on every hypothesis, even the ones she thought were a waste of time. After a few more minutes of discussion, the team decided to disregard Lisa's anomalies. The NUCLEOSAT 2 satellites were ready to become operational and, since the blips had stopped, there was no real need to investigate further. The recent software update to the system may have fixed the problem, whatever it was. Lisa wanted to keep working on this issue, but the team overruled her.

After the meeting, Lisa was annoyed. She followed up in a one-on-one with her supervisor and asked if technicians could be deployed to St. Louis to make measurements at the most common locations of the blips. He replied that he would consider her request, but, since the data did not match any plausible threat patterns, a resource deployment was unlikely.

Lisa knew her data analysis skills were better than anyone else's—even those who outranked her. In graduate school, she had developed algorithms to extract useful information from the Hubble Space Telescope's data streams. The majestic images of distant nebulae and galaxies that the public saw were not simple photographs, but rather the result of Lisa's refined siftings from the mountains of data that Hubble produced each time it turned its gaze to a slender slice of deep space. Serious astronomers didn't need the spectacular images—they worked with raw spectrographic data—but the bosses wanted photos to dazzle the public and Congress to maintain support for NASA funding. The Hubble work was Lisa's master's thesis and she graduated at the top of her class. NNSA recruited her even before her commencement ceremony.

Lisa had gotten her job at NNSA by solving hard problems and she wasn't going to let this one defeat her. She was absolutely certain that her code was clean and the Chinese interference hypothesis seemed pretty unlikely. So she kept working on the St. Louis anomaly in the small amounts of downtime she had from her official responsibilities. She crunched the data over and over, every which way from Sunday, using the math skills that had enabled the Hubble to find useful information in cosmic gas clouds.

Compared to untangling the mysteries of deep space, identifying terrestrial radiation sources should be a walk in the park. There was a logical explanation for everything—

data didn't just appear out of nowhere for no reason. In school, she had learned about Arno Penzias and Robert Wilson who, in the 1960s, worked with early radio telescopes. They figured out that static detected wherever the telescope was aimed was not, as their colleagues had thought, noise generated in the equipment. It turned out to be microwave background radiation, the echoes of the Big Bang—literally evidence of the beginning of time. Penzias and Wilson won the Nobel Prize in physics for their discovery.

However, Lisa also realized that the St. Louis blips might be no more than illusory patterns within random data. She knew how easy it was for us to fool ourselves. Millions of years of evolution had hardwired humans to spot visual cues signifying food or danger on the savannah. Her professors at Carnegie Mellon had emphasized, over and over, that this innate ability often led us to see patterns, and be convinced of them, where none existed.

One Friday evening, Lisa was having drinks with her best friend, Dawn Driscoll, another young, brilliant analyst, who worked at the National Security Agency. Lisa and Dawn had found each other quickly after they moved to DC. They were kindred spirits. Lisa admired Dawn, who was savvier about organizational politics than she was. They were on their second bottle of wine in Dawn's apartment, two nerds watching DVDs of *Sex and the City* and imagining that they were Carrie and Samantha, exchanging quips on the ineptitude and deviousness of men. They were laughing themselves silly.

Lisa and Dawn rarely talked about work. Like everyone else in the intelligence community, they were involved in classified projects, so shop talk was strictly frowned upon.

Lisa had the impression that Dawn worked on super-secret stuff and she knew better than to ask about it. This evening, as Carrie, Samantha, and the pinot grigio worked their magic, Lisa found herself opening up about the problem that had become her 24/7 obsession—the mystery of the St. Louis radiation blips.

"The weirdest thing is the odd sequence. They come in pairs. One will appear, then a few hours or a day later, there will be a second one in the same location. Then, nothing for several days or a week, then another pair pops up. It makes no sense."

Dawn refilled their wine glasses. "Okay. What have you looked into?"

"I've checked out everything. I ran overlays of weather and seismic data. No correlation. I searched the telecom and utility records to see if equipment upgrades or antenna tests could be involved. That was a dead end, too."

Dawn listened quietly and asked a clarifying question now and then. Lisa was relieved to be talking to someone who took her more seriously than the arrogant engineers and supervisors in her department. She knew she should be discreet, but it wasn't even a sanctioned project, just her spare time doodling. Anyway, she and Dawn both had security clearances.

After a while, Dawn said "If it's a human-caused phenomenon, cellphone records may show who was nearby when the radiation events occurred."

"It's the middle of a city! Lots of people would be nearby."

"What if there were people who were present when the events happened and not there at other times? That might tell us something."

"I don't have access to phone records."

"Neither do I…officially."

FRIENDS AND FAMILY

FOR THE FIRST FEW WEEKS after returning from HD, Billy spent a lot of time staring out the window. He had already begun the process of selling his business, the chain of Duke's Digital electronics stores in suburban St. Louis. Without a struggling business to attend to, his phone rarely rang and his email inbox was mostly empty. He didn't have a lot of friends, a reality he had long felt embarrassed about, but which now made the pact of silence about HD easier for him. The peace and quiet was comforting, but what would he do with himself now? He couldn't go back to HD—his ability to cross over had disappeared, as the Knights had told him it would. So, even without their threats, HD was over for him.

Carol returned to her teaching job at Parkway Central Middle School. It was awkward at first—the principal was upset that Carol had disappeared for two weeks the previous October with no warning or communication. Carol gave an evasive explanation that an unexpected family emergency had come up, which was kind of true since she and Billy had been kidnapped and taken to HD by the Knights. The principal relented and stopped asking

22

questions because she needed Carol, who was one of the school's best teachers. Carol believed in hard work and wanted to be busy; dealing with thirteen-year-olds was a welcome distraction from the images of HD, which came to her whenever she had a free moment. She had only seen a brief glimpse of this other world and now it was indelibly under her skin. If she ever got a chance to go back, she would make the most of it.

Meredith, who had spent weeks with Diyami and his family at Cahokia hiding from the Knights, knew that her destiny was intertwined with HD, Cahokia, and Diyami. He had cracked her world wide open and she loved him more than anyone she had ever known. She withdrew from her classes at Webster University so she could help him. His mission gave her an exhilarating purpose, though she couldn't yet see what she was supposed to do to help make it happen.

The three Boustanys made haphazard efforts to reconnect with family and friends, but their hearts weren't in it. They couldn't talk about the most earthshattering experience of their lives. With memories of HD coloring every moment, other people seemed vapid and naïve. Billy, Carol, and Meredith had peeked behind the curtain. Empty conversations with clueless people couldn't compare to that.

Carol didn't breathe a word about HD to her friends from the neighborhood or the other teachers at school. They could see that she had been through some kind of traumatic experience. *What do you expect when she's married to a flake like Billy Boustany? He just walked away from his business without a word of explanation.* Carol had always been loyal to them, so, as curious as they were, they didn't pry or pressure her to confess. Of course, they speculated among themselves—*Did Billy have an affair? Were there financial shenanigans?" Did Meredith have a drug problem or an unwanted pregnancy?*

Meredith was drifting away from her circles of high school and college friends. She and Diyami got together with them a few times. They didn't know what to make of her mysterious new boyfriend, the tall Indian with the tattooed face. He seemed nice enough, but he had appeared out of nowhere. When they went out to bars, he mostly kept to himself. He wasn't good at making conversation with the other guys. He didn't know anything about sports, politics, or TV shows. Occasionally, he would open up and talk his head off about dams or canals or other weird stuff, then sink back into silence. *There must be something there*, Meredith's friends thought. Maybe she liked him as the strong, silent type. He was definitely hot, though the girls had mixed opinions about his facial tattoos. *A bit much, don't you think? It's so rad! Maybe he's ten years ahead of the trend.*

After repeated invitations from Billy's older sister Vera, the family went to a long-delayed dinner at her home. It was a disaster. Carol told Vera that Meredith was bringing a friend, but gave no details. Vera and her husband, Jeff, were shocked when Diyami walked in the door. Whatever they expected Meredith's friend to be, it wasn't this. Their teenage daughters could barely suppress their giggles at his strange appearance. Diyami's precise, deliberate way of talking and moving unsettled them further. He was extremely polite and didn't want to say the wrong thing and upset Meredith's relatives.

Jeff asked Diyami how he knew Meredith. Diyami recounted the cover story that he and Meredith had made up—growing up in Oklahoma, a master's degree in engineering from the University of Oklahoma, and now enrolled in the Webster University business school, where he had met Meredith. Meredith could see the skepticism on Jeff's face so she stepped in to change the subject. "Are you still playing a lot of golf, Jeff?" "Every chance I get," he said. "I had a great game just on Saturday. Hit the best drives of my life." It didn't take much to get Jeff talking about golf.

Carol asked Vera how her son was enjoying his first year away at college. Soon they were deep in conversation about dorm life and annoying roommates. For a little while, Billy made headway with Vera's daughters, using the tried and true "how's school" question that adults relied on with teenagers. After that thread of small talk petered out and the girls drifted away, he sipped a beer, inspected the bookshelves, and was relieved to be left alone.

Before dinner, Jeff gathered everyone in the living room for a group photo. He wanted to try out his new selfie stick. Vera put her arms around Billy and Carol. "It's so wonderful to have the family together again. If only mom and dad were still here. I miss them so much." The kids took more selfies with Diyami and Meredith— they couldn't wait to post pictures of this strange-looking Indian on Facebook for their friends to see.

At the dinner table, Billy announced that he had gotten out of Duke's Digital and the bank was taking over the stores. Vera and Jeff were shocked. The business had been in the family since their father started it in the 1950s.

"What will happen to it?" Vera asked.

"Not my problem." Billy said.

"The end of an era," Vera said, and she began to cry. Being the daughter of the Duke of Discounts had been the only thing that made her feel important during her awkward high school years.

"Give me a break," Billy said. "You were in a big hurry to sell back in '87 when dad died. If I hadn't stepped in, it would have been gone then."

The conversation stopped dead. Vera sobbed. Jeff got up to comfort her and glared at Billy. The teenage girls exchanged glances, totally confused. Carol, who normally was a master of calming tense social situations, couldn't think of anything to say. She smiled a bland smile and kept quiet. Her mind was screaming. *If you only knew what we've seen and what we've been through, none of this crap about the business would mean a damn thing to you.*

The Boustanys and Diyami left as quickly as they could when dinner was over. The attempt to have a normal evening with extended family lay in a smoldering heap. "I'm not doing that again any time soon," Billy said on the drive home.

Not the X-Files

THE FOLLOWING FRIDAY, Lisa and Dawn got together again. "Tonight, we have a true classic. It's rampantly sexist, but still a must-see." announced Dawn, gleefully brandishing a DVD, "*Superbad*!" Somehow, Lisa had never seen it.

Before inserting the movie into the player, Dawn said, "I made a little progress on your St. Louis conundrum. A few hits came up on the phone records."

Lisa's eyes widened. "Really?"

"A single phone was associated with many of the times and locations of several of your events and a second phone on the same account was also there for a few of them."

"Wow! Who?"

"I don't have names or numbers. That kind of unmasking is way above my pay grade. I had to call in a big favor from a friend to get what I got."

"What now?"

"I say we take it up the ladder. Stuff like this doesn't turn up every day. We'll beg forgiveness for the unauthorized search."

Lisa was nervous as she connected her laptop to the conference room projector. Today was a much bigger deal than the meeting with her team the month before. The conference room was filled with more senior level people than she had ever seen in one place, including a deputy director from CIA, Ralph Pellegrini, who far outranked everyone else around the table. Tensions rose in the NNSA building when the higher-ups were told that Pellegrini would attend the meeting. It was extremely unusual for someone at his level—from another agency, no less—to take an interest in their work. Dawn's involvement from NSA added another Pandora's box that contributed to the nervousness of the NNSA managers.

Lisa's supervisor sat her down and warned her that Pellegrini's presence meant that her performance could have major career implications, both for her and her entire team. Pellegrini had a reputation as a world-class bullshit detector, so there was little margin for error. Lisa shrugged his warning off—she always prepared meticulously and was confident about her work.

Lisa began her presentation with visuals of the St. Louis radiation blips— a map and a graph with small bumps indicating the magnitude of the blips. She explained the technical issues about radiation signatures and her noise reduction algorithms. She reviewed her efforts to cross-reference external factors, like weather, routine telecom operations, and even the Chinese satellites. Questions came in from all corners and Lisa adroitly handled every one of them. She glanced surreptitiously at Dawn, who gave her a discreet thumbs up. *This is going great!*

Dawn took over to present her hypothesis about the potential for linking individuals to the blips. Some people in the meeting had not been briefed on her unauthorized discovery that a few phones may be correlated to the mysterious events. They objected to this breach of protocol. Dawn's supervisor from NSA defended her, saying that Dawn had acted within the spirit of the regulations, that no one's identity had been compromised, and that the potential phone linkages may be significant.

Pellegrini spoke up for the first time. The room was quiet. "We shouldn't let the perfect be the enemy of the good. Our procedures support the mission. They don't define it. Ms. McDaniel and Ms. Driscoll were right to take some initiative, even if they were stretching the rules." Lisa and Dawn were encouraged. *Is the deputy director of the CIA on our side?* Their hope faded quickly.

"I have a different problem with this whole discussion," Pellegrini continued. "None of these events, whatever or whoever has caused them, appear to be remotely relevant to the purpose of NUCLEOSAT 2. Ms. McDaniel's presentation makes it clear that the St. Louis signal profiles don't match any conceivable threat. NSA and DOE collect oceans of data every day. Minor discrepancies here and there are inevitable. We can't afford to waste our time on trivialities. Also, there are no grounds here for investigating American citizens. We are governed by the law and the Constitution, after all, and have no authority to conduct domestic surveillance."

Lisa protested, "Sir, there are so many unexplained anomalies here. What will we do the next time something appears outside of our threat profiles?"

"Anomalies alone aren't threats. This isn't *The X-Files.* We're not chasing UFOs. End all work on this matter today.

No phone records will be unmasked. Ms. McDaniel, you and Ms. Driscoll have excellent reputations. Many critical projects need your skills. Go back to them."

Lisa was about to speak again. Dawn kicked her under the table.

Pellegrini stood up. "This meeting is adjourned."

"Sorry," Dawn said to Lisa as she packed up her laptop. "We gave it our best shot."

A few weeks later, Lisa was heating up a bowl of ramen in the office microwave. When she carried it back to her cubicle, a piece of paper was on her keyboard. She unfolded it. A phone number. Area code 314. St. Louis.

An Innocent Abroad

Diyami was eager to get going on his mission to build a new Cahokia in SD, like the one that was his home in HD—a modern, but thoroughly Native American, city and the national center of Native pride and culture. The spirits of Cahokia had spoken to him, but he didn't know where to begin. Could he really do this? Or was he fooling himself? The Cahokian elders in HD, including his mother, had blessed this mission, even though it meant that he would probably never return to HD again. Like Diyami, they didn't want the Native Americans of SD to endure in the barren darkness without a living Cahokia.

The legends of Morning Star and Corn Mother, mythical heroes embodied as two archaeologists who founded HD's new Cahokia in the 1960s, inspired Diyami. Even though Corn Mother was a white woman—Morning Star was an Ojibway—the tales told in Cahokia said they had been guided by the ancient spirits, who spoke to them in their modest bungalow home next to the mounds that remained from the original Cahokia of nine hundred years ago. They traveled across the plains from one Native

31

community to the next, spreading the story of Cahokia and, slowly but surely, convincing their listeners to move to Illinois and build a new city on the site of the ancient metropolis. At first, these Native settlers came in a trickle, then as a mighty river. Like every Cahokia school child, Diyami had grown up with the stories of Morning Star, Corn Mother, and the city's founding. When he was six, he had actually met Corn Mother as an old woman. He never forgot the piercing clarity of her eyes and the warmth of her smile.

Diyami was a civil engineer, a math and science nerd, and the pampered only child of two college professors. He wasn't an orator or a politician—certainly not cut out to be a prophet. He had lived his whole life in HD and he knew nothing about SD. His world had diverged from SD more than a hundred years earlier and gone its own way, with a different history. SD fascinated him as much as his HD world had fascinated Meredith and her parents during the magical summer.

Carol proposed a family project to help Diyami learn what he needed about SD, particularly about the recent history of Native Americans. She asked if he would, at the same time, tell them everything he knew about HD. She came up with a reading list for him, he read voraciously, and they discussed the books often. Meredith taught Diyami how to Google, so he could research Native American nations and communities on his own. He loved it and got easily distracted searching on every topic he could think of. Carol, the teacher, cautioned him, as she did her middle school students, that the internet was full of misinformation and lies. "People say anything to shock or push their agenda. Don't believe everything you read."

Diyami's lessons mostly took place at long dinners where the family cooked, talked, and laughed. He began to pay attention to the news in SD. He was surprised that neither the local St. Louis news nor the national networks said much about Native American issues. "It's like we don't exist." One evening, Diyami asked the Boustanys "who are famous Native Americans today?" They were all silent— they couldn't think of any. It was embarrassing, but that was the reality. Native Americans weren't a big part of contemporary culture.

Also, Diyami was horrified to learn about nuclear weapons, which didn't exist in HD, and was astounded that the Boustanys didn't think about them much.

"Hardly anybody does," Billy said.

"How can you be so calm with unspeakable tools of annihilation hanging over your heads? They could come down on you with no warning."

Billy and Meredith had to admit that Diyami had a point. The nonchalant attitude about nuclear war was pretty strange, when you thought about it. Carol explained, "People can get used to just about anything."

Billy rented movies about Native Americans, like *Little Big Man* and *Dances with Wolves*. Diyami watched them over and over. They covered nineteenth century events that were the same in HD. He described a famous movie from HD, *As Before, So Once More*, that told the story of Morning Star and Corn Mother. "It was a huge hit. I wish I could show it to you."

Diyami was conflicted when he learned about Native American casinos, which didn't exist in HD. On one hand, casinos provided a way for impoverished tribes to earn money. On the other hand, they catered to addiction and greed. At least, the Native Americans were profiting from the weaknesses of the whites this time. Still, the tawdriness of the whole idea disturbed him. Casinos weren't a dignified way to make money and they didn't honor Native cultures. When he and Meredith later visited them on their travels— several of their talks on Cahokia were held in casino meeting rooms—he saw that the benefits of the casinos were not equitably shared. They employed many whites and were often run by white investors. And impoverished natives lived in rundown trailers just a few miles from glitzy casino buildings.

Diyami was also disappointed that almost no one in SD played, or had heard of, chunkey, the game that had originated in ancient Cahokia. In SD, chunkey was just a historical curiosity. In HD, it was a major sport for Native Americans— and even whites played it. The sports pages of newspapers reported on big chunkey tournaments. You could watch games on the moviola. 500 Nations University, where his parents taught, was, of course, a dominant college chunkey power. Diyami went to their games whenever he could.

Diyami was constantly intrigued by the odd customs and quirky language he noticed in SD, "Why do young people refer to something they like as 'sick?' Why do 'I'm up for that' and "I'm down with that' mean the same thing?" "Everywhere we go, people are either taking pictures of what they're doing or sending pictures of something they just did. Who is ever going to have time to look at them all?"

The Boustanys peppered Diyami with questions about every aspect of life in HD. Billy was curious about technology and entertainment. Carol wanted to know the history, the politics, and the trends. When the Knights held Billy and her in the asylum the previous October, they had given them a few books about HD history, which she had managed to bring back to SD. She read them over and over, but longed to know more.

Meredith liked the stories about his childhood. Diyami had grown up watching the news on his parents' moviola, but he hadn't paid much attention to it and was an indifferent history student—he was much more interested in physics and math. Carol wrote down the tidbits of history he remembered, which added to what she had learned from the asylum books:

India was an expansionist power. Having thrown the British out in a long, bloody revolution in the 1930s (the major war of the twentieth century), it became a militant dictatorship, feared and respected. It dominated the countries of Southeast Asia and was a major rival to Russia. Britain held on to Ceylon (Sri Lanka) as an offshore fortress in their ongoing conflict with India.

There was no Bolshevik revolution in Russia. (Diyami was pretty hazy about Russia. "Big country. Makes great electronics. A lot of Russian tourists come over here." was all he knew.)

Argentina and Bolivia merged and became hugely wealthy from mining and minerals. People made jokes about rich Argentinians. All of South America was dominated by the Argentinian confederation.

China was still mostly poor, though the coastal regions were wealthy and had largely seceded from the rest of the country. There were about six independent regions.

The United States had not been involved in major wars in the twentieth century. Diyami was shocked when he learned about the scope and destruction of World War I and World War II in SD.

The U.S. federal government was much smaller in HD. States had more power. Carol surmised that, without major wars, expansion of the federal government never happened.

35

St. Louis' Citizen Shareholder Plan (CSP), that paid annual dividends to every resident, was a model imitated in other cities around the country. St. Louis was also famous as a center of innovation— like Silicon Valley in SD.

A constitutional amendment in the 1980s established Semi-Autonomous City States (SACS) which are allowed expanded local government authority. St. Louis and New York pushed for this amendment and were the first two SACS approved. Other major cities followed, including Chicago, Atlanta, Houston, San Francisco, Boston, and Philadelphia. (Diyami was going from memory—he wasn't exactly sure which cities were on the list.) Cahokia was planning to apply for SACS status.

Transportation was mostly powered by hydrogen and electricity.

High-speed hydrofoil ocean liners competed with airplanes for intercontinental travel.

Television (moviola) had become a big deal by the 1930s.

St. Louis was a music capital. Bands like Milo Riley were famous worldwide and tourists flocked to St. Louis for the music scene. A St. Louis invention, self-teaching musical instruments, was very popular across the country. There was a tradition of people gathering for spontaneous singing in places with good acoustics. Once a song began, strangers would stop and join in. This tradition made St. Louis a center of a cappella music. Music was less important elsewhere in the country.

Ever the history teacher, Carol wanted to write a book about HD. Billy didn't think this was a good idea. It might put them on the Knights' radar. "No problem," said Carol. "We'll publish it as a work of fiction. People love alternate history!"

Billy concentrated on practical matters, like getting a vehicle for Diyami and Meredith to drive on their missions to Indian communities. When Diyami left HD Cahokia, the elders gave him some ancient ceramics to sell for seed money for his new Cahokia project. After Google searches and discreet snooping around, Billy found an antiquities dealer who was willing to buy high-quality artifacts with no documented provenance. The price was lower than Billy and Diyami had hoped, but still enough to cover Diyami's and Meredith's travels for several months, including the price of a used vehicle.

Billy found a great deal on a Dodge van. When they went to look at it, Meredith objected. "No way! I'm not a soccer mom taking kids to school in a minivan." They compromised on a Toyota pickup with a camper shell. Diyami was thinking about how it would look years in the future at a Cahokia museum—like Morning Star's and Corn Mother's green station wagon prominently displayed in the Temple of the Children in HD.

Diyami was completely undocumented—without a driver's license, birth certificate, Social Security number, or anything that made him a real person in the eyes of the law. Billy didn't know what to do about that, but he told Diyami he would think of something. In the meantime, Meredith would have to do all the driving.

One day, Diyami went with Billy to Home Depot to buy a variety of things Billy needed. Diyami roamed the aisles of the store, enthralled with tools, fasteners, door assemblies, and appliances. He was an engineer to the core, fascinated by mechanical devices. Most items were similar to what he knew from HD, but with subtle differences. He had never seen Phillips screwdrivers before. In HD, screwdrivers had square tips that fit into square holes in the screws— a different system from the cross-shaped Phillips bits, but which served the same purpose. They were a small example of how everyday technologies had evolved differently in each world.

In the paint and adhesives aisle, Diyami gleefully waved a roll of gray tape. "This is one of ours!"

"That's duct tape," Billy said. "You can get that anywhere."

"It was invented in my world. We call it "duck" tape because it's waterproof. A small company developed it in secret, patented it, and made a fortune. I read about it in eighth grade, in a book called *City of Inventors*. I loved that book. It made me want to become an engineer. I wonder how this tape got here."

Diyami turned out to be a big help on home improvement projects. He enjoyed construction and fixing things. He had a knack for plumbing—not surprising, given his training as a civil engineer, concentrating on locks, dams, and canals. When Billy had to hire a plumber to repair leaking pipes in a bathroom, Diyami hung out with him for hours, asking questions and making suggestions, which often were very good ones.

At one of the family dinners, they talked about how it felt to find yourself in a new world. Each one shared their memories of those first moments. After many pieces of Meredith's mildly psychoactive taffy, made from a recipe she had learned from two elderly sisters in HD, they came up with the "Stages of Amazement" as a shorthand for describing the sequence of feelings. They laughed themselves silly.

Stages of Amazement:

1. Deer in the Headlights (the WTF moment)
2. Cool! (when you wander around with a big, goofy grin)

3. Nuts? (as in "am I losing my mind?")
4. OMFG! (so what if I'm nuts)
5. Cold Dead Hands (as in "if you want to take HD away from me, you'll have to pry it from my cold dead hands.")
6. Cosmic! ('Cool' times ten—or a hundred)

Meredith took Diyami on long drives around town so he could see what SD looked like. He had a million questions. Why are there so many parking lots everywhere? Why are the sidewalks so empty? Can I get another of those flavored coffee drinks? Other than frequent trips to Starbucks, she didn't have good answers for him.

On a breezy afternoon, Diyami and Meredith were eating lunch in the Delmar Loop, an entertainment and shopping district near Washington University. Meredith snapped a selfie of the two of them in front of the Chuck Berry statue. Out of the blue, he said, "Let's go see the monuments."

"What?"

"You know the big columns, towers, and statues north of downtown."

"Never heard of them."

So, here was another aspect of St. Louis, which Diyami took for granted, that didn't exist in SD.

"Let's drive up Grand and I'll show you."

Meredith hesitated. "I've never gone there. It's dangerous."

"Why?"

That was another question Meredith didn't know how to answer. Since childhood, she had absorbed the belief that most white people in St. Louis held—north St. Louis, populated by Black people, was a scary place. A blank *terra incognita* on the map.

"There's a lot of drugs and crime. We could get carjacked."

"If you haven't been there, how do you know it's dangerous?"

"It's all poor people. Black people." Meredith knew it wasn't cool to admit to prejudice, but her fear was genuine.

Diyami pondered this strange concept. The idea that there was a huge swath of the city where only Black people lived was something he had not experienced.

"Why do they all live there?"

"I don't know." She had never considered that question.

"Now I most certainly want to see it. We'll be fine."

As they headed north on Grand past the Fox Theatre, Powell Hall, and the VA hospital, there were more and more vacant lots, interspersed with occasional fast food restaurants and gas stations. Diyami looked in both directions at every corner to see as much as he could. It was hard for him to make sense of this place, which was so unlike the Grand Avenue that he knew—a bustling, tree-lined boulevard with wide sidewalks and pedestrians at all hours of the day and night.

Meredith also glanced around as she drove the car north, but she was searching for signs of danger. She had crossed into an entirely unfamiliar part of the city, one where she had learned that sensible people didn't venture into. It wasn't only specific warnings from parents and other adults, but also hushed and unspoken assumptions about a place that was rarely mentioned by white people. When she was a teenager and watched the ten o'clock news with her father, North St. Louis locations only came up in the context of burning buildings or crime scenes with flashing police lights and distraught Black people describing some frightening event.

The street became emptier the further they drove in search of Diyami's monuments. On some blocks, there were only one or two buildings left standing. Many of those were boarded up or showed signs of recent fires. Diyami looked up a side street to see a house where only the front wall remained, with a pile of bricks behind it. The second floor windows framed nothing but sky. Diyami was horrified. This part of the city looked like a home whose inhabitants had suddenly fled, leaving behind only pieces of random junk they didn't want. SD St. Louis was stranger than he could have imagined.

"There's a monument!" Diyami said, pointing to a slender structure ahead in the distance. "I knew they were here." It was the Grand Avenue Water Tower, a 154-foot tall white Corinthian column, which had been built in 1871 to hold water in vertical storage to provide pressure to pipes in the area. As Meredith and Diyami approached the SD version of the water tower, the street was eerily still. There were few cars and no pedestrians. The water tower stood in the center of Grand Avenue, which flowed around it to form a graceful traffic circle. Here, the tower's paint was peeling and the circle was bordered by grass-covered vacant lots. In HD, the water tower was the center of a busy neighborhood, known for rowdy street vendors and eccentric artists.

"Stop the car," Diyami said. "I want to take a picture." He had gotten the hang of using the iPhone camera and was quickly becoming a frequent photographer, just like everyone in SD. Meredith pulled over. She waited inside the car and checked her Facebook feed. After a few minutes, she looked up and saw Diyami on the sidewalk. He was talking to two Black men, who looked to be about twenty years old. One was gesturing and pointing. He looked upset. *Uh-oh,* Meredith thought.

A hand pounded on the driver side window. Meredith startled. A young Black woman with braided hair and large hoop earrings gestured to her to lower the window. A jolt of fear shot through Meredith. This was exactly why she shouldn't be in this part of town. Against her better judgment, she rolled the window down a bit.

"Come join us. I've got a J if you want to share."

Through the windshield, Meredith saw Diyami waving for her to come over. She got out of the car and was careful to lock it.

"I'm Jasmine." The girl offered her hand for a shake.

"Meredith."

"Your boyfriend is amaaazing! Where did you find him?"

"At a club."

"Take me to that club," Jasmine joked.

Diyami was talking with two young Black guys. They wore hoodies, baggy pants, and baseball caps.

"Everybody, this is Meredith, who brought me here. Meredith, this is Jamal and Wesley. You already met Jasmine."

Smiles and greetings were exchanged. At six foot three, Diyami was taller than all of them and his facial tattoos and straight black hair down to the middle of his back were unlike anything they had ever seen.

"Your tats are legitimately sick, man." Wesley said.

"Is he really an Indian?" Jamal asked Meredith.

"Yeah," Meredith said.

"I thought Indians only lived out west. You know, chasing wagon trains and shit."

"Diyami is from Cahokia, right near here," Meredith said.

"No way!" Jasmine said. "I went there once with my school. They made this big hill out of dirt."

"My ancestors built that about a thousand years ago," Diyami said. "Many people call it a mound, but to us it's a temple."

"Your people been here that long?" Jamal asked.

"Off and on."

"That is so dope."

"They also built temples near here, but they were torn down when St. Louis was built."

"What were they for?"

"They were holy places and sometimes the kings lived on top of them. Others were mounds where they buried people."

"Here? You mean we're living on top of an Indian graveyard?"

"Maybe there's a curse, like in the movies." Wesley said. They all laughed.

"That explains it," Jamal said.

"Explains what?"

"This place. It sure looks like it's cursed," Jamal waved his hand to indicate the empty neighborhood.

"Diyami wants to build a new Cahokia, a city people can live in today," Meredith said.

"Cool!" "I'm ready!" "Count us in!"

"What's going on around here," Diyami asked.

"Nothing. What you see is what you get," Jamal said.

"I'm leaving as soon as I can get my shit together," Jasmine said. The others agreed with that idea.

A short, sharp blast from a siren surprised them. A police car with flashing blue lights stopped a few feet away. Two officers, one white and one Black, got out. The white officer had his hand near his holster.

"What are you trouble makers doing this time?"

"Nothing, sir. We're just talking." Wesley said.

"You're not allowed to block a public sidewalk."

"There's no one else around. It's not like we're in anybody's way," Jasmine said.

The cops gave them cold, impassive looks, then turned their attention to Meredith and Diyami.

"Do you have business in this area, ma'am?"

"My friend and I came to see the water tower. These people are telling us about the neighborhood."

"May I see your ID?"

Meredith handed her driver's license to the officer. He glanced at it, gave it back to her, then turned to Diyami, studying his tattoos and long hair. "Who are you?"

"Diyami Red Hawk."

"What the hell kind of name is that?"

Diyami looked him straight in the eyes. "Native American."

"ID, please."

Meredith jumped in. "He left it at home, sir. I'm driving, so there's no problem. We're leaving in just a minute."

"I'll let it go this time, but don't come around here again without ID. You should be more careful."

"We will be." Meredith said. Diyami and the officer stared at each other with barely disguised contempt. Meredith put her arm on Diyami's shoulder to gently pull him away from the cop.

The white policeman turned to the others. "Move along now. I don't want to see you here when we come back."

"Yes, sir, officer." Jamal said.

The cops returned to their car and drove away.

"That's exactly why I want to get out of this dump," Jasmine said.

"They were nicer than usual because you were here," Jamal said. "We meant it when we said we want to help you with Cahokia. Don't forget us."

They all exchanged phone numbers, then posed for group selfies.

Meredith and Diyami waved one last time as they got in their car. "Dammit, Diyami," Meredith said. "We can't take a chance on you getting arrested. You have no way of proving who you are. You could be in so much trouble."

Diyami watched the three young people walking away. "Those kids have good hearts, but they're trapped in a dark place. They need a Cahokia, too."

THE PELICAN

ON WEEKENDS THAT FALL AND WINTER, Billy and Carol often drove to South St. Louis to be near the places where Billy had experienced his first glimpses of HD. They liked to eat lunch at the ethnic restaurants on South Grand—Pho Grand, a Vietnamese place, became their favorite—then stroll through Tower Grove Park. One early winter day, Billy spotted a new *For Sale* sign on an empty nineteenth-century building at Grand and Shenandoah. It was the site of Pelican's, Big Bill Boustany's favorite restaurant, famous for seafood. Billy had eaten there many times as a child. At the same location in HD, he had visited the strangest place he had encountered in that world, the Refugees Club, a bizarre, baroque structure that housed a social club for lonely, lost people.

Billy parked the car and he and Carol got out to inspect the boarded-up two-and-a-half story brick building with a conical turret on the corner.

"Let's buy it," Billy said. "It's perfect!"

"Are you out of your mind?"

"We could make an apartment on the second floor and do something with the restaurant space on the first floor."

"You want to run a restaurant?"

"No, I want to live here."

Carol studied the building. Despite being empty, it was sturdy and kind of charming. They had owned a West County suburban home for almost twenty years, which, she had to admit, felt a little sterile after last summer's adventures.

"We can get this place cheap," Billy said. Having run a chain of electronics stores, he knew how real estate worked. He pointed out the great natural light that the tall, second story windows would bring into the apartment. "We could put in skylights, too. And a deck on the back of the second floor." Carol nodded in agreement. She hadn't seen him this excited since they returned from HD for the last time. That night, they told Meredith and Diyami, who liked the plan as well.

Once Billy got an idea in his head, he moved fast. Two weeks later, the building was theirs. He quickly lined up contractors to begin the rehab—new HVAC, plumbing, and electric. They put the West County home on the market. Proceeds from its sale would fund the entire project on South Grand.

Billy and Carol moved into the Pelican building when it was still little more than a construction site. He was impatient to make the break with his former life. The walls were unpainted drywall or newly exposed brick; windows had no moldings; tools were piled in corners; and a film of dust coated everything. The kitchen was functional, though the dining table was a piece of plywood on a couple of sawhorses.

Rehabbing the Pelican building gave Billy and Carol something to think about that wasn't HD. Questions from contractors about doors, windows, insulation, the location of electric outlets, lighting fixtures, and more required daily decisions. Carol took the lead on the interior plans with her arms full of plumbing and lighting catalogs. Structural questions, including the unwelcome discovery of rotting roof joists, were Billy's domain.

Billy wanted to do something with the exterior that would echo the fantastical façade of the Refugees Club in HD, a riotous collage of carved eagles, musical instruments, vines, and fruit. Over a glass of wine one evening, he and Carol came up with the idea—a sculpture, mounted above the roof, of two giant pelicans gliding on outstretched wings. Pelicans were their favorite birds and they wanted to acknowledge the long gone restaurant. Also, two pelicans in formation would be a symbol of the new life that Billy and Carol had begun.

Billy found a local artist who was known for large sculptures. She listened patiently to Billy's description of what he wanted and struggled to make sense out of his awkward sketches. Billy added drawing lessons to the list of things he wished he had done a long time ago. He looked back on his twenty-three years running Duke's Digital as a kind of sleepwalking, when he had plodded from one day to the next, always consumed with immediate crises and challenges, and never deciding what kind of life he wanted to lead or what kind of person he wanted to be. Now he was making up for lost time.

The artist constructed the sections of the two pelicans from scrap metal. She and her assistants, a young man and woman with elaborate tattoos and piercings, bolted a lattice of pipes to the roof and began to attach pieces to it. Each pelican's wingspan was about fifteen feet. Curious onlookers stopped their cars as they drove down Grand

Avenue to ask what the heck was going on. Billy enjoyed the attention for being the ringmaster of this odd circus. It was so completely different from his years of trying to keep Duke's Digital from bleeding customers and cash.

The building inspector, however, was horrified by the monstrosity being attached to the roof of a historic building and stopped the project cold. Billy was forced to bushwhack his way through a thicket of red tape at City Hall. It was rough going until he sought the help of the local alderman, who was amused by the project, though he thought Billy was a little weird. Nevertheless, he was glad that someone was finally putting money into the building, which had been on the verge of decaying into an eyesore.

A New Life

JOHN LITTLE WASN'T USED TO WALKING DOGS. In his seventy years, he had never owned a pet. His mother always said their cramped apartment was no place for dirty, smelly things. Yet here he was following two little corgis with their stubby, comical legs along the tree-lined street where he now lived in a spacious home. It was the same street—Flora Place—where his mother had worked as a maid for Big Bill Boustany, the Duke of Discounts. Well, not quite the same—this Flora Place was in a different world.

John looked forward to his morning strolls. Fresh, new life emerged all around him as spring warmth drew out white dogwood flowers and lavender redbuds. *How did they get that name, they aren't even red.* And it was quiet, so he could think. Less than a year earlier, he had been flat on his back in the VA hospital in the regular world—SD as his friend and former boss Billy Boustany called it. Now, blood and oxygen flowed freely through the stents the doctors had inserted into the blocked arteries around his heart. He felt stronger and clearer every day. Recovering his health was the lesser of the good fortunes that had brought him to this beautiful street on this gorgeous morning. After twenty-eight years, he had reconnected with the one and only love of his life, Leonora Matsui, who owned the large, comfortable home in this amazing world, which Billy had named HD.

John opened the front door and the two corgis scurried into the kitchen to await the snack they had earned. He gave it to them, then went down to the basement to spend the rest of the day happily tinkering with the various devices spread out on his workbench. The odd technologies of HD fascinated him. How did they work? Why had they been designed this way? John explored these questions by taking things apart, then putting them back together. Gradually, he was figuring out the technical contours of a world which had developed on a different path for more than a century.

John found his way to HD through an improbable series of events. In October of the previous year, Billy Boustany and his wife Carol came to him desperate for help to find their daughter Meredith, who had disappeared. They were convinced that she was trapped in HD, probably kidnapped by the Knights of the Carnelian, the secretive organization that dominated HD St. Louis. Billy knew that John himself had visited HD years earlier and that he had once communicated with it via ham radio. John, recovering from his heart attack, didn't want to get involved, despite their pleas. Then, Billy and Carol also disappeared.

John had to do something. He was able to make contact with his long-lost HD love, Leonora, over a tenuous and unreliable radio connection that penetrated the barrier between the two worlds. He and Leonora revisited their old calculations and found a time and place where he could slip across into HD. The strain of that passage on his weakened heart almost did him in. But the stents held.

Leonora's uncle, Martin Matsui, was the member of the Knights of the Carnelian who had given John a stark ultimatum in 1982—abandon your mother and the life you know, join Leonora in HD, and never come home OR do your duty to your mother and never see Leonora again. John decided to stay in SD. His frail mother had no one else. He watched Leonora walk away, escorted by Martin and a pair of bodyguards. It was the worst moment of his life. For twenty-eight years, John hated Martin for forcing him to make that horrible choice.

This time, Martin, now an elder statesman of the Knights, was trying to make things right. He greeted John warmly and apologized for the shabby way he had treated him years earlier. He intervened with the leader of the Knights, a nasty fellow named Giles Monroe, to release Billy, Carol, and Meredith and allow them to return to SD. John was supposed to go back with them. At the last minute, he changed his mind.

Nothing was waiting for John in SD, just the sad little apartment where he had lived his whole life, first with his mother and then alone. He had no friends. As a Black man with a high school education in St. Louis, he never had much of a chance. Leonora was the only person who ever really listened to him, who ever believed in him. When they met again after decades of separation, their connection was undimmed. So he was happy to cast his lot with her.

At Leonora's house, John had time on his hands. Martin suggested that John keep a low profile. No point in poking the beehive that was Giles Monroe. Leonora was busy all day as the Director of Research for the Hydraulic Brick Corporation, the proudest, most successful business in HD St. Louis. She led a team of scientists and engineers who made constant improvements to their flagship product line, electricity-generating "Amperic" bricks. Billions and billions of these bricks powered the global economy.

John's lifelong passion was messing around with electronics and other technologies. Nobody in SD had appreciated the depth of his knowledge. HD, where everything worked differently, presented virgin territory for his inquiries. After he moved to Leonora's house, creating the basement workshop was an obvious next step. He needed tools and stuff to work on. "I know just where to go. You'll love it," Leonora said.

The next Saturday morning, they got into her car, a robin's egg blue ovoid with three wheels splayed out on stainless steel struts. "My team members got tired of my old, beat-up vehicle and nagged me to get something better," she said as they sped west on Chippewa. John winced as Leonora weaved through the traffic, dodging the hordes of young people on scooters. He couldn't get used to the way people drove in HD. They crossed a bridge over the River Des Peres, a picturesque stream that meandered through the city. It was dotted with canoes and pleasure boats. Fly fishermen stood in the shallows and flicked their lines through the air.

Leonora made a left turn into an industrial area with long, low buildings and parked. John saw a large structure ahead. A sign over the entrance said "Mechanical Market." The peaked roof covered four square blocks. It was supported by slender steel columns and trusses. Clerestory windows brought natural light to the interior. The walls were thin curtains of pale green bricks.

Inside, John was like a kid in a candy store. There were aisles upon aisles of booths and shops. Men in aprons pushed carts filled with radios, power tools, and coils of wire. Customers inspected the wares and haggled with vendors. One booth sold screws, bolts, and fasteners. The next sold used moviolas. The one after that had bins full of gears and camshafts. Another aisle contained nothing but fuel cells and batteries in a dizzying variety of shapes and sizes. John and Leonora wandered around for two hours. He was loaded down with parts and tools when they left.

The Mechanical Market, with its cornucopia of HD technology, became John's second home. He came by streetcar at least twice a week while Leonora was at work. Mornings were the best time. He browsed the aisles to check out the latest treasures for sale. New items arrived early and often the best were gone by noon. John struck up conversations with vendors, who became his instructors in the technology of HD.

Terminology was his first lesson. Everything had a different name. The HD word "computer" meant a self-contained device that used sensors, servomotors, and actuators in various combinations to translate inputs into motion. One of the most common types of computers were the boxes that automatically furled and unfurled awnings and shutters based on the changing angle of the sun. These provided shade on every major street in the city.

HD did have analog "difference engines"—DEs for short—which were similar to SD personal computers, but less versatile. Various models were designed for specific tasks— one for writing, another for calculations, and still another for managing lists. To John, it was a cumbersome arrangement.

"Scrolls" were coiled metal or plastic strips, covered with notches and pinholes. They were miniaturized versions of player piano rolls, explained one of the vendors. Scrolls held stored programs that managed the operations of many different machines—from electric power transformers to radios, elevators, and automobiles.

"Ghost keys" were virtual keyboards projected in space by rotating prism devices. The user wore reflective gloves to type in mid-air. They worked well, but took a little getting used to. Similar devices guided students' hands in automated music lessons.

Once, John needed to buy an oscilloscope to test the circuits of a radio he was building from a pile of parts. No one at the market knew what an "oscilloscope" was. Then he saw a vendor at one booth studying waveforms on a screen as he used small electrodes to probe a device. John innocently asked him what he was doing. "Making some final adjustments with my trusty old wave tracer," the man said. "It's outdated, but it still works for me." *Aha!* thought John, *a wave tracer is an oscilloscope.*

After a few weeks of wandering around the Mechanical Market, John came to a startling realization: Digital processing and storage of information were unknown in HD. Everything was analog and physical. These technologies had been refined and miniaturized to an amazing degree—the inner workings of a moviola looked like an expensive Swiss watch—but they were inherently limited. No scroll could ever match the speed and versatility of random access memory. Nor was there any concept of digital communication networks. HD had an excellent analog telephone system and sophisticated fax machines, but no websites or email.

That night, John's conversation with Leonora lasted almost until dawn. He sketched out the fundamentals of digital technology and the possibilities it opened up—the internet, online databases, search engines, e-commerce, and much more.

"Why didn't you tell me about this years ago?"

"We had computers in 1982, but networking was just getting started. Now, everything is digital and connected. It's moving at an unbelievable pace."

Leonora's head was spinning. She had never conceived of such a thing.

John listened to music as he worked in the basement. Bach, his favorite, often played on the classical music radio station. In his old life, John had also enjoyed jazz as a background for the delicate tasks of electronics repair. But jazz didn't exist in this new HD world. There was some interesting popular music that was a little like jazz, but to John, who had the sounds of Duke Ellington, Ella Fitzgerald, and John Coltrane etched in his heart, it wasn't the same. There was one single audiocassette of Duke Ellington in all of HD. John had given it to Leonora when she left SD for the last time in 1982, along with his Sony Walkman. John tried to play it every now and then, but it was distorted and unlistenable. The strong magnetic flux of the barrier that kept the two worlds apart had partially erased it when she crossed into HD.

By setting up this basement workshop, John recreated the familiar environment of his windowless repair room in the Duke of Discounts store. He had a long, cluttered workbench with tools, measurement instruments and half-assembled electronic devices. Bins with drawers holding parts and components were attached to a wall. With his mother's help, John had gotten the job at the Duke of Discounts soon after his discharge from the Army in the early 1960s. He worked alone in the back room of the store, repairing TVs, radios and stereos. It was a crappy job with no chance for advancement, but John accepted it as the best that he was likely to find. Lily's words, repeated endlessly throughout his childhood, had smothered his confidence. "Black men and big ideas—a surefire recipe for trouble!" He worked in that little repair room for more than twenty years.

Today, John was taking apart a television, or "moviola" as it was called in HD. It had neither an LED display nor a cathode ray tube, the common technologies in SD. Instead, there was a frosted glass screen and, behind it, an assembly of miniature prisms that rotated on a shaft. A second assembly of shutters opened and closed many times a second, selectively shining colored lights on the prisms, in response to the signal received, to create the image on the screen. To his repairman's eyes, the mechanism looked like a disaster waiting to happen, prone to frequent misalignments and breakdowns. But these devices were everywhere, so they must work reasonably well. John used a jeweler's screwdriver to take the prism assembly apart and examined the pieces with a microscope he had recently purchased. The precision of the tiny metal, ceramic, and glass components was impressive. The guy who sold him the moviola said "quality parts and high grade lubrication oils inside a sealed housing is the only way to go." The HD manufacturing workmanship was far better than anything he had ever seen. That's what made the overly complex device practical. Still, all the intricacy would be unnecessary if they only had the solid state electronics and integrated circuits John had worked with in SD in the 1980s. But no one in HD had heard of such things.

John began the most challenging task. Could he put the moviola back together again? With Bach's *Goldberg Variations* providing the soundtrack, he worked slowly and meticulously, placing components, tightening screws, and inserting wires. When he finished, he had used every one of the parts laid out on the workbench—always a good sign. He plugged it in and went through the calibration protocol the salesman had shown him. A game show appeared on the screen in full color.

John looked at his watch. It was late afternoon. Leonora was due home soon and she would probably be worn out. John and Leonora lived for their evenings together. While he started dinner, she played with the dogs to wash away the stress of the day. Then, their conversations usually lasted late into the night. Individually, they were both technical wizards. But when they began bouncing ideas of each other, magic could happen. When most evenings came to an end, they happily fell into bed filled with new insights and plans. John had lived a long life of solitude and disappointment; his relationship with Leonora was the most glorious, exhilarating thing he had ever experienced. He didn't need anyone else.

After dinner, Leonora leaned across the table and spoke in a hushed, conspiratorial tone, "I am about to describe an ultra-level secret project," Leonora said. "You can never tell anyone about this."

"Who am I going to tell?" John replied. "You're the only person I know in this entire world."

"I've explained how Amperic bricks generate electricity through thermal expansion and contraction. Hydraulic invented them in the 1940s and they have been our biggest product ever since. They're the world's leading source of power."

"Yes. I remember."

"We have learned that the bricks may eventually stop working. Their output appears to degrade over time, on a scale of decades. The buildings outfitted with Amperics in the first years now only generate about half as much electricity as they did originally. And the rate of decay may be accelerating as they age."

"What can be done about it?"

"That's the problem. You can't replace all the bricks on a huge building. Far too expensive. The company is doing everything it can to keep the problem out of public awareness. They have acknowledged that decay affects the earliest versions of the bricks and say that newer formulations provide steady power indefinitely. However, my team's internal research shows this is not true. Over the next ten or twenty years, large portions of our installed base around the world will begin to experience significant degradation."

"Have you found a solution?"

"Not yet. We're trying everything, no matter how far-fetched. Coatings, injections, high-frequency vibrations, you name it. The executives are terrified. If knowledge gets out that all of our bricks decay and we can't fix it, the company could be destroyed. The pressure is incredible. My team has been working on this full time for two years."

"Does anything look promising?"

"It's hard to tell. How do you run experiments on a phenomenon that may not show up for fifty years?"

John closed his eyes and pondered. Leonora let him think undisturbed. She had learned that his deep silences meant that something brilliant might come out. After a minute, he opened his eyes.

"With a mathematical model of long-term decay and the effects of different potential treatments, you should be able to simulate the electric efficiency of a brick over a period of fifty years or so. That could tell you which treatments were most likely to work."

"The decay process is extremely complex, John. Just running the calculations for a simulation like that could take years—we can't wait that long."

"You need a computer. My kind of computer."

DUMPSTER DIVING

"THANK YOU FOR MEETING WITH ME, Mr. Boustany." The young woman was sitting across from Billy at the City Diner, a few blocks from his new home in the Pelican building. Every time he went to this place, he thought of the magical night the year before when he danced to the music of Milo Riley at the street supper in HD. It happened right at this location on Grand Avenue.

"You said you're writing a book about my father?" Billy asked.

"Not exactly. I'm writing about the broader history of 1970s and 1980s television pitchmen. Every city had a figure like your father, each with his own story. They make a fascinating window into a changing America."

"What was your name again?"

"Lisa Moon."

"I'm happy to help you Lisa, if I can. Fire away."

"I've seen some of your father's commercials on YouTube and read local newspaper articles about him from those days. I was hoping you could tell me about what he was really like."

"He was a guy trying to build a business out of nothing."

"The commercials are hysterical. Do you have a favorite?"

"The wedding ad is the one people still talk about."

"Was he funny in person?"

"No. It was all an act. He was kind of a jerk, actually."

Lisa scribbled notes on a pad of paper.

"Hey, don't print that. Off the record. I had a difficult relationship with the old man. Recently, I've developed more respect for him."

"Why?"

"I learned about some of what he had to do to keep his business—and our family—going."

"What was that?"

"It's kind of private."

"OK. You took over the stores. Why?"

"Dad died suddenly. I had no choice."

"Then you shut the business down last year."

"Again, I had no choice. Amazon was killing us."

"I spoke to one of your long time employees, Dennis Healy. He knew your dad."

"Yeah."

"He told me you were very distracted during the last months before you closed the business."

'So what?"

"He said you disappeared for days at a time."

Billy got annoyed. "What does this have to do with your book about my father?"

Lisa stammered, "I'm, uhh, just trying to understand the full story...of your dad, the store, and his ads."

Billy stood up. He was pissed. "I don't know who the hell you are or what you want. My life is none of your business!" He stormed out of the diner.

Lisa was taken aback. *I guess I'm a better data analyst than I am a spy.*

"We don't have to be scared of everything just because we have a secret," Carol said.

Billy had told her about the disturbing 'interview' he had at the City Diner. "I didn't like where she was going. Something's not right."

"Maybe she was just being thorough in her research."

"Or she works for the Knights and was trying to get me to spill the beans, so they would have an excuse to grab us again."

Over the next week, Billy began to see—or imagine—more and more signs that he was being watched. Cars were parked on Shenandoah across from his building with people sitting in them. On the way home from the hardware store, the same car was behind him almost the whole way. Driving down Grand, at the corner of Gravois, he saw a woman taking a photo of the South Side National Bank building, the place where he had first learned to cross over to HD. With the traffic moving, he couldn't stop, but it sure looked like Lisa what's-her-name who had interviewed him.

If the Knights were watching him, that would really piss him off. Billy and his family had scrupulously followed the rule that Martin had laid out when he sent them all home from HD—no talking to anyone about HD, ever.

Carol worried that Billy was getting paranoid. But even she was a little unsettled by the coincidences. One morning, as she was making coffee in the partially-done second floor kitchen, she looked out the back window and saw a person rooting around in their trash can.

"Billy! There's another homeless guy out back." She shouted. Carol didn't enjoy the close proximity to poverty that was part of the bargain of living in this neighborhood. Billy shuffled out of the bedroom in his bathrobe. "I'll take care of it."

He went downstairs and opened the back door. "Hey, move along. This is private property." The person turned toward him. It was a woman. She looked familiar. Billy dashed up to her. "Goddammit! It's you again." Lisa McDaniel was startled. She started to back away, but Billy grabbed her arm. "I told you to leave me alone! You want to talk? Now we'll talk!" He pushed her towards the door.

Carol hurried down to the back door. She could see the fear in the young woman's eyes. "Billy, calm down."

"She's the one who tried to trick me with her bullshit story about writing a book."

"I'm sorry. I'll leave you alone. I won't come back," Lisa said. She was trembling.

"Did the Knights send you?" demanded Billy. He noticed that she had a device on a strap over her shoulder. She was holding something that looked like a microphone in one hand.

"Who?"

"The Knights. Are they going to kidnap us again?"

"I don't know what you're talking about."

Carol sensed it was time to calm things down. "Let's go inside and talk this over."

The three of them sat at the plywood sheet dining room table. Carol poured cups of coffee. Lisa looked like a mouse who had been trapped by a cat. Billy was steaming mad.

"What the hell do you want from us?" he asked. Lisa was silent. She took slow, deep breaths to avoid hyperventilating.

"What's your name?" Carol asked.

"Lisa McDaniel."

"That's not the name you gave me last week," Billy interjected. He pointed to the device hanging from her shoulder. "What's this?"

"A Geiger counter. For detecting radiation."

"You were looking for radiation? Here?"

"Yes," Lisa whispered. She was mortified that she had been caught. "I'm really sorry. I won't bother you ever again."

"Is that what Giles Monroe is into these days? Radiation? Or maybe you work for Martin Matsui. Nice guy, but he might be double crossing us."

Carol took stock of the situation. Billy's paranoia had been right. They were being watched. But something didn't add up. Lisa looked genuinely terrified.

"Lisa, we're not going to hurt you. We're not going to call the police. But we need to know why you're here. It's important."

Billy took Carol's cue and spoke more softly. "It's OK to talk about the Knights. We know."

"Who do you work for?" Carol asked.

"Federal government. National Nuclear Security Agency."

"Nuclear security? Are you kidding?"

"We noticed some events around here that happened last summer. It appeared that you might be involved."

"What events?"

"Short bursts of weak radiation."

"So the government is watching us?" Billy asked. This was quickly becoming worse than he and Carol had imagined.

"No. Just me. My superiors told me to stop—that it was a waste of resources. But I wanted to see if I could figure out what had happened. I'm really, really sorry. I should have let it go."

Lisa took a deep breath, then began to explain the situation about the radiation blips that had happened in this area and their odd timing. For some reason, she trusted these people—at least a little bit. She was careful not to mention NUCLEOSAT 2, which was top secret, or the sifting of telecom records that had led to Billy's phone number. She didn't want to get herself in any more trouble than she already was.

Billy and Carol listened intently. They glanced at each other from time to time, but didn't say anything. They both began to think that this young woman was telling the truth and was probably not a threat.

Lisa finished her story. "Thanks for listening. I'm not here to cause any problems. I only want to understand what caused the radiation bursts. Can you help me at all?"

"You're right. Some pretty crazy stuff happened last summer," Billy said. "But we didn't notice anything to do with radiation."

"None of it is any threat to the government, or national security, or anything like that," Carol said. "No laws were broken. No harm was done."

"You mentioned someone called the Knights. Who are they?"

"We can't go into that. Just like you can't tell us everything you know," Billy said.

"Are you going to report us to the government?" Carol asked.

"No! I'm not even supposed to be here. I'm just a number cruncher who got curious."

The tension dropped. Carol offered Lisa breakfast. In between apologies, Lisa told them more about her work, though without divulging anything classified. "I basically sit at a computer all day, looking at data and developing models and algorithms to make sense of it. You might think it sounds pretty dull, but it's satisfying to me, like doing a giant puzzle."

Later, Billy asked Lisa how to reach her. "Carol and I need time to digest what you said. I don't know if we can help you or not." Lisa gave him a P.O. box number in Maryland. "It's safer than using the phone."

"Do we need to be safe?"

"It can't hurt. I go to the box regularly."

Billy had one final question, "Is the radiation dangerous?

"Probably not. It was weak and didn't appear to contain heavy elements. Just nitrogen and oxygen. Basically irradiated air."

They shook hands and Lisa left. Billy and Carol cleared the breakfast dishes from the table.

"I think she's harmless," Billy said. "But somebody noticed what we were doing."

"Does this mean the cat's out of the bag?"

"Maybe."

ON THE ROAD

MEREDITH AND DIYAMI PREPARED for their first trip to speak to Indian communities about Cahokia. Diyami wanted to start by visiting the tribes in Oklahoma believed to be descended from the people of Cahokia and the Mississippian culture: Omaha, Osage, Ponca, Kaw, and Quapaw.

For three days, Diyami hunched over his laptop from early in the morning until late at night. Meredith had shown him how to use PowerPoint and he quickly got the hang of creating slides with pictures and text. He tuned out every distraction. He didn't hear when Billy asked him a question. Carol had to tap him on the shoulder to get him to join them for dinner. Diyami wanted his presentation to be absolutely perfect. In graduate school, he had learned to approach civil engineering projects by working methodically from problem to cause to solution. Convincing people to move to Cahokia to build a new Native American city shouldn't be so different from designing the locks, dams, and pumps of a canal.

Every time Meredith asked him how the presentation was going, he put her off. "Let me get it right first, then I'll show it to you." Finally, on the third night, he was finished. "You're going to love it," he said with a big grin. He showed her the title slide, *Cahokia: An Ancient City. Can it Live Again?*" She nodded, "Not bad." He advanced through several slides about the origin and early history of Cahokia. Each one had two or three small pictures and large blocks of tiny text.

"Don't put all those words on the screen. Nobody will read them."

"I have a lot to say."

"Focus on what's important."

"It's all important."

She became frustrated as he went through more slides.

"How many slides are there?"

"Ninety-seven."

"That's way too long! It will take two hours, minimum. You'll lose people long before the end."

Diyami's enthusiasm evaporated. He had worked so hard and she hated it. Meredith saw his disappointment. She took a deep breath and they started to cut the presentation down together. "The first rule of PowerPoint is to have as few words on the screen as possible. Let's make your paragraphs into bullet points."

"What's a bullet point?"

Diyami's engineer mind resisted every edit, but Meredith persevered. After a few hours, they had the presentation down to fifty slides. It was a lot better and they both realized they needed each other if this quest was ever going to succeed.

Billy and Carol waved goodbye as Diyami and Meredith drove off in the pickup truck. "What do you think is going to happen?" Carol asked.

"They're going to eat him alive out there. He doesn't have a clue how to sell his idea. He has stars in his eyes."

"I hope it doesn't crush his spirit."

"It's the only way to learn. He'll figure it out."

"Meredith is as gung ho as he is. It could be rough on her, too."

"She wanted an adventure. She's going to get one."

Meredith checked the cable from the laptop, clicked on the presentation, and focused the projector. The title slide appeared. Diyami paced back and forth as he reviewed his notes. It was time for the meeting to start, but only four people sat in the folding chairs of the meeting room. A middle-aged woman said, "Please wait a few more minutes. The birthday party down the hall is just finishing up." After ten more minutes, there were now seven people in the audience. A few were eating cake off paper plates. The woman nodded to Diyami that it was okay for him to begin.

He introduced himself and his "colleague" Meredith. He opened with a question, "What do you know about Cahokia?"

"It was a long time ago." "They built big mounds." "I visited there once. Excellent museum."

Diyami was pleased that there was at least some awareness of Cahokia.

"I have lived near Cahokia for many years. I know it like the back of my hand. It is far more important than most people think." He reviewed the history of Cahokia's settlement, from about 800 CE to about 1350 or 1400. The most significant period was between 1050 and 1250, the "peak of Cahokian civilization," when it was larger than London or Paris were at the same time. While Diyami spoke, Meredith advanced the slides as they had rehearsed.

"The main pyramid at Cahokia, which we call Monk's Mound, was the largest pyramid north of Mexico and the third largest in all of the Western Hemisphere. We know that Cahokia's cultural and religious influence stretched from Wisconsin to Louisiana."

"Around 1050, the city as we know it was built very quickly on top of an earlier, smaller city. We don't know why this happened. Some call it the Big Bang. What we do know is that Chinese astrologers saw a supernova, the explosion of a dying star, in the sky in 1054. It created a bright star that was visible day and night for almost a month. Was this heavenly sign the inspiration for the major construction at Cahokia? Maybe or maybe not, but it shows how quickly a city can be built."

Diyami ended his talk with the question that he and Meredith had worked out, "Wouldn't it be wonderful if we had a city like Cahokia again? I think it can be done." The last slide filled the screen with the question.

The room lights came on and people began to leave. A few came up to thank Diyami for his presentation. "Very educational." "It's important to know more about our history." The man who had visited Cahokia was eager to talk about his trip there. "I also went to the St. Louis Arch. The view from the top is spectacular." He was the only one who wrote his email address on Meredith's sheet. As they packed up the equipment, Meredith could see that Diyami was disappointed. "We got the first one under our belts," she said cheerfully. "They'll get better as we go."

But they didn't. Two weeks of traveling and speaking to small groups across Oklahoma yielded little response. Most of the talks ended with fewer people in the room at the end than were there at the beginning. Some stayed out of courtesy, others out of pity for this awkward, earnest young man. Then they shuffled out of the room without making conversation or eye contact. Diyami and Meredith collected a few email addresses on their clipboard, but their follow-up emails were mostly met with silence.

They were learning the many faces of rejection.

When people aren't interested in a pitch, there are a hundred ways to say "no," without ever uttering the word. They look out the window, check their phone, remember another appointment they have to get to, make a joke that isn't funny, or say something encouraging, then never again respond to messages or calls.

Diyami began to wonder what if he failed to attract even a single migrant to Cahokia? After these first meetings and presentations, this seemed like a distinct possibility. A few of the people in his talks made critical remarks, but most seemed bored or confused. He appreciated it when someone told him his plan was the stupidest thing they had ever heard. That was better than no reaction at all, or slipping out of the room before he finished. Did they see him as a fool? Or just another con man? One of the long parade of whites and Indians over the centuries who spun sweet fantasies to hide schemes to trick them out of their lands and money?

One young man, after hearing Diyami's pitch, "Nice idea, but aren't you a few hundred years too late for something like this?"

Another, "The whites pushed us out of every place they wanted. Why would they let us go back to Cahokia?"

To most, the pitch sounded implausible. "You want me to move to somewhere I've barely heard of, where no Indians live, to build an 'Indian city?' I don't think so. Piss off the white people who don't want us there? Not likely. I'm trying to make a buck, get my kids a decent education, and enjoy life. And you're asking me to give up everything I have for your pie in the sky dream?"

Diyami longed to tell them the real story of where he came from and how glorious New Cahokia was. But then they would certainly see him as a crazy person.

When he spoke in an Osage community, Diyami was hindered by the fact that no one knew who he was. He said he was an Osage, and he could speak the language (fairly well, actually), but he wasn't on the list of enrolled Osage Nation members. He and Meredith had made up a plausible-sounding cover story that his grandfather left Oklahoma, moved to Europe, and didn't bother to keep up with the tribe. People sensed that something was off. Native Americans had learned the hard way not to trust anyone until they earned that trust.

The white girlfriend added to their suspicion. Was she just another New Age idealist with a romantic idea of Indians? These people, with all their earnest, misguided ideas, were usually a waste of time.

As the days of rejection wore on, Diyami longed to be back in HD, a place where life made sense, where Natives had carved out a space of real dignity and showed that they could play the whites' game and win, without abandoning their souls. Why couldn't anyone over here see that? Was coming to SD for this lonely mission the stupidest thing he had ever done?

During drives across the prairie from one reservation or urban low income neighborhood to another, Diyami had his first encounters with the poverty of many of the Native communities. He had led a comfortable, privileged life, so he had no experience with the crushing despair of people who have little education or opportunity. Some were only one small step away from being just another lost soul at the bottom of the American ladder. Their Indian heritage kept them afloat—but just barely. White people no longer saw them as antagonists, but simply ignored them—out of sight, out of mind.

As she drove, Meredith said, "These people didn't grow up like you. Their parents aren't college professors with PhDs. They've never lived in a world where Indians have built something to be proud of. Their past was taken away and their future looks pretty bleak. You have to find a way to meet them where they are."

Meredith cringed from the back of the room as Diyami gave another of his awkward talks. She noticed every person who stared at their phone, whispered with a friend, or sneaked away as Diyami droned on. It hurt her to see him flailing up there. It brought back the memory of an open mike comedy night she had attended at college. Inept, would-be comedians bombed while half-drunk students heckled and laughed at them. Even her friends thought it was hilarious to make fun of kids they would walk past on campus the next day. She could see the embarrassment of the comedians as they scurried off the stage in shame. Meredith was ashamed of herself because she had joined in the sarcasm and mockery, following the lead of her friends. She learned something that she didn't usually pay much attention to—people can be really mean.

This was a hundred times worse. It was Diyami up there. He was so sincere and trying to do something important. Meredith was angry at the audience for tuning him out, but also at him. Couldn't he find a way to break through? Diyami was methodical. He wasn't very good at reading the room and adjusting on the fly. He ploughed ahead and stuck with his plan, even when it wasn't working.

Later, as she and Diyami packed up the laptop and projector, she could see the discouragement in his eyes.

"How do you think it went?" he asked.

"I saw heads nodding, so they were listening."

"I couldn't see them very well because of the light from the projector."

Meredith searched for something positive to say. "I thought the question about where the Cahokians went was good. And your answer was perfect."

"Thanks," said Diyami.

They walked out to the pickup. Diyami looked across the huge parking lot of the casino and up into the cloudless sky. This was the eighth or ninth talk they had given and it hadn't gone any better than the ones before. A handful of people, a couple of desultory questions, a few email addresses collected on the clipboard. Nothing like the stories of Morning Star and Corn Mother he had learned in school and from his parents. What was he doing wrong? Was he the right person for this? Why had the spirits pointed him in this direction, only to abandon him?

Meredith put her hand on his shoulder. He turned toward her. He had the most mournful expression she had ever seen. "This is a disaster. I wish I had never come," he said.

Meredith was furious. "You want to quit? No way!"

"You're not alone in a strange world."

"Alone? What about me?"

That evening they were supposed to speak to a Kaw Nation group at the Southwind Casino in Newkirk, Oklahoma. When they arrived, the front desk clerk pointed them to a multipurpose room. As they set up their equipment, Diyami sank into a depression. He couldn't face going through this one more time. The audience filed in, about a dozen people, mostly middle-aged women. Diyami whispered to Meredith, "I can't."

"We have to. They have come to hear you."

"Please tell them it's canceled."

"We have come this far. I'm not going to let you give up."

Diyami just shook his head. Meredith was both exasperated and worried by Diyami's bleak mood. If he was abandoning his dream, what the hell was she supposed to do? But the time had come. The audience was getting restless. Diyami was slumped in his chair next to the computer. He stared at the floor. Meredith picked up the remote control and turned on the title slide, *Cahokia: An Ancient City. Can It Live Again?*

"Good afternoon. Mr. Red Hawk was supposed to speak to you today, but he is feeling under the weather. My name is Meredith Boustany. We don't want to disappoint you, so I will do my best to fill in for him." Meredith had no idea what to say next. She looked at the faces of the audience. Most were blank and polite, revealing nothing. One older woman in the back row looked directly at Meredith. Her faced beamed with a broad smile and gentle, welcoming eyes. She reminded Meredith of her grandmother, who had died when she was four. Meredith felt surrounded by a warm glow of pure love. The words began to pour out:

"Nine hundred years ago, there was a great city just a few hours' drive from where we are today. It was larger than London or Paris. It was beautiful. People came from hundreds of miles around to trade, to dance, and to worship. Your ancestors built it. My ancestors didn't know a thing about it. Mr. Red Hawk—Diyami—believes we need Cahokia again. For your children, for your grandchildren, for the Native people all across this country. Cahokia—a new Cahokia—can be a blessing for this entire land."

She went on. She flipped through Diyami's slides, but she said a lot less about the old Cahokia and a lot more about what a dream can do. About how it might be time for Native peoples to, once again, build the most beautiful city in the world. "There's nothing to stop us but ourselves."

Diyami watched, mesmerized. *Where is this coming from?* Meredith kept on spinning silken words that filled the room like strings of sparkling lights. When the last slide came up, she said, "I want to leave you with a saying about Cahokia that Diyami taught me, 'As Before, So Once More.'"

The room buzzed with excited murmurs. Hands shot up. Almost everyone had a question. Meredith did her best to answer. After a few minutes, it was time to leave. Another meeting was scheduled for the room. The people crowded around Meredith and Diyami. Diyami accepted handshakes, but stayed quiet. Meredith held the spotlight. Women hugged her, one after another. Meredith looked for the woman from the back row. But she wasn't there.

After Meredith's success, Diyami sank even further into doubt and despair. She made connecting look so easy—why couldn't he do that? He was letting down his parents, the spirits, and all of Cahokia. At least, his parents didn't know how badly he was failing. The whole project of enlisting members of various tribes to come to Illinois to build a new Native American city seemed to be dying of its own weight. What made him, a person who knew nothing about the Indians in this world, think he could pull this off?

On the drive back to St. Louis, Diyami was silent for hours. He stared out the window at the mile markers shooting by.

Meredith held back tears as they sped through the night on I-44, east of Springfield. The grand mission had turned into a bitter joke. She tried to engage him.

"Diyami, this is so not working. We only get one chance with these groups. If you bore them to death, they'll never let us come back."

"You don't understand Native people," he said.

"I understand people. I can see when you're losing them."

"I'm teaching them. That takes time."

"Don't 'teach' them, sell them. Get them excited about Cahokia."

Diyami didn't say anything.

"We've got to try something different, Diyami."

"What?"

"I don't know. Whatever it is that Indians do when they need a kick in the butt."

Diyami looked out the window into the darkness.

"How about letting my dad talk to you? He's been selling his whole life, and his dad before him."

"I don't want to do that."

"Not a choice. We're doing it."

They sat around the plywood table in the Pelican apartment—Billy, Carol, Meredith, and Diyami, who felt like he was the dunce in a remedial class. Billy saw that Diyami didn't want to be there, so he tried to ease him gently into the conversation.

"Selling is all about solving the customer's problem. You've got an incredible product, but your customers don't know they need it. What problem can Cahokia solve for them?"

"Native people knowing their history and coming together."

"Do they want to know their history?"

"Doesn't everybody?"

"Not necessarily. You've got to figure out what's bothering them. What's stopping them from having a better life?"

"How do I figure that out?"

"You listen. People don't like to be sold a product, but they love talking about themselves. You need to find their FUD—F-U-D, fear, uncertainty, and doubt. What is the FUD in their lives?"

"So I go out to talk about Cahokia and then don't talk about Cahokia?"

"Exactly. The more you let the customer talk, the more you will sell."

Diyami stood up. He was upset. "I'm sure this works fine for selling televisions and computers, but it's not me! It's not Cahokia!" He stormed out of the room and down the stairs. They heard the front door slam. Meredith looked panicked. She started to run after him. Billy stopped her. "Let me handle this."

Billy caught up with Diyami on the sidewalk. Diyami was agitated. Billy didn't say a word.

"I want to go home, Mr. Boustany."

"I bet you do."

"Meredith must be so angry with me."

"I know what that's like."

"I never should have come over here. I'm no salesman. I can't be like you."

"I wasn't a salesman either. All I knew about selling was what my father did. And I hated that."

"So what did you do?"

"I stumbled and failed. I ended up face down in the mud. The only options left were the bad ones, the stupid ones, and the ones I was scared of. So I tried them all."

Diyami began to calm down. After a little while, he said, "What if I don't have any options?"

"Sometimes, you just have to jump in the river and see where it takes you."

In that moment, it came to Diyami—the river.

Billy and Carol were cleaning up the kitchen after Diyami and Meredith left. His mood had brightened and Meredith was relieved, but a bit confused by Diyami's new plan.

"What did you say to him?" Carol asked.

"Nothing in particular. I just let him know I understood how he felt."

She gave him a hug. "Billy Boustany, there's hope for you yet."

THE RIVER

MEREDITH AND DIYAMI UNTIED THE ROPES and bungee cords, wrestled the canoe off the top of the camper shell, and set it on the sloping stone levee below the Arch. They had borrowed it from her aunt Anita, who hadn't used it for years. Meredith had invented a story about being invited on a Current River float trip with some friends.

"Are you sure about this?" she asked Diyami as they loaded the canoe with gear. "No one floats the Mississippi. It's way too dangerous."

"I'll be fine. Meet me in Cairo in four days."

"You don't have enough food."

"I'm fasting. That's how it's done."

They embraced. Meredith didn't want to let him out of her arms, but she knew Diyami's mind was made up. He pushed off from the levee and waved back to her. He hadn't been in a canoe for a few years and never on the Mississippi. The canoe wobbled as he caught the current. He paddled with swift strokes to avoid the line of barges moored below the Poplar Street Bridge. The vision quest had begun.

All afternoon he dodged giant tows that were everywhere in the St. Louis part of the river. Each one consisted of a diesel-powered towboat pushing a formation of steel barges lashed together, as many as seven wide by five long. These several-hundred foot long behemoths churned up and down the channel relentlessly. Even if the towboat pilot saw Diyami, there was no way he could maneuver around a tiny canoe. Diyami found himself being drawn by the current into the path of a massive tow coming towards him from behind. The pilot sounded a screeching horn. Diyami paddled furiously to avoid being sucked under the front end of a barge. Then, as the tow passed, it threw off six-foot high waves that threatened to swamp him. Water sloshed over the side as the canoe bucked up and down. After that, he hugged the riverbank through the industrial landscape that stretched for twenty miles below the Arch. Abandoned factories, rusty cranes, and huge storage tanks tagged with graffiti.

By late afternoon, Diyami passed under the Jefferson Barracks bridge. He got too close to the current that swirled past one leg of the bridge. He almost hit the pile of driftwood logs clumped up against the concrete pylon. His canoe was spun around and he careened down the river backward until he was able to orient it again.

He entered a more natural landscape, with sandy banks, sycamores, and willows. The skeletons of human structures began to fade away and no tows were nearby. For the first time, Diyami relaxed and admired the shoreline sliding by. He coasted with his paddle on his knees. He closed his eyes and felt the smooth, silent motion of the river beneath him. He absorbed its deep, inexorable power and felt a kinship with the ancient Cahokian traders who traveled the Mississippi in canoes laden with ceremonial items of copper, shell, and clay as they spread the stories of Morning Star, Corn Mother, and the Hero Twins across the continent. A ray of sun slipped through the clouds to sparkle the waters ahead of him. Surely, he would find a vision to guide him out of the hole he was in.

As the sun got low, he found a place on the Illinois side to pull ashore and camp. He hauled the canoe out of the water and tied it to a tree trunk that stuck out of the mud. He set up his tent, which was also borrowed from Meredith's aunt. His engineer's mind effortlessly solved the tangle of rods, stakes, and elastic cords. *If only convincing people to build a city were this easy,* he thought as he gathered firewood.

He built a fire and gazed out over the river. Orange and lavender shades of dusk were reflected in the smooth water sliding downstream, like sheets of stained glass. On the far bank, the lights of a massive power plant formed a castle in the evening haze. Diyami could hear its roar and clank and see the smoke, tinted by the sunset, rising from its two-hundred foot tall stacks. Coal scraped from the earth arrived on mile-long, snaking trains to be devoured by this ever-hungry beast. A spider web of steel towers and wires fed its power to the lights of St. Louis in the distance. Diyami was both fascinated and repelled as he contemplated the spectacle. *How did people allow this to defile the sacred river?* In HD, centralized electrical generation facilities existed only in history books. The Amperic brick revolution had made them obsolete by enabling every building and home to produce its own power, with surpluses to manufacture fuel for transportation.

He boiled water for tea, but made no dinner because he was fasting to ready himself for the vision he sought. He had foolishly thought he could fulfill his mission all on his own. He had rushed out to talk to Indians about Cahokia before he was ready and had failed miserably. Now he had to open his heart and beg the Great Mystery for guidance. That is what his mother had done back in his beautiful Cahokia. Would the spirits listen to him, a stranger alone in this strange land?

In the last few months, Diyami had drained his own abilities dry. He didn't know what to do next. Meredith had found a way to inspire an audience, but he couldn't. Had the spirits helped her and abandoned him? Why? As Diyami sipped his tea, he wondered what the vision would feel like. Would it descend from the sky in radiant glory? Would euphoria bubble up from inside? Would it sneak up on him?

The first time he felt the spirits calling him, on his visit to Cahokia in SD the previous year, he had distinctly heard the whispering from beneath the ground. He couldn't make out the words, but he had absolute clarity about what they meant, *build a city to free the people from this darkness.* He hadn't expected those voices and wasn't prepared to receive them. But they came nonetheless. A vision, by definition, must be something surprising, not what you could figure out on your own. How do you prepare for a surprise?

Maybe preparation had nothing to do with it. Whether the spirits spoke to you or not was up to them, not to you. He had been taught as a child about the importance of a vision quest, which was a requirement for every senior in his high school. But, like most of his friends, he didn't take it seriously. He spent a couple of nights alone in the woods thinking about ice cream and girls. Now he was trying again for a vision, out here on the river. Was he doing it right? He wished his mother were here to point him on the correct path.

As the colors faded in the western sky, Diyami heard a humming. The sound came from every direction. Could this be the first hint of his vision? He felt a pinprick on his neck, then another on his arm. He slapped his arm, then brushed his face. Mosquitoes! He retreated into the tent and zipped it up tight. The humming grew louder. He spread his sleeping bag on the foam pad he had brought. The darkness deepened and he fell asleep.

Diyami awoke in the night to flashes of lightning and claps of thunder. Rain and wind pummeled the tent. He went outside to bring in the rest of his gear, flip the canoe over, and make sure it was far enough from the water. Back inside the tent, he slept a deep, dreamless sleep.

The next morning, Diyami felt refreshed, though his shoulders ached from the first day's hard paddling. The morning was clear and bright. The power plant still roared on the opposite bank. Brown water moved swiftly past his campsite. The river had risen more than a foot. He packed the canoe and headed out. Branches, logs, and even entire trees were being swept downstream in the current. He had to maneuver carefully to avoid them. A tiny branch poking out of the water could mean a submerged tree trunk hidden inches below the surface.

Diyami focused his full attention on keeping the canoe away from snags. Thoughts about the nature of visions vanished. All he wanted was to avoid capsizing. He worked his way out to the center of the channel where he had more room to maneuver and there were fewer obstructions. Rising waters didn't stop the towboat traffic, but now Diyami was more confident in his ability to stay out of their way. By late morning, he could paddle comfortably and relax enough to enjoy the beauty unfolding around him. Flocks of ducks flew in V-formations. Eagles soared and circled. Great blue herons flapped their long wings as they left one tree to perch in another. Diyami felt he was seeing the world of his ancestors once again—except, of course, for the tows of barges pushing up and down the river with brute diesel force, and the occasional speedboat.

With the strong current, he made about seventy miles that day and was satisfied when he landed for the night on a sandy beach below a low bluff on the western bank. He pitched camp in a grassy meadow and built a fire. He held to his fast and only brewed tea. A steady breeze from the north kept the mosquitoes away.

A long tow of barges chugged slowly past, pushing upstream. The lights on the towboat twinkled merrily. Diyami heard faint wisps of country music and imagined the crew members playing cards. He felt lonelier than ever before. He wished Meredith were with him to share the sights of this day. He vowed to bring her here soon. They would cook a big meal over the fire—it wouldn't be a vision quest—and laugh and talk until they fell into their sleeping bags.

Night fell and thousands of stars came out. The Milky Way, which the Cahokians called the Path of Souls, stretched from one horizon to the other. Diyami saw a meteor streak through it, a fresh soul on its journey to the World Above. This was the perfect moment for a vision. He smiled, tended to the fire, and waited patiently. But nothing happened. Sometime after midnight, he realized he had been dozing off, so he crawled inside the tent and went to sleep.

The air was still the next morning. Diyami's hunger cut deeply. Meredith had insisted he bring along a few granola bars, just in case, and he wanted one more than anything. But he hadn't uprooted his whole life and come to a new world, only to give up now. He studied his map to see what the river had in store for him today. He was on schedule to make Cairo tomorrow and rendezvous with Meredith as planned. Not much time left for a vision. *Come on, spirits!* The map showed that the river split into two channels about thirty miles downstream, separated by a long string of islands. He would take the narrow channel on the left, where the tows didn't travel.

The current slowed as he entered the channel that afternoon. It was almost a backwater, but the map assured Diyami that it wasn't a dead end and would rejoin the main river several miles downstream. Wildlife abounded. Turtles sunning on logs plopped into the water as Diyami passed. Dragonflies hovered over irises and meadow grass on the bank. A lone hawk perched high in a tree. Diyami spotted a few deer watching him from the woods on the east bank. They brought back memories of the managed deer parks that surrounded his Cahokia and provided the venison that was a trademark of the city's cuisine. He could almost taste the juicy grilled steaks from his favorite café.

The sky grew overcast. Mist floated above the water ahead of the canoe. Before long, he was drifting through a thick fog. The trees on either side of the channel were no more than faint gray silhouettes. He picked his way gingerly and made slow progress forward. Frogs chirped in the shallows. The canoe got hung up on a tree trunk hidden beneath the surface. Diyami had to push on the log with his paddle to get over it. He couldn't see any more than twenty feet in any direction and couldn't tell what was in front of him. It was time to stop.

He pulled the canoe onto a muddy beach on the island. An open space in a grove of sycamores looked just right for a campsite. He secured the canoe, pitched his tent, and gathered a large pile of firewood. He was determined to sit in quiet contemplation all night, if that is what it took for a vision to come.

He had gotten to the point in his fast where he didn't feel hunger. A little loopy and weak, but otherwise just fine. He lit the fire, sat back, and savored a sip of water from his canteen. Owls hooted in the trees as the fire blazed. He ruminated, once again, over his troubles of the past months. Where had he gone wrong? He had expected that the whites of St. Louis and Collinsville would be against the new Cahokia. They would resent the influx of Native Americans, the state would not want to give up the park, and zoning disputes would come up. Billy and Carol had taught him a new word, "NIMBYism" (for Not In My Back Yard), to describe the opposition that would surely arise. But he hadn't gotten far enough for any of that to matter. The project was dying because of something Diyami had never expected—the indifference of Indians to the idea of Cahokia. How many meetings had he been to? How many miles driving to faraway reservations? What did he have to show for it? To use one of Meredith's expressions, it was a "nothing burger." This failure baffled and depressed him. He wanted to weep.

The fire settled into a glowing pile of logs and coals, red and orange with licks of flame popping up. Soft pulsing heat in the layers of coals reminded him of a city, bustling with people and life. The Cahokia he dreamed of was down there in the embers. As he gazed into the fire, his depression drifted up with the smoke and he felt at peace. Finally.

A loud crash erupted in the darkness off to the right. Something large was pushing through the underbrush. A man emerged into the circle of fire light. "What the hell are you doing on MY island?"

Diyami stood up. "I'm sorry, sir. I'm just camping here for the night."

"I don't remember you asking permission to camp."

"It didn't look like the island belonged to anyone."

"Uh-huh," said the man in a harsh, gravelly voice. He was big and broad, with a shapeless, floppy hat and a dirty, ragged coat that hung loosely from his shoulders. He was holding a large cloth sack. "What does it look like now?" he bellowed.

"I don't know. An island." Diyami was irritated by this obnoxious visitor.

"Wrong. MY island!"

The island man paced around the fire, peering at Diyami's tent and gear. He lifted the flap of the tent with a long walking stick.

"I'm hungry. What's for dinner?"

"I wasn't making dinner. I'm fasting tonight."

The island man stared at him. He tilted his head and pursed his lips as he tried to make sense of Diyami's words.

"Well, I'm hungry. What's for MY dinner?"

"I don't know."

"You intrude on my island, you don't offer me anything to eat, and you answer my questions with "I don't know." So you're both rude and ignorant."

"I'm sorry. I don't want to offend you. But I didn't bring food."

The island man began to rummage through Diyami's duffle bag. Diyami opened his mouth to protest, then realized it was useless. He just wanted this loudmouth jerk to leave, so he could regain the serenity of the evening. The island man pulled more and more out of the bag, inspecting each item to see if it was edible, before dropping it on the ground. He held up a plastic grocery bag in triumph.

"Aha!" He took out two cans of Dinty Moore Beef Stew. "Just enough for me. Maybe now you can learn how to treat a guest properly." He tossed Diyami a piece of paper from the bag. "A note from your mother." Diyami unfolded it. *For emergencies. Stay safe. Love, Meredith.*

The island man placed the cans in the coals to heat up. "Fasting is for fools. A warrior needs strength. On the other hand, a fool can learn something now and then. So, what are you, a warrior or a fool?"

Diyami said nothing. *What kind of question was that?*

"Just as I thought," said the island man, "you're neither. That makes you useless."

Diyami found a metal plate, spoon, and can opener in the bag. He turned the cans so they would heat evenly. The island man watched with piercing dark eyes.

"The *wasichus* come to this island to get drunk, shoot their guns, and scare the animals. They make very poor company. I hope you're better."

Diyami opened the cans and poured the stew onto the plate. The island man took it and began to shovel stew into his mouth. He slobbered as he ate and bits of food dribbled onto his filthy coat. Diyami got his first good look at him. He had long, greasy black hair, his face was blotchy, his lips were red and thick, and his teeth discolored. A few were missing.

"I'm thirsty!" announced the island man. Diyami handed him his canteen and watched him take a sloppy swig. He tried to make conversation.

"Do you live on this island?"

"I come and I go."

"Do you have a boat?"

"Don't need a boat."

"Do you swim across the river?"

"Do you ever stop asking questions?"

The island man licked the last bits of beef stew off his plate and let out a loud belch. "Why again are you here?"

Diyami decided he might as well tell the truth to this guy. Maybe then he would leave. "I'm looking for a vision."

The island man laughed so hard that tears welled up in his eyes. "Why do you, of all people, deserve a vision?"

Diyami started to speak, but the island man held up his hand to stop him. "I know. 'The spirits sent me on a mission, but I'm failing.' Been there, done that. Why should anyone care about your failures?"

"I don't want to dishonor my family."

"You left them. They have no idea whether you're failing or not."

How does this guy know that? Diyami got angry. He stood over the seated man. "Leave me alone! I didn't ask for your advice."

The island man jumped up. He loomed over Diyami (who was himself six-foot-three). He glowered at Diyami, their faces inches apart. "Yes. You. DID!"

Diyami was astounded. He sat back down by the fire. He was shaking. The island man sat down and reached for his sack. "Some people can't see a vision until it smacks them in the face." He took a long pipe, carved from red stone, out of the sack. "Let's have a smoke." He filled it with tobacco and lit it with a stick from the fire. He took a slow puff, then handed the pipe to Diyami. "Sometimes the spirits really piss me off. First, they give you a job, then they don't tell you how to do it."

Diyami quietly accepted the pipe and smoked. He didn't know what to say.

The island man spoke in a softer tone. "Your heart is pure and you are clever. But can you be both a warrior, who fights, and a fool, who listens with an empty mind? So, one more time, why do you deserve a vision?"

"Because the people are lost and suffering."

The island man nodded approval. "The words of a warrior are few and well chosen. They reach into the hearts of the people. Smoke is the Great Spirit's breath. With a pipe in our hands, we cannot but speak the truth."

They smoked and talked for quite a while. The island man told many stories.

"One spring day, a young man went hunting with his friends. The winter had been long and their people were hungry. They walked for hours through melting snow, but found no game. The young man spotted a buck with broad antlers in the distance. He chased it, but could not get close enough to launch an arrow. The buck ran further and further into the forest. After a while, the young man was lost. He did not see or hear his companions. He did not call to them, lest he scare the buck away. He was alone in the dark forest when night fell. As the moon rose, he saw he was in a clearing, with the river on one side and a curve of smooth hills surrounding him on the other. Hungry and exhausted, he sat on the ground. The hills spoke to him: 'Long ago, people lived in this great city. They knew the power of this place and they were fed. Because you persevered, we will teach you our power.' The young man stood up and saw the buck in the clearing. He gave the proper thanks, then shot an arrow that killed it. In the morning, he carried the buck back to his village. People rejoiced. He had returned and they could eat."

"Another time, the people were surrounded by birds wherever they went. The birds chirped sweetly all the time and, before long, the people were bewitched. They searched for birds everywhere so they could listen to the chirping. Husbands, wives, children all stopped speaking to each other. They cared only for the chirping. They forgot to eat and were starving. A wise woman brought the people food, but they did not see her. She had to learn the songs of birds to talk to them."

"A different young man sat down by the great river. 'You are so slow,' he said to the river. 'You wander back and forth.' 'What's the hurry?' said the river. 'Watching you makes me dizzy,' the man said. 'I will help you.' The man dug a trench, long and straight. 'Go this way,' he said. 'I don't want to,' said the river. 'You must,' said the man and he pushed the river into the trench. The calm river grew angry. It churned and frothed and dragged trees and villages into the trench. The man howled in terror. The river leapt out of the trench and back into its old channel. It became calm and smooth again. 'My way is to yield to every rock and branch,' said the river. 'I do not care about twists and turns. I will get to the sea in due time. You should follow this path.'"

After midnight, the island man opened a different pouch of tobacco. He brushed his hair out of his eyes as he filled the pipe. Diyami noticed his ear for the first time. A little face was growing out of it with eyes darting and tongue wagging. Before Diyami could make sense of this bizarre sight, the island man offered him the pipe. This smoke was stronger and with one puff Diyami felt woozy. He saw the little face staring at him before he fell asleep.

The island man took a bundle out of his sack and placed it on a stone near the fire. It was wrapped in soft leather and bound with colored rope. He slid the pipe into the bundle, then stood up and began to sing. He raised his arms and danced slowly around the fire. His shadow rippled across the sycamores. The ragged sleeves of his coat made his outstretched arms look like wings. After three times around the fire, he bent down to whisper in the ear of the sleeping Diyami, "First be a warrior, then a fool."

He picked up his sack and walking stick. He poked the stick into the red coals, sending a spray of sparks and embers into the air. When they burned out, the island man was gone.

Diyami awoke as a shaft of sunlight pierced the tree canopy and shined on his face. He was curled up in the dirt, trying to keep warm. The fire was out. He looked around and saw that he was alone. A leather bundle lay on a stone by the fire ring. His back was stiff when he stood up to get the bundle. He untied its intricate knots and unfolded the leather on the ground. The island man's red pipe was there, along with a gourd rattle and pouches of tobacco and herbs. The last object was a dagger with a flaked obsidian blade, shiny and black. Diyami held it up, ran his finger over its glistening surface, and felt its sharp edge.

He drank water from his canteen. His quest had succeeded. Diyami mulled over the island man's words. He didn't want to forget one moment of this experience. He didn't understand the stories yet but knew they would guide him in the future. As he packed the canoe, he tied up the bundle and lay the dagger on top so he could admire it as he paddled. He pushed off into the channel. The river was especially beautiful this light-filled morning. Green and blue dragonflies hovered among cattails in the shallows. Diyami took a few strokes into the gentle current. He should reach Cairo by afternoon.

He felt a bump from below. A log? He didn't see anything in the brown, cloudy water. Another bump. There was a swirl of movement in the water. Then a third bump tipped the canoe to one side and water poured over the right gunwale. Diyami paddled hard back to the shore of the island. He hopped out and his feet sank into the soft mud. The water was up to his knees and his feet were stuck. He pushed the bow of the canoe up onto a sandy beach. Something bumped the back of his leg. He turned and saw a long shape in the murky water, like a log. He reached down to push it away. It was smooth and soft. Writhing violently. Too thick to be a snake, too smooth to be an alligator. He shoved it away, then fell over with his feet still stuck in the mud. Something grabbed onto his arm and began to pull him into deeper water. It tugged hard enough to free his feet from the mud.

Diyami dropped his paddle into the canoe with a clank. He splashed and twisted, struggling to keep his head above water. The creature tugged harder. Diyami saw that his arm was caught in the wide, toothless mouth of a huge catfish. Seven feet long and a foot thick, with a broad, flat head and eyes spaced far apart. It made a clicking sound, like a loud drum. Diyami kicked it, but it didn't let go. He flailed with his free arm and found a submerged branch. He held it tight, but it snapped in two when the fish yanked him further into the deep. He poked the sharp end of the branch into the creature's side and it let go.

Diyami swam to the surface and angled upstream towards the beached canoe. He was desperate to reach it before the fish came back. He found secure footing on a rock in shallow water near the shore. He stood up and held onto the canoe. His chest heaved. He couldn't catch his breath.

The catfish clamped down on Diyami's ankle and pulled his leg out from under him. Diyami grabbed the dagger from the top of his pack, just before the monster dragged him into the current. Diyami plunged the dagger into its eye. It convulsed and twisted in a death throe. The drumming sound was deafening. Then the monster went silent and limp. Diyami's foot found a rock. Holding onto the dagger, still stuck in the monster's head, he staggered to the shore. The catfish lodged against a log in the shallow water. Its shiny skin glistened green and blue in the sunlight. Red blood oozed from its eye and drifted downstream in a plume.

Diyami extracted the dagger and collapsed onto the sand. He lay there for several minutes, staring at the sky, until his heart calmed its frantic beating. He sat up and was suddenly ravenous with hunger. He thought of the granola bars in his pack, but they would not be enough.

He built a fire on the beach, then picked up his dagger and walked over to the dead fish a few feet away. He stood over it for a moment and raised his hands in thanks. Though it had almost destroyed him, it had done him a great service. He cut a big piece of flesh out of its side, skewered it on a stick, and grilled it over the flames. He savored the smoky smell. He squatted on his haunches and looked out over the river as he took the first bite. It was the most delicious thing he had ever tasted. He tore at the flesh again and again. Then his teeth bit into something hard and sharp. He reached into his mouth and pulled it out—a hand-flaked stone arrowhead.

Diyami pondered the arrowhead in his hand. He knew it was a precious gift. *How long has this fish lived in the river? Who fought with it before I did?* He felt connected to the deep past. His quest had succeeded.

A hawk was perched on the top branch of a tree above him. It cocked its head to peer at the scene below. Then it spread its wings and flew away into the morning sun.

Before he set off for Cairo, Diyami put the arrowhead in one of the small leather pouches from the island man's bundle. He attached it to a cord and made a necklace. He wore that necklace every day for the rest of his life.

Meredith was standing on the boat ramp late that afternoon when Diyami steered the canoe to shore. She held the bow as he got out, then threw her arms around him. "You look like hell," she said.

"I feel wonderful." He hugged her tight.

They stopped at a diner for something to eat. Diyami ordered fried catfish for both of them. Meredith peppered him with questions about his voyage. "Did you find your vision?"

"Yes."

"What was it like?"

"A spirit visited me last night. He told me stories and gave me gifts. Then a river monster almost drowned me before I killed it."

He showed her the arrowhead.

"What did you learn?"

"I can't put it into words yet, but it was everything I need."

After their plates of catfish and French fries arrived, she said, "I had a great idea while you were gone. I don't know why I didn't think of it before. Twitter. It lets you send messages from your phone to all your followers. We can get hundreds of followers, maybe thousands. I created handles for us, @CornMother for me and @MorningStar for you. I have already gotten a ton of responses." She showed the phone to Diyami. He saw the logo of the little blue bird.

After Diyami's experience on the river, he and Meredith embarked on their longest road trip so far to speak to the Lakota, Hidatsa, and Mandan nations in North and South Dakota. Diyami was profoundly affected by the poverty of the first reservation they visited. Trailers and cheap, flimsy houses. Trash-strewn yards where dogs snuffle through garbage, tearing at the black plastic trash bags to get to the clumps of macaroni and cheese inside. Cluttered kitchens with dishes piled high and young children in diapers and T-shirts, hypnotized by cartoons on TV. Rustbucket cars with blotchy, faded paint jobs, missing hubcaps and torn upholstery. Teenagers waiting for something interesting to happen.

Diyami grew up with order and purpose and cleanliness. That's what his Cahokia was all about. Gleaming white buildings, concentric canals, the symmetry of the Grand Plaza. To him, respect, cooperation, and thoughtful actions were what it meant to be a Native American. These people didn't seem to live that way. What could he say to inspire them or, at least, to suggest that another path might be achievable?

He was nervous before the first talk. There were about a dozen people in the room, who were outnumbered by empty chairs. Most were middle aged adults, with a few teenagers and young people sprinkled in. In the back, an old man was hunched over in a wheelchair. Would the vision from the river help Diyami connect with them?

He closed his eyes for a moment and took a deep breath. Images of the island man and the patient, ever-yielding, unstoppable river came to him. His talk flowed in a new direction.

"Cities were not invented by the white man. Though their cities are a scourge on Mother Earth, filthy, full of death, destruction, and misery. Many of us have thought that we had only two choices: to adopt the white man's way of life and live in their world, or to stay on reservations, where we are close to the land, but are stuck in places the white man doesn't want. We have fought long and hard to reclaim our sovereignty, but most of America still thinks of us as relics of a lost world. What if we could bring that world back to a life that matters today? We once had our own great city—and we can build one again. A city in our image. A city that nourishes life and beauty, and lives in harmony with Mother Earth. A city that shows everyone who we are and what we can do. The modern world isn't going away. Our children must live in it. Let's allow them to do so in a way that makes them proud. That is the dream of Cahokia. You can build it. Let's claim it."

The audience stayed with him. Afterwards, several people gathered around Diyami to ask questions.

A woman about sixty years old came up to him. She was pushing the old man in the wheelchair. She introduced him as her father, one of the elders in the community. "He wants to meet you," she said. The old man was staring blankly at the floor. "Here is Mr. Red Hawk, pop." He labored to lift his head up to look at Diyami with cloudy eyes. His gnarled hand took hold of Diyami's hand with a surprisingly strong grip. He muttered something in a barely audible voice. Diyami was puzzled. The daughter explained, "His speech has been impaired since his stroke. Most people can't understand him." She bent down closer to the old man's face, "Can you say that again, pop?"

He spoke a little louder, "Uhhr-ing aar."

"I think he said 'Morning Star.' I don't know what that means."

Diyami knelt in front of the old man, looked right into his eyes, and squeezed his hand back. "Yes. Thank you. We are here. Together."

The old man spoke again. This time with excitement, loud enough for everyone in the room to hear, "Uhhr-ing aar! Uhhr-ing aar!"

The room fell quiet.

"Uhhr-ing aar! Uhhr-ing aar!"

Meredith, who was talking to someone else, turned to see Diyami and the old man.

"Uhhr-ing aar! Uhhr-ing aar!"

That night Diyami and Meredith drifted off to sleep under the pickup's camper shell with their arms entwined around each other. A great weight had been lifted.

The next morning, Diyami's phone buzzed. He read the screen. "It's the person who set up our meeting last night. He wants to know if we can stay over. More people want to hear us."

This time, the room was full—about fifty people. They paid close attention to Diyami's words. Several lingered afterwards to ask questions to Diyami and Meredith. The signup sheet filled with email addresses. After most of the people left and Diyami was putting away the laptop and projector, a man in a suit approached. He was about forty years old, short and stocky, with a wide smile and a ponytail of black hair. He introduced himself as Stan Huffman, a lawyer who represented several tribes on casino matters and other business. "I don't know why, but I'm intrigued by your project."

He asked Diyami and Meredith to join him for dinner in the casino restaurant nearby. They talked for hours. Stan was as outgoing as Diyami was introverted. He had vaguely heard of Cahokia, but had never been there. He was from Minneapolis, with mixed Lakota, Cheyenne, and Menominee ancestry and had gone to law school at the University of Minnesota.

Diyami and Meredith could hardly believe they were finally speaking with someone who showed a genuine curiosity about what they were doing. Diyami started slow, then, halfway through the main course, everything began to pour out.

"There could be a hundred thousand people living at Cahokia in ten years. Businesses, apartment buildings, even a university. Everything will be designed on Native principles, oriented to the four directions...The wide open Grand Plaza will be the center of the city...It will be clean and quiet—no cars—and we will build a canal to connect Cahokia with the waters of the Mississippi."

"That's quite a plan, Diyami," said Stan. "How did you come up with it?"

"He has a vision," Meredith said. "When Diyami talks, it's like he has already been there."

Stan asked a lot of questions and was favorably impressed by their answers. He liked Diyami's confidence and logical approach to his dream of an Indian city. Every time Stan asked how something in the new Cahokia would work, Diyami had an answer that sounded pretty good. Stan was a student of Native languages and knew a little Osage—the Osage Nation had been a client in the past. He made a comment using one of the basic phrases he knew and Diyami responded in perfect Osage.

At the same time, there was something odd about Diyami, but Stan couldn't put his finger on it. During the dinner, Diyami made some unusual word choices. He said that he wished their pickup had a "retractor." Meredith softly corrected him, "sunroof." He said that she did the "steering" on their travels. He told the waiter that he wanted the frozen yogurt with raspberries for dessert—but he pronounced it *yah-gurt*. Stan made a lame joke about Tonto and the Lone Ranger and Diyami drew a blank. He didn't get the reference. *Sure, he's too young to have seen the old TV show, but everybody knows that one....*

Stan also wondered what Meredith was doing there. They seemed like an improbable couple. How had she hooked up with Diyami? She said she and Diyami had met in St. Louis, but Stan suspected there was more to the story than that.

By the time dessert and coffee came, Stan decided that he liked these two idealistic kids, though he doubted they realized what they were up against. "You're going to have to fight the government and you'll need a lot of money. My work is all about money, getting it to those who deserve it and keeping it away from those who don't." He had spent years handling the business affairs of Indian casinos and was getting burned out. He needed something new to focus on.

"I don't like the casinos," said Diyami. Meredith gave him a dirty look. *Don't offend this guy who can help us.* "They're all about weakness and greed."

"Diyami, you're not old enough to know what it was like before. The casinos lifted a lot of our people out of poverty."

"There's a better way." Diyami peered fiercely at Stan. "I know there is."

"At least, with the casinos, it's us making money, rather than the other way around."

"Money is important. But do we have to lose our way on this earth to earn it?"

This kid's got guts. thought Stan. That was good enough for him. He told Meredith and Diyami that, by coincidence, he was going to be in St. Louis the following week. One of his tribal clients owned a trucking company and was looking for a site for a new terminal and warehouse. St. Louis was a promising location, at the confluence of three interstate highways.

"Can you show me around Cahokia?"

After Stan drove off in his Mercedes, Meredith and Diyami hugged each other in the casino parking lot. It was happening!

"There will be three rings of concentric canals for transportation within the city. They will connect with the larger canal to the Mississippi."

Diyami, Meredith, and Stan were standing atop Monk's Mound in Cahokia on a blustery spring day with clouds scudding across the blue sky. Downtown St. Louis and the Arch were visible a few miles to the west. Diyami pointed out the future locations of various features.

Meredith gestured to the small museum a few hundred yards to the south. "We'll build a new pyramid—transparent, covered with glass—out there. It will mark the other end of the Grand Plaza."

"What about over there?" Stan asked, pointing to a run-down trailer park a few hundred yards from Monk's Mound.

"That's where we will put the university," said Diyami.

"Listening to you, I can almost see it," Stan said. "But you realize that this is a historic site, owned by the state of Illinois. How are they going to let you do this?"

"We hoped you could figure that out." Meredith said. Stan laughed.

Stan's education, business experience, and personality all attuned him to small details which often revealed the key to people or problems he was dealing with. Since the first night, he had felt a tug of doubt about Diyami. The missed jokes, the odd turns of phrase, the hints of weird innocence and naivete. Diyami said he was an Osage with relatives in Oklahoma. Stan had put in a call to a clerk at the Osage Nation headquarters. There was a Red Hawk family, but no Diyami Red Hawk. The clerk gave Stan the number of an elder Red Hawk, who had a minor position with the tribal government. The elder said "who?" As far as he knew, there had never been a Diyami in the family.

Stan, Diyami, and Meredith began to walk down the long staircase toward the base of the mound. Stan couldn't contain his doubts any longer. *Best to get them out in the open.* "Sorry, but your story doesn't add up. What are you not telling me?"

"Nothing. We're trying to get Cahokia off the ground."

Meredith sensed the challenge and stepped in "Is something the matter, Stan?"

"The Osage Nation has never heard of you, Diyami. You're not an enrolled member of the tribe."

"My grandfather was in the military, then settled in Europe. I grew up overseas. I've never gotten around to registering with the Osage."

"Why didn't you clear that up? If you're not enrolled, you're an outsider. You can't claim your rights. Every Indian with any sense knows that."

"Aren't you being a little paranoid?" said Meredith to Stan.

"I like this Cahokia idea and I want to work with you guys, but I need to be comfortable that I'm not getting mixed up in a cult. I learned something a long time ago, 'Don't try to bullshit a bullshitter.' Our people have been scammed for centuries. Mostly by whites," Stan gave Meredith a sharp look, "but also by Indians. Maybe you want to be a messiah. That's fine. But are you Sitting Bull or Charles Manson?"

Stan saw the blank look on Diyami's face at Manson's name. He had no idea who that was. They reached the bottom of the staircase. Diyami stopped and took a moment to calm himself.

"You're right. There is more. But if I told you, you wouldn't believe me."

"Try me."

Meredith stepped in. "Not now. Give us time. How about tomorrow?"

"OK. But this better be fucking good."

That night, Meredith and Diyami had an emergency meeting with Billy and Carol. What should they tell Stan? Billy didn't want them to say anything. The family had kept the secret and the Knights had left them alone. Why mess that up? Carol pointed out that Stan's help might be the key to getting the new Cahokia off the ground. Based on what Diyami and Meredith said about him, she was ready to trust him. Billy saw Meredith's plaintive look. If the others were willing to take this chance, he could too. He knew that Cahokia was a big deal.

"Okay. Invite him here for dinner tomorrow. I want to meet him. If I'm comfortable, we'll tell him, though I have no clue how that will go."

Stan stood outside the Pelican building, looking up at the huge metal birds that hovered above the roof. *What kind of an evening is this going to be?*

Inside, Meredith's parents appeared to be perfectly normal. No cultish or fanatical vibe. Her father, Billy, was charming and funny—he got every one of Stan's pop culture references. Her mother, Carol, asked a lot of questions about Stan's background and education. She wasn't grilling him; she seemed to be genuinely interested. For a schoolteacher, she had a decent grasp of basic legal concepts. Billy brought out lamb kebabs, couscous, and salad for dinner. Stan relaxed and began to enjoy himself. Still, he was waiting for the promised revelation of Diyami's secret.

Meredith and Diyami cleared the dinner plates, then Meredith returned with a tray of wrapped candies. "My homemade taffy," she said. "I guarantee you'll like it."

Stan took a piece and popped it into his mouth. "That's incredible."

"Secret recipe," said Meredith with a sly grin.

Everyone had some taffy and the pleasant conversation continued. After Stan told a particularly funny story, Billy nodded to Carol. She pushed a dollar bill across the table to Stan. "Here's a retainer. You represent us now. Everything we say is covered by attorney-client privilege."

Billy refilled Stan's water glass. "Stan, what do you know about neutrinos?"

"Nothing that I'm aware of."

"Neutrinos are subatomic particles with no charge. Their mass is so tiny as to be practically zero. Trillions of neutrinos pass through your body every second. You don't notice them, but they are every bit as real as you are."

"Okay. So what?"

"The same principle applies to more than neutrinos."

Billy asked Stan to imagine a whole world intertwined with ours, but completely undetectable—most of the time. How was it separated? Images and metaphors can't do it justice. Billy explained his membrane theory—a diaphanous membrane is everywhere—and his carousel theory—millions of carousels spinning in unison.

"Maybe both theories are true, maybe neither. Take your pick about which one to believe, but I'm telling you that this other world is absolutely real. We've been there."

"And I grew up there," Diyami said.

Billy, Carol, Meredith, and Diyami were all eager to tell Stan about the two worlds. They got so excited that their words piled up on top of each other. They hadn't spoken to anyone about this in the months since the original events. It was a relief to lift the burden of secrecy. Stan wasn't so sure he wanted to be on the receiving end of their pent-up enthusiasm, but it was one hell of a story. Their descriptions of this other world were remarkably consistent. Stan was moved when Diyami explained that the new Cahokia already existed fully and that he had made it his mission to bring it to the Indians of this bleak world.

"You gave up everything and everyone you knew?" Stan asked. He opened his third piece of taffy.

"I heard the calls from the spirits. I could not ignore them."

Carol showed Stan a few artifacts supposedly brought back from this other world—beer coasters, books, and postcards. Meredith cleared the table and Diyami unrolled maps, architectural plans, and engineering drawings of the fabled Cahokia, including elevations of the 'Temple of the Children,' a huge glass pyramid with museums, offices, and a high school inside. Stan could hardly believe his eyes.

He pressed them about the possibility of taking people to the other world—or "HD," as Billy called it. Wouldn't that be the best way to prove that it was real? Billy assured him that they had considered every angle and that they knew of no way to cross over again. He also explained about the Knights and their threats to keep visitors out at all costs. Diyami scoffed at the mention of the Knights. Cahokians weren't afraid of them.

Stan's head was spinning. He didn't know what to make of these people. They were either:

A. fantastic liars with wild imaginations,

B. seriously delusional, suffering from some kind of group hallucination, or

C. telling the truth.

Option C seemed to be the least likely, even though their consistent, detailed story about another world that overlayed our own and which already had a shining, spectacular Cahokia was the most amazing thing he had ever heard. As the night wore on, Stan was running out of ways to dismiss this far-fetched tale. All of this could be fake, but why would they go through so much trouble?

Stan couldn't stop thinking about one thing that Billy said, "HD is the coolest place I have ever been—by far. I would do anything to see it again." Meredith agreed, "It's totally amazing."

When they said goodbye to Stan on the sidewalk in front of the Pelican building, Diyami and Meredith advised him to take time to digest everything. They would check in with him in a few days. Billy thanked him for coming and said he looked forward to seeing him again. Carol gave him a hug and whispered in his ear, "Remember, attorney-client privilege."

As the Boustanys and Diyami were cleaning up the dinner table after Stan's departure, Meredith said, "Did you see the look on his face? Stage One, Deer in the Headlights."

"If you ask me," Billy said "He was in Stage Three by the end." They all laughed. "I think he got to Stage Four," Carol said.

Meredith texted Stan a few times over the next week, but he didn't respond. She and Diyami began to worry. "Maybe we scared him off." He was their best hope for an ally to get the Cahokia project going.

After another week, she and Diyami got a text from Stan. "Sorry. Very busy here. Can you meet me at Cahokia on Tuesday? Foot of Monk's Mound. 2 PM? I have news."

Diyami and Meredith saw Stan getting out of his car in the parking lot next to the mound. They shook hands. Meredith expected that he was going to tell them that he wanted no part of their crazy scheme. Instead, he greeted them warmly. "Let's walk over to the trailer park."

When they got there, he asked Diyami, "So this is where your university is?"

"Yes," Diyami said.

Stan looked around at the dilapidated trailers. "You're standing on the first piece of Cahokia land owned by Native Americans in a few hundred years."

"Who owns it?" Meredith asked.

"We do!" said Stan, breaking into a broad grin. "Remember my tribal client who wants to build a freight terminal? They authorized me to buy this property for a headquarters building. They did it in the form of an investment in the *ABSOM Cahokia Native Development Corporation.*"

"What's that?" Diyami asked.

"Something I just set up. Meredith and I are on the board of directors. You will be too, Diyami—as soon as we can make you into a legal person." Meredith practically jumped into Stan's arms.

On the way back to the parking lot, Stan explained his strategy for making Diyami legal. "First we'll get you listed as an enrolled member of the Osage Nation. Then we can get you a Social Security number." Stan asked if Diyami knew the name of an ancestor who the Osage could identify in this world. Diyami remembered what his father had told him about the family, "My great-grandfather, George Morrison Red Hawk, was born in 1895. In those days, the Indian agents made sure everyone had an English name." Meredith pointed out that HD and SD split in 1904 or 1905, so someone born in 1895 would have lived in both worlds. That information was puzzling to Stan. He added it to the growing list of paradoxes that he had decided to accept as true.

"I'll get to work on your tribal membership."

SCANDAL

GILES MONROE WAS BOILING MAD. If it weren't for his dark skin, his face would be red with rage.

He had a full day of meetings ahead of him to address the problems of "the trade"—the Knights' secret program to steal intellectual property from SD and sell it to companies in HD. Today's meetings were going to be challenging under the best of circumstances. Then, just as Giles was about to leave home, something slid under his front door. It was the latest edition of a trashy gossip rag he rarely read, the *Weekly Whirl*. A huge headline across the front page screamed:

TYCOON'S 'HEROIC RESCUE' WAS A FRAUD!

Only a few short months ago, industrialist Giles Monroe was hailed throughout the city as a hero for saving two children from being run over by a gang on speeding scooters. Citizens were captivated by the heart-rending images of him hobbling on crutches from injuries he suffered in the rescue. In dramatic testimony to the Board of Alderman, carried live on moviola, he demanded new laws to combat the growing menace of reckless scooters.

The Whirl has learned that Monroe's entire story was a pack of lies. His famous smashed kneecaps were actually caused by an angry mother beating him with a baseball bat after an unsavory incident with her daughter. The altercation occurred outside Whittemore's Bar, in the 3500 block of Gravois. The Whirl interviewed several people, including Mary Jo Robinson, the manager of Whittemore's, who said, "The woman really let Mr. Monroe have it. He screamed and crumpled pitifully to the sidewalk. She was mad as hell." Other witnesses asserted that two lowlife miscreants working for Monroe were in the process of kidnapping the daughter. Police arrived on the scene within minutes, but the alleged knee basher, her child, and two other companions had already fled.

The Whirl conducted an exhaustive investigation to locate the unidentified woman and her daughter, who was described as being approximately twenty years old. They have disappeared without a trace.

The Whirl also contacted the parents of the two children who were purportedly rescued from the scooters by Monroe and who were prominently featured in news stories at the time. Their parents refused to speak with our reporter. They referred all questions to their attorney, Raymond Sadecki, of the Maxvill, Javier, and Flood law firm, located on the 75th floor of the Hydraulic Building, just below Mr. Monroe's opulent office suite. Mr. Sadecki had no comment. "Our policy is not to dignify scurrilous rumors."

On behalf of the citizens of our fair city, the Whirl has one question for Giles Monroe: WHEN WILL YOU APOLOGIZE FOR YOUR DASTARDLY DECEPTION?

Giles crumpled the newspaper and threw it in the trash. *Billy Boustany and his wretched family were an annoyance—though a very painful one—last year. Now, that sorry episode is making my life difficult again. They won't get away with it this time.*

Giles entered the wood-paneled conference room for his first meeting. He quickly noticed that the others present, members of the inner circle of the Knights of the Carnelian, avoided eye contact with him and pretended to be studying the papers on the table in front of them. Martin Matsui, the longest-serving member of the group, was the last to arrive. He nodded to Giles, then took his seat. Giles knew they had all read the story in the *Weekly Whirl*. The news had spread like wildfire through the upper ranks of the Knights, the secret society, led by Giles, which controlled every aspect of business and political life in HD St. Louis. Giles did not acknowledge the obvious tension hanging over the room. He called the meeting to order.

Jim Hines, who created the modern organization of the Knights, started "the trade" back in 1941, soon after he discovered the pills that enabled travel between HD St. Louis and its companion city in the SD world. Knowledge of this other world, and the means for traveling there, was the Knights' most closely guarded secret. No one else in the booming city had any idea that a parallel city existed alongside theirs.

For decades, the trade brought untold riches to HD St. Louis. Stolen products included everything from zippers—which revolutionized the clothing industry in the 1940s—to advanced machine tools, drill bits, pesticides, and techniques for molding high-impact plastics. These products contributed to St. Louis' spectacular growth and its reputation as the "city of inventors." Only the Knights around this table, and their predecessors, knew the true origin of these "golden eggs." But the harvest had begun to decline. Over the last few years, the Knights' spies hadn't found much of value that HD companies could use. The products they brought back fell into two categories—either they were trivial with limited economic potential, like an electric toothbrush, or they were something that couldn't be replicated. Would today's candidates be any different?

A young member of the Knights nervously began his presentation. He had recently returned from a mission to SD and he was excited by his latest find. It was a new device, the "iPhone," that people over there were clamoring for. Despite its name, it was far more than a telephone. This small white slab could write letters, show photos, play music, display maps, and do a hundred other things. "Like everyone over there, I became addicted and spent hours a day playing with it." He laid two of the devices on the table for everyone to see. The cover of one of them was removed to display its inner workings. "There are no moving parts. It's amazing."

"Let me demonstrate how it works," he said. He held up the second device and gestured for everyone to gather around to see its screen. He squeezed a button and the black glass turned into a screen with rows of colorful symbols. "Touching this symbol lets you write a letter. They call it 'email.'"

"How does the person get the letter?"

"It shows up on their iPhone instantly, like a telegram." He tapped another symbol. "This one can show a map of where the phone is located anywhere in the world. You type in your destination and it gives you directions."

"Show me directions to a beach with palm trees," said one of the senior Knights, with a chuckle.

"I can't. It needs a signal to work."

Jennifer Logan, a high-ranking Knight who ran a large engineering company, said "What you have here is an excellent radio with no radio stations. It's useless."

"We have radio stations," Giles said.

"This will require special radio stations. Probably a different one for each function," she replied.

"What? I'm not going to build a bunch of special radio stations just to make this little trinket work! That would cost a fortune." harrumphed Giles. "Does anybody think this is a worthwhile idea for us?" He looked around the table. If one of the Knights was going to challenge his authority in light of this morning's scandal, now was the time. No one said a word.

Giles turned to the humiliated young Knight. "Nice try, son. Next time, bring me something we can make money with."

The rest of the day didn't go any better. A parade of products that had little potential and generated no interest from the Knights who represented St. Louis' major businesses. Giles grew more and more frustrated. As he adjourned the meeting, he said, "The trade is in real trouble. We need a radically new approach to get the money flowing again. Right now, I don't know what that is, but I promise you I will find it." He was already working on a new idea that would assure the Knights' dominance, but it was too soon to say anything.

The other Knights gathered their papers and filed out of the conference room. None lingered to make small talk with Giles. Martin studied their faces as they left. They would be jabbering about the *Weekly Whirl* article as soon as they were out of earshot. But, once again, they were afraid to confront Giles.

Only Giles and Martin were left. "As the saying goes, don't let the bastards get you down." Martin said.

"Ridiculous lies. The press doesn't treat me fairly."

"It will soon be forgotten."

"I could shut that paper down tomorrow."

"Not worth it. We have important work. The city needs you."

"Someone will pay dearly for this," Giles seethed.

Martin knew that Giles would never admit anything and would lash out sooner or later. Martin had butted heads with Giles several times over the years, but he was getting too old for the drama. Giles would be Giles. Martin exchanged a few parting pleasantries with him and walked slowly to the elevator. He was saddened by the decline of the Knights from the vision of Jim Hines to the naked greed and petty resentments of Giles Monroe. Martin's beloved organization, which did so much good for the city, was becoming little more than a snake pit of gangsters. He braced for the trouble that would surely come.

A young woman holding a clutch of files got off the elevator, nodded to Martin as she passed him, and walked into the conference room with a limp. She approached Giles.

"I have set up the meeting, sir. They will be here day after tomorrow."

"Will there be someone with the authority to make decisions and follow through?"

"Yes."

"Well done, Ada. Once again, you have proved your worth."

This was the first good news Giles had heard all day.

Martin Matsui walked up the steps to Leonora's front door very carefully. At seventy-seven, he wasn't taking any chances with having a fall. He rang the doorbell. When Leonora opened the door, he waved to his driver to leave. Leonora gave him a big hug. Once inside, Martin shook hands with John, "So good to see you, Mr. Little. I hope you're enjoying your time with us."

They sat in the living room, where Leonora poured glasses of wine. "Argentinian, the expensive stuff," Martin said with a twinkle in his eye. "You are always the perfect hostess."

"I've missed you, Uncle Martin."

"And I have missed both of you. Thank you for inviting me. These days, few people do."

They sipped and chatted for a while, then moved into the dining room for dinner. After the meal, Martin said, "There are rumblings around town. I fear for the future."

He showed Leonora and John the *Weekly Whirl* article that had come out just that morning. They had not seen it.

"I hope this doesn't come back to haunt your friend, Mr. Boustany." Martin said. "You never know what Giles will do when he's backed into a corner. In the past, I have been able to restrain his excesses, but I won't always be here."

Leonora changed the subject to the reason she had asked Martin to come—the problem with the Amperic bricks. He was already aware of it. She marveled that there was almost nothing she could tell Martin that he didn't already know.

"I am certain you will find a solution. You always do." he said.

"This is the hardest thing I have ever worked on."

"I have faith in you."

"John has come up with a fresh approach."

"Excellent, Mr. Little! I thought your brilliance would rub off on us somehow. What is it?"

"Actually, the solution may lie over there."

"Really? In the other world?"

"Yes."

"What is it that Mr. Boustany calls it?"

"SD."

"Ahh, yes. And what are we?"

"HD."

"Of course. I remember now. And he thought that HD was the better place."

"Most of the time."

"I must say that the cuisine over there is exceptional. I still find myself thinking of your mother's pecan pie, John."

Leonora and John described their new strategy for computer simulations to model long-term effects of different brick treatments. "Without the simulations, we have no way to find out which treatments and formulas will extend the life of the bricks the most."

"We need equipment that doesn't exist here."

Martin listened. Leonora had a hazy awareness that the Knights knew how to bring products over from SD, but she didn't know that Martin had been deeply involved in doing it for decades. Even though she was his niece, there were secrets Martin had sworn to protect and could never divulge.

"I must have very specific items or it won't work," John said.

Martin thought of the recent disappointments of the trade, like this morning's debacle with the little white slab.

That's what happens when people don't understand science and technology. To tightly control knowledge of the other world, the Knights had done everything using their own members, who were little more than ambitious amateurs. That strategy had worked for many years. Jim Hines could pull it off. Now, the well-connected young Knights, who Giles Monroe chose for their obedience, not for their intelligence, were in over their heads.

The Amperic brick problem could ruin St. Louis. Who did Martin trust to solve it—the hothead Giles and his sycophants, or Leonora and John?

"This has been a lovely evening, but it's getting late for me." he said. "Can you phone my driver to pick me up?"

At the front door, Leonora asked one more time. "Can you help us, Uncle Martin?"

"You make a very difficult request. It boggles the mind of an old man."

Leonora and John were dejected after Martin left without offering help. What would they do now with no way to get a computer from SD?

A few days later, the doorbell rang. John answered. A man in a chauffeur's uniform was holding a ribboned box. "This is for Miss Matsui." John set the box on the hall table, then returned to his basement workshop.

When she got home, Leonora picked up the box. White cardboard, stamped with a logo in gold, *Everything, since 1965,* and a curly pink ribbon. She opened the attached card. *Happy birthday, from Uncle Martin.* That made her worry. Her birthday wasn't for several months. Was Uncle Martin's memory slipping? Inside the box, she found an assortment of brightly colored pieces of taffy, individually wrapped in wax paper. She picked one up and felt something hard beneath. She lifted out a small glass bottle filled with little white pills. There was another note: *One to go, one to return. These pack quite a wallop. Use them wisely. I can't get you any more.*

You Never Can Tell

BILLY POSITIONED THE LADDER, then climbed it with paintbrush and can. If all went well, he would finish painting the wall that separated the bedroom from the living area before Carol got home from teaching. He and she had been living in the new apartment in the Pelican building amid bare drywall and stripes of joint compound for too long. Just as he made his first careful brushstroke, the phone rang. *Goddammit!* He thought about letting it ring, but out of habit he scrambled down the ladder to answer.

He didn't recognize the area code on the number before he accepted the call.

"Hello. I'm looking for Bill Boustany."

"That's me."

"You're a hard man to find."

"I like it that way."

"I tried to contact you at your store."

"Not my store any more."

"That's what they said. They were very reluctant to give me your number. My name is Wendell McMillan. I'm a ham radio operator in Montana. Last night, I was contacted by a guy I used to talk with a lot, but who I hadn't heard from in almost a year. John Little."

That name got Billy's attention.

"It was an awful connection. I could barely make out what he was saying. He wants you to be on the radio at nine o'clock tonight. He said it's very important and you would know the channel. He tried to tell me your phone number, but the interference got bad and I couldn't hear him anymore."

Billy thanked him, then hung up.

The paint job would have to wait. Billy rummaged through the stack of boxes in the corner to find John's old Heathkit shortwave set and logbooks. *I hope this damn thing still works.*

As nine o'clock approached, Billy and Carol sat anxiously by the radio. She squeezed his hand. He prayed he was tuned to the right channel. He found the notation and the comment "unusual call" in John's logbook from 1982. The radio was picking up a mixture of wheezes, chirps, and clicks. Precisely at nine, they heard a faint voice through the noise, "This is John calling Billy, John calling Billy." The pitch oscillated from high to low and back again.

"This is Billy."

"We need your help. I can't go into it now, but Leonora is coming to you soon."

"Are you OK?"

"Yes. My heart is doing well, but I'm not going to take a chance with traveling."

"Tell her to cross as far away as she can. I can pick her up anywhere. There are people who noticed what was going on last year."

"Okay. This is John signing off."

Billy and Carol looked at each other with wide grins. HD wasn't done with them after all.

When Billy and Carol pulled up, Leonora was standing in the parking lot of a McDonald's near the Alton, Illinois train station. She was holding a suitcase and was relieved to see familiar faces, even though she had only met them briefly, in HD Cahokia many months ago.

"We came as fast as we could," Billy said as he put her suitcase in the back of his car. "It's almost thirty miles. Fortunately, not much traffic on a Saturday morning." Carol gave Leonora a long hug.

"John said you wanted me to cross far from St. Louis. This is the last stop on the commuter train."

As they drove over the bridge back to Missouri, Leonora looked out the window, eagerly drinking in every building, every passing car. It felt miraculous to be in the other world again. "I was only here once, in 1982, with John."

"We'll show you everything. First, let's go to our place."

On the way to Billy and Carol's apartment. Leonora explained her purpose, to buy computer parts for an important project she and John were working on. "He gave me a list of what he needs and told me exactly where to get them."

When they arrived at the Pelican building, Leonora said, "This is where the Refugees Club is."

"I know," Billy said. "I was there."

In the apartment, they talked for hours. Billy and Carol knew almost nothing about Leonora—just that she and her uncle, Martin Matsui, had engineered their rescue from the Knights, and that, somehow, she knew John from long ago. And she knew very little about them. John told her that he had known Billy since Billy was a child in the repair room at the Duke of Discounts and that his mother had worked for Billy's family. Billy was floored when Leonora said that she been to the store and met his father back in 1982.

Billy recounted his exploits in HD the previous year—what he had seen, his encounter with the Knights, Meredith's connection with Diyami and Cahokia, how Giles Monroe had them kidnapped—the event that had led John to reach out to Leonora after so many years.

Carol said, "We're not big fans of that guy Monroe."

"You may not have heard the last of him." Leonora opened her suitcase and took out the copy of the *Weekly Whirl*. "This caused quite a stir just last week."

Carol let out a loud guffaw when she read the article. "Hah! So now I'm famous in HD, even if only as an 'angry mother.' That's priceless."

"Uncle Martin says Giles is furious about this. Be careful. He might come looking for you."

As the day wore on, the conversation came around to the subject of John. During all the years she had been separated from him, Leonora kept the story of their lost love to herself. No one in HD would have understood. Now, she was talking to someone who had known him for decades. A dam burst inside her and her deep love and admiration for him came gushing out. Leonora described how John had discovered the dynamic principle of the barrier between the two worlds, how he was making a detailed study of HD technology, and his plan for computer simulations to help solve the biggest challenge her company faced.

Billy and Carol were flabbergasted to hear Leonora talk about John as a brilliant genius. To Billy, he had been the quiet, humble man who repaired TVs and stereos in the back of his father's store. How had Billy—and everyone—underestimated him so? He had written John off as no more than a background figure in his own personal drama of rescuing his father's business. John had never gotten a decent break from anyone, except this woman from another world. Words from Billy's father washed over him. *Don't be a pushover or the bastards will stomp all over you.* Had Billy been one of the bastards stomping on John? He hoped that helping Leonora and John now would give him a chance to atone for the past.

Billy asked, "Why didn't you come back over here to look for him years ago?"

"First, I was afraid of the threats from the Knights. Then I didn't know how—any ability I had to cross had long vanished. Until a few days ago, when Uncle Martin gave me the pills."

"What pills?"

"Take one and you can cross over. Take another and you come back. They are the Knights' deepest secret."

"They gave us those when they kidnapped us!" Carol said. "And Martin gave them to us when we came back from Cahokia. I thought they were tranquilizers."

"They make the crossing happen," Leonora said.

"You have them?" asked Billy.

"A few."

It was late in the afternoon. They were all exhausted from the intense conversation. Carol made a pot of herbal tea and put out plates of food for a simple dinner, which included Meredith's taffy. They agreed to go shopping tomorrow for the items John needed. Meredith and Diyami were out west meeting with Native groups and weren't due back for a few days, so Leonora could stay in the spare bedroom.

"I am going out for a bit before it gets dark," Leonora said. "I live in this neighborhood. I want to see what it's like over here."

"Where?" asked Billy.

"Flora Place."

"I grew up on Flora Place!"

"I know."

"We'll come with you," Carol said.

"Thank you, but I would like some time alone. This has been quite a day."

After Leonora left, Billy and Carol puttered around the kitchen, cleaning up in silence. Carol washed the dishes in the sink—the dishwasher wasn't hooked up yet. Billy swept the floor, then took out the trash. When he came back up the stairs, Billy said, "Are you thinking what I'm thinking?"

"Probably."

"It changes everything."

"No shit. Those pills could take us back to HD."

"But is that a good idea? Our friend Giles is already pissed at us. Leonora said so. He would go ballistic if he found out we were there."

"All I know is that you dream about going back every day. I've seen that look on your face a hundred times, but I never thought it could happen."

"I'd prefer not to get kidnapped again."

"Are we any safer here? The Knights think we have no ability to cross over. So, actually, HD is the last place they would expect us to be, even if Giles does want to go after us."

She had a pretty good point, Billy had to admit. Carol then played her trump card.

"Last year, you hid HD from me for months. You got to wander around and see the sights. I didn't. Don't I deserve the same?"

"Sure, Carol. But it's a huge risk. Those people don't mess around. If they grab us again, Martin and Leonora won't be able to get us out of it."

"Billy, if we pass up a chance to go, we'll regret it for the rest of our lives."

"Leonora only has a few pills. What makes you think she'll give any to us?"

"She came here for our help. I bet she'll part with some."

Billy started to warm up to the idea. "We could do a lot better job of staying out of sight now. Wearing their clothes and avoiding places like the Hydraulic building. And if they spot us, we pop a pill and we're out of there."

Carol made one last point. "Diyami and Meredith could use a few pills too. You know how much he misses his family and Cahokia."

That sealed the deal. They agreed to ask Leonora when she returned.

Leonora walked the six blocks north on Grand from Billy and Carol's apartment to Flora Place. She saw a mix of familiar and unfamiliar buildings. The ornate mansions of Compton Heights to the east were just as she knew them. On the west side of Grand, instead of the elegant terrace of the Azalea Tea Palace, where she and John often went for breakfast on weekends (if the wait for a table wasn't too long), she saw a row of nondescript buildings with a variety of small businesses and an ugly church. She was surprised that the sidewalks were empty on this pleasant evening. The entrance to Flora Place was marked by the same arched gateway as in her world.

In 2000, Leonora was promoted to the top research and development position at Hydraulic. The Knights had either forgiven or forgotten (it wasn't clear which) her transgression in 1982, when she accidentally made forbidden contact with the other world. Hydraulic needed her to supply the innovations that drove the continuing growth of the Amperic brick business, so no one objected to her promotion. She rewarded herself by buying a beautiful home on Flora Place. It was much too large for a person living alone, but she wanted it.

For the first few years, the house was the site of lavish parties, which became legendary all over town. Leonora delighted in bringing together a mélange of artists, entrepreneurs, and creative thinkers for long, champagne-soaked evenings. Many careers were born from chance encounters at 'Leonora parties.' They provided a distraction from the loneliness she still felt over the loss of John. Eventually, she grew tired of them and threw herself deeper into her work. When the top executives at Hydraulic turned to her to save the company from the existential threat of dwindling efficiency of Amperic brick power generation, there were never enough hours in the day.

Then, John reappeared in her life and she felt alive once more.

Leonora turned into Flora Place. It looked the same as her Flora Place. The canopy of trees formed a comforting, leafy cocoon. The brick and limestone-faced homes were the ones that she knew, with a handful of more recent additions. The most noticeable difference were the unusual cars parked along the street. Strolling west, she imagined that John was, at this very moment, on the same street in HD, out with the corgis for their evening walk. Was he walking alongside her or was he going in the opposite direction, passing invisibly through her? The idea sent a shiver up her spine, but, actually, there wasn't even the tiniest hint that a second world lay superimposed on top of this one. *How strange this business of two worlds!* When you were in one, you were in it all the way—until a little pill or a radio weak spot flipped you into the other. Leonora had left John in her world less than twelve hours earlier, but already she missed him terribly.

These musings were calming to her, so she kept walking the length of Flora Place up to where it ended at Tower Grove Avenue, across from the Missouri Botanical Garden. Maybe she could get a glass of wine at one of the restaurants inside the Garden.

As she approached Tower Grove, dusk was settling in and the colors were slowly thinning into gray. She saw the stone building at the entrance to the Garden, but here it didn't appear to be an entrance. The colonnade was filled in with floor to ceiling glass walls and the interior was brightly lit. Behind the entrance building, a curved, transparent structure with a lattice work of metal hexagons loomed like a giant net. Very odd, she thought.

Well-dressed people sat at tables inside the bright-lit entrance building. Leonora crossed the street, but couldn't find a door to go inside. She was tired, so she sat on a low stone wall just outside the glass wall. She saw a young woman in a white dress seated next to a man in formal wear with a huge grin on his face. It wasn't a restaurant; it was a wedding reception! Leonora was sitting no more than ten feet away from the glass. She was in the dark and the room was brightly lit. She could see the people inside perfectly, but if they looked in her direction, they would only see their own reflections. She could observe undetected, though the sounds were muffled by the glass. It was like she was watching a play performed by a cast of SD actors.

Various people took turns speaking into a microphone. The guests laughed and raised their glasses as frequent toasts were offered. Two gray-haired men passed the microphone back and forth. Their banter evoked mild chuckles from the audience. They appeared to be the fathers of the bride and groom, though Leonora couldn't tell which might be which. A young woman took the microphone—the maid of honor, maybe the bride's sister—there was a definite resemblance. She brimmed with earnest love and good wishes for the couple.

Next came a young man with swagger and a winning smile—the best man, no doubt. He held the microphone like a pro and launched into a series of quips and jokes. Leonora couldn't make out what he was saying, but she detected his English accent. The guests laughed at his every line. At the end, he raised his glass to the couple. The whole room joined in the toast, then applauded.

As Leonora watched the reception, she saw that these people seemed genuinely happy. For the bride and groom and their families, this evening would long be remembered. Would they be more or less happy if they knew what she knew? That another world existed where their lives were mere phantoms. The Knights were doing everything they could to suppress that knowledge. They ripped her and John apart, terrified Billy, Carol, and Meredith, and did who knows what else for decades—all for the purpose of keeping a secret. Was it worth it? Didn't people in both worlds deserve to know that the other existed? Would that knowledge lead to something good, or not? Or should these people be left alone to live their own lives without the burden of mind-bending revelations? She would have to talk to John about these questions. He always saw things clearly.

The reception guests got up from the tables and drifted out to the terrace on the other side of the building. Music began to play. A voice announced—she could understand it over the loudspeaker—"We're going to begin with a song by a local singer-songwriter." The music had a bouncy, lilting melody. Leonora listened as she watched a few people begin to dance. She could only make out snippets of the lyrics. Something about teenagers and old folks wishing them well—a sweet song, full of hope. Leonora tapped her foot in the darkness as she watched the dancers through the glass, both the graceful ones and the awkward ones. This bride and groom weren't teenagers, but Leonora wished them well.

Billy and Carol were relieved when Leonora finally returned to the Pelican building. "After it got dark, we were worried about you."

"I had a long, lovely walk."

"We want to help you and John," Billy said. "But we have a question."

"How many pills do you have?" Carol asked.

"Not that many."

"Can you give us some? We would do anything to visit HD one more time. Meredith and Diyami will want to also. He thought he would never see his family again. You're our only chance."

"Do you think it's wise to go there when the Knights are upset?"

131

"You said Giles may come after us here. So we might actually be safer there. He doesn't think we have the power to cross."

"Now we know how to blend in."

Leonora had to consider this proposition carefully. She only had the one bottle of pills. She knew what John would want her to do—be generous with their friends. "I can give you enough for a few round trips."

"And some extras? You never can tell what might happen."

"Yes. Some extras also."

The next morning, they went over John's list of items needed. "He said to get two of everything so there are spares." The list:

> Case
> Motherboard
> CPU (Processor)
> Graphics Card (if not integrated with the CPU)
> RAM, 4 GB, 8 GB is better
> Storage Device (SSD best, 512 GB or more)
> CD/DVD Drive
> Cooling Fan
> Power Supply
> Mouse and Keyboard (I jury-rigged my own, but just in case)
> Cables to connect everything
> Software (all on CD, so it won't be erased when crossing)
> Windows
> Excel/Microsoft Office

Acrobat
Data Modeling software (ask which is the best)
Manuals for software (PDF or print)
I don't need a display. I have already built one.
Go to Gateway Electronics. They will take care of you. Use my name if you need to.
P.S. Get yourself a new shortwave radio. Don't trust my old piece of crap.

Billy was impressed by John's thoroughness. And he was looking forward to buying computer equipment, rather than trying to sell it.

Leonora opened a small pouch. "This should be enough to pay for everything." She poured an assortment of coins onto the table. They were twenty-dollar gold pieces from the nineteenth century. "Looks like more than enough," said Billy. "The store won't know what to do with these. I'll pay by credit card and take the coins for reimbursement."

"After we finish shopping, we will take you on a tour around town," Carol said.

Leonora was fascinated by Gateway Electronics. It was SD's version of the Mechanical Market. Billy took charge as they collected the items on the list. The terminology was incomprehensible to her. She said to the salesman "John Little told me this was the best place to come."

The salesman brightened at the mention of John's name. "He hasn't been in for quite a while."

"He moved out of town," Leonora said.

As they carried everything out to Billy's car, Leonora said that she wanted to go to a music store. "John gave me a list of CDs he wants."

"I know just the place," Billy said.

At a store called Euclid Records, Leonora approached a clerk, a tall man who seemed to be in charge. She explained that she needed to get jazz CDs for a friend. She showed him John's list of artists: Duke Ellington, Count Basie, Ella Fitzgerald, Miles Davis, John Coltrane. "I don't know much about jazz. Can you help me choose the best ones?" He was very patient as he led her around the store. Before long, they had a small stack of CDs on the checkout counter. "What's your name?" asked Leonora.

"Steve."

"I really appreciate your help, Steve. I don't know what I would have done."

"You're welcome. We're here to help people find the music they love."

"One more thing. Yesterday, I heard a catchy song and I can't get the tune out of my head. It was something about teenagers, old folks, and c'est la vie. Do you know that one?"

Steve nodded and went over to the shelves. He came back with a CD, *Chuck Berry: The Definitive Collection.* "Your song is track 26, *You Never Can Tell.*

"Thank you! I was afraid it was by someone no one had heard of. Are his other songs good?"

"Everybody likes them. My favorites are *Maybellene* and *Johnny B. Goode.*"

"I will be sure to listen to them."

Steve watched Leonora leave with a shopping bag full of CDs. He had never before had a customer who didn't know who Chuck Berry was.

GUEST SPEAKERS

IT WAS HAPPENING AGAIN. Jamal Henderson came up against the same wall every time he began something risky. At first, he would be excited and confident. Then, even if he was doing fine, he got cold feet and started to talk himself out of it. *This is going to take too long and be too hard…. No way I can do it right…I'm not good enough…who's going to pay attention me anyway?*

When he was a kid, it was pickup basketball at the playground. In high school, it was an advanced class that his teacher urged him to take. Now it was a course at Forest Park Community College—*Start a Business and Change Your Life.* Jamal had done pretty well in the introductory business administration courses on spreadsheets, finance, and marketing. The teachers complimented him and suggested he take this advanced course. Jamal liked the idea of being his own boss and making some real money, but a few weeks into the course, he was getting nervous. He was comfortable when he was given assignments, but this course required mostly independent work. Each student was supposed to identify a business they wanted to launch, then develop a business plan to be critiqued by both the teacher and the other students. The teacher began each class with an inspirational saying, like "I can't teach you anything, but I can help you learn." or "Think small, and big things happen." He spent more time in class asking questions and putting people on the spot than teaching them stuff.

All the other students got going on their businesses—like a hair salon, a bicycle shop, a home care service for senior citizens, a barbecue restaurant—right from the get go, but Jamal couldn't decide what his business would be. He considered a DJ service (*Partying is my profession!*), a video game store (*No lame games here!*), a car wash (*We make your ride fly.*), and a dozen more ideas. But he found something wrong with each one. The pressure Jamal felt to get going on his project was becoming intolerable and he was running out of time. That's when dropping the class began to seem like a good idea. Maybe he wasn't cut out for this. The problem was that his mother was on his case to finish what he started. His uncle Alonzo, a local politician, was right there with her. "Get a degree and then I can help you find something."

Jamal dragged himself to class one Friday. It was the last place he wanted to be. He was ready to drop the course, but not to face his mother's anger. The teacher started off with another of his sayings, "Do good and do well." He looked right at Jamal. "Mr. Henderson, what do you think that means?"

"I don't know. Do something good and make some money while you're doing it?"

"Exactly! You have just defined social entrepreneurship. Today we're going to explore social entrepreneurship and Tuesday two guest speakers will tell us about their very exciting and original venture."

Jamal perked up. Maybe a social-whatever type business would be better for him than the other dumbass ideas he had been thinking about. He paid attention and took notes the whole hour and decided he would come to listen to the speakers.

When Jamal entered the classroom on Tuesday, he was floored. The two visitors talking to the teacher were the Indian and the white girl he had met a few months earlier. He took his usual seat in the back row and said to the students next to him—the hair salon girl and the bicycle shop guy—"I know these dudes! They're totally dope." Jamal waved to Diyami, who nodded back to him and smiled.

The teacher introduced Meredith and Diyami. Meredith had been his student at Webster University.

"Meredith comes from a family of entrepreneurs. Her grandfather started a well-known store called the Duke of Discounts in the 1950s—ask your parents about it. Her father rebranded it as Duke's Digital and ran it until last year. Now she and her partner Diyami Red Hawk have embarked on a unique venture in social entrepreneurship."

Diyami talked about the ancient history of Cahokia and about their project to rejuvenate the city. Meredith talked about the investments they had secured from a tribal corporation to build a freight terminal near Cahokia. "Creating jobs is an important part of our strategy."

The teacher asked a question, "What's your elevator pitch?" He was always preaching that every entrepreneur needed a perfectly-honed elevator pitch. Diyami looked puzzled. Meredith whispered in his ear what an elevator pitch was. He thought for a moment, then said, "We're building a modern city that honors Native American heritage, culture, and values."

A student asked what their unique value proposition was. This was another concept the teacher had drilled into them. Diyami answered, "I can see a new Cahokia in my heart and I know Native people, and all people, need it."

Another student asked, "What's your competition?"

"Apathy is our competition."

Diyami and Meredith talked and answered questions until the end of the class. They were a big hit. The teacher had to cut the conversation off when time ran out. Jamal worked his way toward the front of the room. Meredith saw that he was shy about approaching them, so she waved him over and hugged him warmly. "What a surprise. It's so good to see you again."

"I love what you're doing. Like I said last time, if you need any help, give me a buzz."

"When the moment ripens," Diyami said. "The winding river will reach the sea."

Jamal wasn't sure what Diyami meant, but it sounded positive. Meredith tapped Diyami on his shoulder. "We need to go. I just got this text from my mom." She showed him her phone.

Come to the Pelican ASAP. Important.

Lost

At the Pelican, Billy went for the big reveal. He slowly opened his hand to show Diyami and Meredith the little bottle of pills. "With these puppies we can go back to HD!" He got a kick out of the look on their faces. Diyami was elated at the idea of basking once more in the warmth of his home. He had given up all hope of ever seeing Cahokia or his family again. Now he could. So much had changed for him in less than a year. Meredith was thrilled that she could see the magnificent city once more. Carol repeated Leonora's caution to use this limited resource wisely. "We can travel back and forth a few times and that's it."

"We have to bring Stan," Meredith said. This no-nonsense Indian lawyer had gone out on a limb to help them achieve a dream he didn't fully understand. "That's your call," Carol said.

Diyami sent Stan a text.

When can you come to Cahokia? We have big news.

Stan was there in two days, after wrapping up a series of meetings in Washington on behalf of his tribal clients.

He sat with Diyami and Meredith in the beat-up trailer that had been converted into the temporary office of the ABSOM Cahokia Native Development Corporation.

"What's the problem?" he asked.

"No problem. Everything is going fine," said Meredith.

"OK. So why am I here?"

"Something very good is about to happen," Diyami said. "We want you to come with us for a few days."

"Sorry, no way. I'm up to my ears in bureaucratic bullshit."

"This is more important. I promise you will thank us."

"Turn off your phone and leave it here," Meredith said.

"I need to be available to my clients."

"Not as much as you need what we're about to do."

After a little more haggling, Stan reluctantly agreed to whatever it was Diyami and Meredith wanted. They didn't explain—they wanted to surprise him. They went outside the trailer to a nearby stand of trees. Diyami held a leather bundle, wrapped with colored rope. He calculated that this spot lined up with the 500 Nations University building in HD.

Diyami opened a small metal case and took out three little white pills. He held them in his palm. "One for each of us. Swallow, then close your eyes."

"You might feel dizzy or nauseous," Meredith said. "Don't worry, it will pass."

Diyami and Meredith each picked a pill out of Diyami's hand. Stan shook his head. "What kind of crazy shit are you two getting me into?" He reluctantly picked the last pill.

"We take them together," Diyami said. "All is blessed by the Great Mystery." They swallowed the pills, then held hands in a circle.

Within a few seconds, Stan felt a sharp headache. Everything went dark and he doubled over and fell to the ground in a fetal position. Diyami and Meredith helped him back to his feet. The headache was subsiding. He had broken out into a sweat.

"Take your time," Diyami said.

They were in a large, windowless room with a concrete floor.

"Where are we?" asked Stan.

"Lower level of the university."

Meredith held up a bandana. "Let me put this over your eyes. You'll be glad I did." She smiled mischievously. She had learned the power of the big reveal from her father. Stan allowed her to blindfold him. They each held one of his hands and began to walk. He heard a door open and then felt the warmth of the sun on his face. They walked another fifty feet or so. Stan heard people talking and laughing nearby.

"Behold, my friend," said Diyami as he removed the blindfold. Stan blinked. He was standing in a wide open space, flat like a giant manicured field. Monk's Mound was in front of him, but it wasn't covered in grass. The edges were straight and well-defined. The surface was dark, smoothly-packed earth. A small structure stood on the top. White buildings lined the horizon beyond the mound. Stan turned. Sun glinted off a huge glass pyramid at the far end of the field. It was shaped like the mound, but was about forty stories tall. Smaller structures were visible inside it. Stan turned to see the large, gleaming white building he had just walked out of. Green vines draped terraces on several levels. A group of young people were lounging in the grass. They were still engaged in their happy conversation. Stan kept turning and looking this way and that. Diyami and Meredith enjoyed his luscious bewilderment.

Stan could barely believe what he was seeing. It was all real—every word they had said to him. The Native American metropolis was alive! He sank to his knees in the grass. Tears of joy streamed down his face.

"Stage Two," Meredith said.

"I'd say Stage Four coming soon," replied Diyami.

Juliet Red Hawk's arms enveloped Diyami in a tight embrace seconds after she opened the door. "Herbert! Herbert! Come here!" He dropped his book and rushed to the front entrance of their apartment. There was Diyami, the son he thought he would never see again. And Meredith. And someone else, whom he barely noticed. Herbert clasped Diyami in his own hug and slapped him on the back.

"What happened? How did you get here?"

"We received a wonderful gift," Diyami said.

They went into the living room and sat down. Diyami explained the barest outline of all that had happened in the last year. Juliet held his hands and beamed with joy. Diyami introduced Stan as the person who was helping them get New Cahokia off the ground in SD. "It was a miracle when we met him." Stan did his best to politely greet Herbert and Juliet, but his head was still swimming with shock. He knew that, logically, he was in the other world, but all his senses were swirling in agitation. It didn't feel like it could be real. His eyes wandered to the bookshelves, the carpet, and the furniture. Meredith noticed his distress and said, "Let me show you the view." In a daze, Stan followed her through the sliding glass door onto the patio.

"I felt the same way the first time I crossed over. Take your time and allow your mind to catch up."

They looked out over the expanse of the Grand Plaza. Monk's Mound was to the right. "They call it the Temple of the Ancestors." And the massive glass pyramid was to the left. "That's the Temple of the Children. We'll take the elevator to the top. It's the best place to see the whole city".

Stan took slow, deep breaths and began to calm down. "H-H-How can this be happening?"

"We are the lucky few. Hardly anyone knows about this. Now you can see why Diyami wants to build a new Cahokia."

Meredith pointed out some other landmarks and told him about the Three Worlds Festival last fall, when the plaza was filled with thousands of revelers and dancers. After a little while, they went back inside to join the others. Diyami and his parents were deep in conversation. A tray with glasses and a pitcher of water was on the coffee table. Stan filled a glass and drained it in one long swallow. He was completely dehydrated.

They remained in the apartment for the rest of the day and evening. Diyami told his parents about his encounters with the river spirit and the catfish, unwrapped the bundle, and showed them the pipe, dagger, and arrowhead. This was the first Stan had heard about Diyami's vision quest. He would have been astonished, if he were not already amazed beyond comprehension. Juliet lit the pipe and held it aloft with two hands to welcome the return of their son, his dear companion, and their new friend. They passed the pipe around. Later, Herbert grilled venison and Stan got his first taste of Kahok Beer.

The conversation lasted deep into the night and ranged far and wide. Diyami recounted his challenges in promoting a new Cahokia in SD. "I couldn't get through to anyone. One day, Meredith took over and showed me the way. After my vision, Stan came to us." Herbert and Juliet wanted to know about the state of Natives in SD. Stan did his best to explain a hundred years of history, how Native nations had been beaten down, then had regained some pride and power. Like Diyami, they found the story of Indian casinos to be distasteful. "It's sad if we have to do that to provide for our people," Juliet said.

Stan learned that Herbert was a linguist at 500 Nations University and had developed Modern Cahokian, a common language for the people of many tribes who migrated to Cahokia. "It's a synthesis based on several Dhegihan Siouan languages—analogous to Esperanto, which is a synthesis of European languages." It was now taught in the schools of Cahokia and Herbert had great hope that there would soon be a generation that spoke Cahokian as a first language. Juliet was a professor of microbiology and also a spirit speaker, who had the gift of communicating with the ancient spirits of Cahokia. Stan had never been much of a spiritual person—he was more comfortable in the world of treaties, statutes, and contract negotiations—but, after today, anything seemed possible.

Meredith asked Herbert and Juliet to tell Stan the story of the founding of new Cahokia by Morning Star and Corn Mother. "My dad and I were blown away when we heard it." The story blew Stan away too. Now, he fully appreciated what Diyami was trying to do. During this long evening of dinner and conversation with the Red Hawks, he sensed that something ancient, noble, and good was calling to him.

Stan awoke to the smell of coffee. He had slept like a rock, even though the sofa in Herbert and Juliet's living room wasn't very comfortable. *Having your mind blown can take it right out of you,* he thought. The others were already up and soon they were all eating breakfast on the patio. Meredith offered to take Stan on a tour of the sights of Cahokia. "The Red Hawks have a lot to talk about," she said. Herbert and Juliet lent clothes to Stan and Meredith, so they would fit in better when they went out in public.

They walked out of the building and stepped onto the edge of the Grand Plaza. It was a bright early summer morning. Several groups of chunkey players were scattered across the plaza, running with long sticks and shouting. Coaches were blowing whistles. "They always like to practice early," Meredith said. She suggested that they first go to see the Temple of the Children. Stan kept turning his head this way and that as they walked, drinking in every sensation. Meredith told him how she had first come to Cahokia with her father the previous summer and was later stuck here for a few weeks with no way to get home. That's when Diyami accepted his calling from the spirits to build a new Cahokia in SD.

The Temple of the Children looked even more impressive the closer they got. People streamed in and out the tall doors. Stan saw that they were mostly Native Americans. Many had facial tattoos like Diyami's. Some were dressed with a traditional flair, with beaded vests, bone necklaces, or a feather pinned in their hair. But it didn't seem like they were going to a powwow or ceremony—they looked like people on their way to a day at the office.

Inside, Meredith pointed out the museum and shops on the ground floor, workplaces that took up fifteen or twenty stories, and the high school on the upper floors. "The museum is totally awesome!" she said. "We'll check it out after we go to the top."

Stan and Meredith stood on the elevator platform with about a dozen other people. A recorded voice said, first in Cahokian, then in English, "Stand back from the edge. Please hold onto your children and belongings." With a whoosh, the platform accelerated straight up. The ground fell away and the vista expanded through the glass walls of the pyramid. Stan looked up and saw the roof slide open just before the elevator reached it. They were in a broad open space at the very top. From this height, Stan saw the layout of the city—the Grand Plaza in front of them with the Temple of the Ancestors at the far end. A tall pole at the center of the plaza marked the formal chunkey field. White buildings lined both sides of the plaza. Beyond, the city was laid out in concentric circles linked by lakes and canals. The university was on the east and commercial areas on the south. Residential neighborhoods were on the west and north, with smaller pyramids and parks interspersed between houses and apartments. Meredith pointed out the St. Louis skyline six miles to the west. "They don't have the Arch over here. That freaked me out the first time!"

They stayed on the roof for quite a while. Stan couldn't get enough. Eventually, Meredith persuaded him to go down to look at the museum. "Something tells me this won't be your last visit here," she said with a laugh.

The museum was spectacular. One wing was devoted to ancient history. With art and artifacts, it covered the sweep of Native peoples from the first migrants who crossed from Asia fifteen thousand years ago up to European contact in the sixteenth century. The other wing told the story of modern Cahokia, beginning with Corn Mother and Morning Star, incarnated as two archaeologists, in the 1950s. An animated map traced the travels of the Cahokian pioneers, who came from Native nations across North

America to build the city. Stan looked at every exhibit and read every word of every plaque until he was worn out. Meredith suggested lunch in the museum café. As they ate, she told him that it was impossible to take pictures because phones and cameras stopped working when you crossed over from SD. "Some kind of magnetic thing. My dad can explain it better than me."

After lunch, they went into the gift shop. Stan picked up a stack of postcards and a few books.

"Will these make it back to SD in one piece?"

"Yes, but keep them to yourself. People would be extremely confused by them."

After paying for the postcards and books, Stan said, "I'd like to explore on my own for a while. I can find my way back to the apartment later." Meredith understood. "It's hard to get enough of this place."

Stan took off. He walked west into the residential districts of Cahokia, without a map or a plan. Wandering alone through the cities he visited had long been one of his favorite ways to relax. His work required travel all over the country, so he explored places from New York and Boston to San Francisco and New Orleans, and many more. He took a European vacation where unstructured days in obscure neighborhoods of Amsterdam, Barcelona, and Paris were his fondest memories.

Stan followed a street that led away from the Grand Plaza, turned at a narrow side alleyway, then crossed a bridge over a canal. He was in a neighborhood of two- and three-story white buildings. Some had shops facing the street, others had blank walls on the first floor and windows above. Tall trees, probably growing in courtyards, poked over the roofs. Shopkeepers and pedestrians smiled and nodded to him as he passed. At first, he was struck by two things. There were no cars, only open golf cart-like trams, and no one was using a cell phone. It was quiet and peaceful. He felt a deep sense of harmony everywhere he looked. Intricate friezes were painted around doors and windows. He recognized designs from several tribal traditions—stylized birds, fish, and bears. He rounded one more corner and saw a small park with grass and a playground. A conical mound was at its center. A sign identified it as an ancient mound, believed to date from around 950. A group of children ran around playing tag while their parents sat on benches, watching and talking. He listened to the children's shouts and realized they were speaking a mix of English and Cahokian—part of that first generation of Cahokian speakers Herbert had described.

Stan took his time and looked into shop windows as he walked—a craft store, a tattoo parlor, a photography studio, a bank. After an hour or so of wandering, he went into a flower shop, where he struck up a conversation with the owner as she arranged bouquets. She asked him where he was from and gave him a quizzical look when he said "Minneapolis."

"I meant what's your heritage?"

"Menominee, Cheyenne, Lakota."

"I'm a Seneca, from western New York. Are you moving to Cahokia?"

"No, this is my first visit."

"It won't be your last. Cahokia gets in your blood. The next thing you know, it feels like home."

He told her he was getting hungry and asked for a suggestion. She pointed him to a café that served sandwiches and homemade pawpaw ice cream. It turned out to be as delicious as she said. As he walked further, Stan kept asking himself *How can we build a place like this?*

How can we not try?

The afternoon shadows were getting longer. It was time for him to get back to Diyami's parents' apartment, before they began to worry about him. He retraced his steps on the street that had led him to the sandwich shop. From there, he could follow the canal back to the Grand Plaza. But he couldn't find it. After a few more blocks, he realized that this wasn't the street he had been on earlier. He walked up a cross street which led to a small square with benches. A group of musicians was playing drums and flutes. Two elderly women at a table were teaching children how to weave baskets. Looking for the canal, he tried a different street, which turned out to be a dead end. He went back to the square and followed yet another street, which led him to a new group of houses. Now he had no idea which way to go.

Stan was lost in a backwater neighborhood of a Native American city on a Friday afternoon. It was the best day of his life.

Meredith watched Stan walk away through the crowd in front of the Temple of the Children. She enjoyed sharing in his first experience of HD Cahokia. *Stan is a good guy. We're so lucky we found him.*

Diyami wasn't expecting her back for a while, so she had time to herself. She knew exactly what she wanted to do. She hurried out onto the Grand Plaza, then turned left to follow a street across three canals. She soon reached the edge of the city where there was a busy wharf at the end of a long canal that led to the west. A sleek hydrofoil, the *Morning Star*, pulled in and unloaded passengers. Tram taxi drivers called out their destinations. Vendors hawked souvenirs and snacks. She joined a group waiting to board the next scheduled departure to St. Louis.

Thirty minutes later, Meredith was walking across the Eads Bridge into downtown St. Louis. She remembered being here with Diyami on their first day together. The gleaming, multicolored spire of the Hydraulic Building rose above the forest of skyscrapers. Barges and excursion boats traversed the river below. She reached the Missouri side of the bridge and headed into the noisy, bustling streets of downtown.

Meredith loved this place, which thrilled her compared to the low-energy downtown of the St. Louis where she had grown up. But it also brought back the panic she felt when agents of the Knights had kidnapped her off one of these streets. She pushed that thought away and concentrated on her goal for today—to see the two people she missed most in all of HD.

The bell jingled as she opened the shop's front door, which was etched with the name *Everything, since 1965.* Inside, an elderly woman was dusting shelves of knickknacks and curios with a feather duster. A second elderly woman sat behind a counter reading a magazine. Meredith walked in with a big smile. The woman with the feather duster, Churcha Crockett, saw her, shouted "Meredith, my dear!" then enveloped her in a warm embrace. The other woman, Scienca Crockett, looked up from her magazine.

"Meredith, Meredith, sweet Meredith," Churcha said as she hugged her tight. "We've missed you so much."

"I've missed you too."

"I also need a hug," said Scienca, "but I'm on a leash."

Meredith ran to the counter and leaned over to hug Scienca. A thin plastic tube ran under Scienca's nose and was connected to an oxygen tank next to her chair. "What happened?" Meredith asked.

"The doctors say it's a touch of emphysema, but what do they know." She held up a long cigarette holder with a plastic cigarette inserted. "I'm reduced to pretending to smoke this fake."

"Tell us about your exciting life out there in California," Churcha said.

"What about your beau? We remember that tall, handsome Cahokian gentleman." Scienca said.

"We are still together."

"Have you set the wedding date?"

Meredith blushed. "We haven't talked about that yet."

"Don't let him get away," Scienca said, waving her finger. "He's a keeper!"

"I've thought about you every day," Meredith said. "I was afraid I would never get back here to see you."

"Nothing can keep us apart, my dear," said Churcha.

"We have a new flavor, coconut lime," Scienca said as she handed Meredith a wrapped piece of taffy. The sisters, whom Meredith thought of as the taffy ladies, had taught her how to make their special, South African style taffy the previous summer.

"One of our most loyal customers asked for a special flavor and this is what we created."

"I love it. Your finest." said Meredith as she chewed.

"What wonderful adventures have you been up to?"

Meredith described her travels around the west with her 'beau' and working on a big project with him in 'California'—Churcha and Scienca didn't know about the SD world. They doted on every word she said. She asked them how they were doing.

"Other than this foolishness," said Scienca, pointing to the oxygen tube, "nothing has changed."

"Our lives are quite dull, compared to yours," said Churcha.

They talked and laughed for quite a while. Meredith basked in the warmth of their complete and unconditional love. When the time came for her to leave, she could barely hold back her emotions.

Churcha gave her a box of the coconut lime taffy. "We're always together in each other's hearts. All will be well, dear Meredith."

As she left the shop, Meredith looked back one last time. They both beamed at her. Churcha blew her a kiss.

Out on the sidewalk, she burst into tears.

The next morning, Diyami, Meredith, and Stan prepared for their trip back to SD. Diyami told his father to buy a shortwave radio transmitter.

"Under the right conditions, we can talk by radio. I will have one at this location on the other side."

"How will I know when to use it?"

"I'll be on every night at eight. Leonora Matsui will get instructions to you with the frequency. But some nights will be clearer than others. Interference comes and goes. Be patient, and keep trying. And, just to be safe, let's talk in Cahokian."

Out on the patio, Juliet conducted a small ceremony of thanks and blessings for a safe journey. Stan took a final look over the Grand Plaza.

Ten minutes later, they were back in SD.

Giles Monroe waited patiently. It had been a most frustrating week. All he wanted was a little peace and quiet. He looked forward to his Friday evening ritual—a glass of wine and contemplation of his prime number. His numerologist had taught him a new method of assigning a musical note to each digit, the lowest for 1 and the highest for 9, then humming the melody of each six-digit "word" within the number. If he emptied his mind, he might be able to perceive the meanings within the melodies. Giles had tried it once without much success, but the numerologist said that practice was essential. He hoped tonight would go better. He needed all the guidance the numbers could give him as he pursued the delicate negotiations with his new partner.

Churcha and Scienca finished up with other customers. Scienca turned to Giles. "Your taffy is ready, Mr. Monroe." She set a small, white box on the counter. "The new coconut lime flavor you requested."

"Our lovely young friend, Meredith, was here earlier," Churcha said. "We gave her a taste and she thought it was heavenly."

"We were so thrilled to see her. She hadn't come in for months," Scienca added as she tied a ribbon around the box of taffy.

"Her father wasn't with her this time," mused Churcha. "He's a busy man out there in California."

Giles smiled as he thanked Churcha and Scienca for his taffy. Inside, he was fuming. *They're back! What trouble will these people cause me now? I never should have let them go.*

ANOTHER DAY AT THE OFFICE

STAN WAS A BUNDLE of metastasizing energy as he paced back and forth in the trailer that was the temporary headquarters of the ABSOM Cahokia Native Development Corporation.

"We'll apply right away for federal recognition as an Indian nation or tribe. The process will take a long time, but we'll need it to file a claim to the state park someday."

"But there's no Cahokian tribe," Diyami said. "What is the basis for recognition?"

Stan pointed out the window to Monk's Mound. "It's right there. Obviously, this was a sacred site, even if it was abandoned before the Europeans showed up. Based on archaeology and linguistics, we can make a plausible claim that several tribes, including the Osage, are descendants of the people of Cahokia. Also, we need a daily presence here, like an office manager, so the ABSOM Cahokia Native Development Corporation looks like more than empty words on a piece of paper."

"Meredith and I have to keep traveling to spread the news about Cahokia."

"There must be someone."

"We know a young man from St. Louis," Meredith said. "He seems to be smart and enthusiastic."

"Is he an Indian?"

"No. He's Black."

"An Indian would be better, but another minority won't hurt. Hire him!"

Stan continued his rapid drumbeat of ideas. "What about economic development? There have to be jobs if we want people to move here. The freight terminal is a start, but won't be enough."

"No casinos!" insisted Diyami.

"Then we'll have to find something else, but I have no idea what that would be."

Diyami closed his eyes for a moment. "The opportunity will arise when the Great Mystery opens the way."

I dropped out of my classes to become an office manager and this *is the office? My mother is going to kill me.* Jamal Henderson followed Diyami and Meredith into the trailer. It had seen better days. There were two decrepit desks, file cabinets, a lumpy brown sofa, a bulletin board, a small refrigerator and a microwave. Diyami turned a knob on the window-mounted air conditioner, and it wheezed into life. He was still fascinated by this remarkable technology, so different from the air cooling systems in HD. "Meredith and I are going to Wisconsin for three days. We need you to just be here. Answer calls and help anybody who comes in."

"Some truck drivers from the freight company are due here tomorrow. Make sure they know they've found the right place and help them out anyway you can," Meredith said.

"What freight company?" Jamal asked.

"Eagle Transportation. That's who's paying for all this.

155

Our attorney, Stan Huffman, set everything up. They're going to build a freight terminal near here."

"That's all you want me to do? Just welcome these guys?"

"Can you work on our mailing list? There are a lot of names that need to go into the spreadsheet."

"Sure. No problem. At the community college, I learned how to do Excel, PowerPoint, all that shit."

"That would be so great. I thought I was going to have to do it all myself." She showed him how to log into the laptop and gave him a file folder with handwritten signup sheets.

"We have a long drive today," Diyami said. "We should leave." He saw that Jamal was overwhelmed by the hasty introduction to the job. "I know this place doesn't look like much, but remember, we're doing something big and important. We need you."

On her way to the pickup, Meredith said, "Check out the Cahokia PowerPoints we made. You'll enjoy them."

Jamal watched them drive off. *What have I gotten myself into?*

The next morning, after dropping off his mother for her shift at the hospital, Jamal returned to the trailer. He cleaned up the place as best he could, then entered all the names and addresses in Meredith's folder into the mailing list spreadsheet. He noticed the addresses were mostly from places he had never heard of in Oklahoma, North Dakota, and South Dakota. Some of the names were regular ones, while others were Indian names, like Tallchief, Blackbird, and Yellow Robe. Then he looked at the PowerPoints, which were about the history of Cahokia and how it could be a big deal again. It was all brand new to him, but he liked it—making something out of nothing.

The blast of an air horn shook Jamal. He opened the door and saw a huge eighteen-wheeler truck pulled to the side of the road next to the trailer. "Is this ABSOM Cahokia?" a guy yelled from the cab.

"Yeah."

"We've been looking for you for half an hour. Where do you want me to park this thing?"

"Back there, I guess." Jamal pointed to an open space next to other abandoned mobile homes on the lot. The driver turned into the space and a guy jumped out of the right side of the cab. He was an Indian, but unlike Diyami, without tattoos (Diyami was the only Indian Jamal had ever met).

"Are you Red Hawk?" the guy asked.

"He's not here. I'm Jamal."

"I'm Bert. We've had a long day. Got anything to drink?"

"Cold soda inside."

Another Indian, Bert's partner Vince, soon joined them.

"This place needs a sign," Vince said.

Jamal, Bert, and Vince sat in the breeze from the wheezy air conditioner, sipped soda, and talked. They asked him what there was to do in St. Louis and the conversation turned to music, sports, and girls. Jamal realized that these Indians were a lot like the guys he knew from his neighborhood.

The next day was more of the same. The first truck left and two others arrived. Jamal had to show them where to park and answer their questions as best he could. He didn't know if this is what he was supposed to be doing, but everyone seemed satisfied. On the third day, he was relieved when Diyami and Meredith returned and took charge. Meredith loved his idea for a sign and she drove with him to the copy shop and hardware store. He finished the sign in a few hours. It looked great, with a silhouette of Monk's Mound above the words "ABSOM Cahokia Native Development Corporation." One of the truck drivers took a picture of Diyami, Meredith, and Jamal standing next to it. Meredith posted the photo on Twitter.

Later that afternoon, Diyami wanted to show the truck drivers around Cahokia and he asked Jamal to join them. Standing at the top of Monk's Mound, Diyami pointed out the ancient landmarks and described his ideas for the new city. "We can build neighborhoods over here and connect them with canals, so people can get around the city without cars. On the other side of the Grand Plaza, we will have a university, a Native American university. People will come from all over." The drivers listened and asked many questions. Diyami led a brief ceremony of offerings to the four directions. He chanted in an Indian language. The drivers, guys who had shot the breeze with Jamal about basketball and hip-hop just an hour earlier, seemed to know how to participate. Jamal was unsure of what to do, so he stood awkwardly off to one side—but he watched and listened carefully. As they walked back down the mound, Jamal said to Diyami, "Man, when you talk about this city, it sounds like it's almost real."

"It is real."

That evening, Jamal was bursting with enthusiasm for Cahokia as he ate dinner at home with his mother. "Diyami wants to build a place for his people, with a university, houses, canals, and everything. He is deep! And these Indians are driving in big trucks from all over."

"Do you know what those trucks are carrying?" his mother asked.

"What does that matter?"

"I hope it isn't drugs."

"C'mon, mom. These people are on the up and up."

"How do you know? You're telling me about strangers with trucks and money. Sometimes, when something seems too good to be true, that's what it is."

The next day, Meredith took Jamal to see the Cahokia Museum, which was just a few hundred yards away from the trailer, on the Grand Plaza. He loved the movie *City of the Sun*, which evoked the world of ancient Cahokia. They wandered through the exhibits of pottery, tools, and daily life. In the life-sized diorama of Cahokian houses, she showed him the seated figure of a young man who looked almost exactly like Diyami. "You should have seen his face when I showed this to him last year."

"That's crazy!" Jamal said. "Last year was the first time he saw it?"

"Yep." They both thought that was pretty funny.

One afternoon, a curious staff member from the historic site dropped by the trailer. "I saw your sign and wondered what was going on here." Diyami sat down with her on the lumpy sofa and explained, in very general terms, what **ABSOM** Cahokia Native Development Corporation was doing. "We're funded by a Native American tribal corporation to work on economic development in this area. We're looking at several opportunities. The first will probably be a freight terminal for truck traffic. There's quite a bit of vacant land available just to the west of the historic site, with good access to the interstate." Stan had coached him on what to say if people asked about the project—*be honest, but don't go into details. Avoid any mention of building a new city. It's far too soon for that.*

"Why do you call it **ABSOM** Cahokia?"

"To honor the heritage and traditions. As Before, So Once More."

The staff member listened politely, but she was skeptical. *What is going on here?*

A few days later, the office was quiet. Diyami and Meredith had appointments in St. Louis and would arrive in an hour or so. Jamal was transferring more names and email addresses into the spreadsheet. He was getting the hang of this job and he was starting to enjoy it. He wanted to go back to the museum at lunch. He could get a hot dog at the snack bar and revisit the exhibit on archaeologists' methods, which was one of his favorites. *It's sick how much they can figure out by sifting through dirt.*

He heard some cars pull up outside the trailer and footsteps as people got out. A voice said, "Stand over here by the sign, so we're ready when the cameras arrive." Jamal went to the window and peeked through the blinds. There were about a dozen people. Most were white, a few were Black. One woman took signs out the back of an SUV and handed them to the others. As the people stood in a line next to the road, Jamal read the hand-lettered signs:

Indians Go Home

Don't Gamble with Our Future

Casinos = Crime

NO CasiNO

You Cannot Serve Both God and Money
-Matthew 6:24

The protesters began to walk back and forth in front of the trailer. They chanted, "Indian gambling, evil and sick. You can't fool us with your trick."

A familiar panic rose up inside of Jamal. He was bullied a lot as a kid and confrontation terrified him. In the school of hard knocks that was his neighborhood, he had gotten knocked around too many times. There was no way to escape—the trailer's only door opened to right where the protesters were marching. He didn't think they knew that someone was in the trailer. He backed away from the window and hunched down on the floor.

A TV news van arrived. The reporter and cameraperson got out and started to film the chanting demonstrators. A gray-haired white woman, who appeared to be in charge, greeted the reporter and thanked him for coming. The reporter got the cameraperson to frame a shot with the trailer and protesters in the background, then started to interview her.

"Who do you represent and why are you here today?"

"We're the CCC, the Concerned Citizens of Collinsville. Our community is under siege by strangers who don't know anything about us or our values. They're trying to force an alien system on us—casino gambling— that we don't want. They should go back where they came from and leave us alone."

"Has ABSOM Cahokia announced plans for a casino?"

"They don't have to. We know what they're doing. It's the same everywhere they go."

Jamal called Diyami. "We got a big problem. There are people outside marching and carrying signs, and they're mad. The news is here, too. You need to come quick."

"What are they mad about?"

"They think we're building a casino."

"That's absurd. I don't want anything to do with casinos."

161

Outside, the chanting grew louder as the people intensified their protest to impress the TV camera.

Jamal had to raise his voice. "You have to get over here and tell them that."

"We're coming as fast as we can, but it will be a little while. Can you talk to them?"

"Me? Who the fuck is going to listen to me?"

"Just try to settle things down until Meredith and I get there."

"I don't know what to say."

"There's no one else, Jamal. You can do it."

This was his worst nightmare, to step into the jaws of an angry mob.

"We need you," Meredith said.

Jamal closed his eyes. "OK. I'll give it a shot."

The crowd had grown as passersby parked their cars to see what all the commotion was about. When Jamal opened the door, the chanting stopped as the protesters turned to look at the Black man standing on the trailer's tiny porch. They hadn't realized that anyone was inside. The TV reporter gestured for the camera to be pointed at Jamal.

"Hello, everybody. I'm Jamal Henderson of the ABSOM Cahokia Native Development Corporation. Thank you for coming today."

"Where are the Indians? Are they afraid of us?"

"Mr. Diyami Red Hawk wants to talk with you. He is on his way and will be here soon. One thing I can tell you is that he doesn't like casinos any more than you do. We are not building a casino."

"That's a lie! You can't trust Indians," the woman leading the protest shouted. The chanting began again. "No casino in Collinsville! No casino in Collinsville!"

Jamal waved his hand to quiet them.

"I understand you got to make noise sometimes to get people's attention. Nothing wrong with that. I'm a Black man from St. Louis. I know a thing or two about who to trust and who not to trust. And I trust Diyami Red Hawk. The Indians were here a thousand years ago, long before any of us. They want to be here a thousand years from now. Mr. Red Hawk isn't going to do anything that will mess this place up."

"They're heathens! The Bible says gambling is a sin."

"I believe in the Bible. I grew up in the church. You can ask my momma. We all have to find the path the Lord wants us to take. Mr. Red Hawk is a spiritual man. His path is not about hurting anybody or taking advantage of anybody."

The temperature of the anger among the protesters lowered a bit.

"If they're not building a casino, what are they doing here?"

Jamal explained what he knew about the plans for a trucking terminal on the vacant properties near the interstate. "There's going to be good jobs, honest work." He answered a few more questions, then did an interview with the TV reporter. Most of the protesters put down their signs and waited for Diyami. Sensing that the excitement was over, some of the onlookers got back in their cars and drove away. Jamal was feeling better as he talked to the reporter. He looked forward to seeing his mother's reaction when he was on TV that evening.

Diyami and Meredith arrived. All eyes were on Jamal and the reporter, so no one noticed them at first. They listened until Jamal's interview was over, then Diyami walked through the protesters and put his hand on Jamal's shoulder, "Thank you, my brother. Well done."

Diyami stepped up onto the trailer's porch and addressed the crowd. He drew upon the public speaking experience he had gained in the past few months to calm everybody down and answer their questions. A little while later, he was exchanging phone numbers and shaking hands with the gray-haired woman.

The ABSOM Cahokia Native Development Corporation had weathered its first crisis.

RETURN

THE TAXI PULLED INTO THE PARKING LOT of the Chesterfield Montessori School on Ladue Road, which was deserted on a Sunday.

"Are you sure this is where you want to be?" the driver asked.

"Yes," Billy said. "A friend is going to pick us up."

Carol and Billy watched the taxi drive away. They walked around to the back of the school, each pulling a small, wheeled suitcase like they were going on vacation. To fit in, he had on his floppy HD hat and she was wearing the same loose dress she wore for her first visit to HD last year. They decided on this place with Leonora when they drove her around West County a week earlier. It was only a few hundred yards from Billy and Carol's old house, which they had sold over the winter to move to the Pelican building. Like everywhere in SD, Leonora commented on how different this suburban area, with ranch houses and broad lawns, was from HD. "Lots of crawler-builts around here," she said.

"What's a crawler-built?" Carol asked.

"Inexpensive high-rise apartments, for people who can't afford to live closer in."

"Why do you call them that?"

"Each building has a vertical track up one side, so it's easy to mount a crane that crawls up and lifts additional blocks into place. They keep adding levels to keep up with demand. Some started out as eight stories and are now thirty or thirty-five."

Leonora had crossed back into HD from this place and suggested that they use it as well. Billy still wanted to do the crossings away from the city, in case anyone was watching.

"How will you find us?" he had asked Leonora as they agreed upon the time for the crossing.

"You'll see a park near here with a tall, bladed tower. You can't miss it. Stand by the road at the base."

Behind the school, there was no one in sight.

"I never thought it could happen, but here we go," Billy said.

"Are you nervous?"

"If we get caught, we may never see home again. On the other hand...no more 'coulda, woulda, shoulda.'"

"Bon voyage," Carol said with a big smile.

They held hands tightly, then swallowed the pills. After a brief spasm of headaches and vertigo, they were underneath a canopy of trees in HD. Children laughed and shouted in a playground about fifty yards away. Billy and Carol walked to an open space, where they saw the crawler-builts—Jenga-like towers of varying heights that surrounded the park. A slender cylindrical spire about thirty stories tall was on the opposite side of the playground. Long blades spun slowly two-thirds of the way up, like a horizontal wind turbine which bathed the area in a cool breeze. They found the road and waited, trying to look as inconspicuous as possible.

After a few minutes, a light blue, three-wheeled car approached. Leonora lowered the window and waved to Billy and Carol. The door slid open and they hopped inside. John, wearing a fashionable HD jumpsuit, greeted them with a big smile. The sights flew by on the harrowing trip to Flora Place—Leonora drove fast and talked nonstop. Carol and Billy had many questions—they hadn't seen this part of HD before—but couldn't get in a word edgewise. When they arrived at Leonora's house, Billy noticed the HD version of his childhood home just down the block. It looked exactly the same, except for the big awnings that shaded the front windows. What would his life have been like if he had grown up in that house, rather than in SD? It freaked him out to be face-to-face with the randomness of everything.

Inside Leonora's, they relaxed with iced tea and sandwiches. Her elegant home was quite a step up from the cramped, cluttered apartment on Enright Avenue in SD where John had lived his whole life. Billy was still getting used to thinking of John in this new life.

"There's so much I want to see," Carol said, "especially a bookstore." She talked about her desire to learn as much as she could about HD and its history.

"I'll take you up to Seven Wonders," Leonora said. "A bookstore there has everything you can dream of."

"What's Seven Wonders?"

"A bohemian neighborhood. Very colorful. We'll go soon."

"Today, let's get you what you need to fit in," John said. He and Leonora had assembled several sets of clothes for both Billy and Carol, who had given Leonora their sizes when she was in SD. "That includes ID cards in case the police or anyone else stops you. We're going to see a guy at my favorite place."

John led Billy and Carol through the maze of shops and stalls underneath the cavernous roof of the Mechanical Marketplace. "It's amazing what I've found here. An education in the technology of this world." Billy had little idea of what the piles of odd equipment and parts on tables were for. At a far corner of the Marketplace, John took them to the back of a shop, then through a curtain into a dimly lit room. A wiry man with a stringy beard looked up from his desk.

"Sergei, these are the friends I told you about. They need some of your best identification cards."

"CSP memberships, Yohn?" asked Sergei in a thick Russian accent.

"Yes."

"For collecting payments or for identification only?"

"Identification only." John and Sergei agreed upon a price. Sergei asked what names should go on the cards. John suggested 'William Duke' and 'Carol Duke'—Billy got a chuckle out of those—and an address on Accomac Street. "It's an apartment where Leonora used to live. She still owns it."

Sergei took photographs of Billy and Carol with a large bellows camera, then told them to come back in twenty minutes. John took them up and down more of the many aisles of the Marketplace. As he pointed things out, he talked about the different design approaches of HD and SD.

"Everything here has intricate moving assemblies, discrete electronic components, and prisms. No integrated circuits, digital devices, or what we think of as software. That's why I needed the computer parts and software from SD. When we get home, I'll show you what I've built."

Carol asked about something she saw in one stall, which looked like a typewriter attached to a frame with levers and metal beads on wires.

"That's a calculator. Very fast, if you know how to operate it. Like a semi-automated abacus."

"Stage Four," Billy said to Carol. She laughed.

When they returned to Sergei's shop, he handed them two official-looking plastic cards with their photos and the logo "Citizen Shareholder Plan."

"Don't try to use these at a payment office or bank. Those are the only places that will spot them as fake."

Over dinner that evening, Leonora advised Billy and Carol to avoid walking on Flora Place. "I'm a public person, so someone may notice unusual visitors. It's better to go in and out through the back alley. I don't expect a problem, but let's not attract attention."

The next day, the first order of business for Billy and Carol was to explore the city. Billy had done quite a bit of that the previous year, but Carol had not. When his adventures began, he had avoided telling her about them, out of fear that she would think he was crazy—he spent a lot of time wondering that himself. Billy had only revealed HD to Carol, and taken her there, after Meredith disappeared. So Carol's first experience of HD was the frantic search to find her daughter and get her back.

Billy's secrecy created a rift between Carol and him, which was taking a while to heal. Today was his opportunity to complete the repair. Billy wanted to show her the places in HD St. Louis that had dazzled him the most. "I have a great day planned. Just you and me." So, wearing the HD clothes that Leonora had gotten for them and with their fake IDs, they set off.

They walked along Grand Avenue, hand in hand, on a sunny morning. The first place they stopped was the Refugees Club, which was on the same site as the Pelican building in SD. He had once tried to describe to her its bizarre façade, a riotous mix of giant carved eagles, musical instruments, vines, and a large clock, but he couldn't do it justice. Carol marveled at its overwhelming weirdness.

"If we took those pills right now," Billy said, "we would be standing in front of home."

"So I guess that makes us the neutrinos." Carol said. Now she understood why Billy had wanted to move to this spot.

They went inside. They stood in an enormous skylit room, three stories tall, with fig trees in planters, library tables, and a shuffleboard court. Small groups of people around the room sat in conversation or playing board games. A woman, who seemed to be responsible for visitors, welcomed Billy and Carol. She explained that the Refugees Club was a social organization that provided comfort and companionship to lonely and lost people—those who couldn't adapt to the pace and harshness of the modern world. She asked them the three questions that embodied the club's philosophy: "Are you far from home? Are you alone? Do you despair? You are welcome here." Carol talked with her for a while. Billy, who had engaged in a similar conversation the year before, hung back. Carol thanked the woman for her time and accepted some Refugees Club literature.

Outside, Carol shook her head. "This place is like a mashup of Alcoholics Anonymous, a church, and a book club. Wonderful, but very, very strange."

"Let's walk south, "Billy said. "I'll show you where the street supper was. We can go to Whittemore's Bar on Gravois, and then take the streetcar downtown. It's an incredible ride."

"Hold it right there," Carol said. "I know you want to show me all the places I missed last year. But that's not what I want. Let's go this way." She pointed north. "The best thing you can do is to let me decide where we go. We can discover some new places together."

Carol started walking up the sidewalk. Billy, flummoxed, tagged along. "Where are we headed?"

"Central West End."

They hopped on a Grand Avenue streetcar and rode it to Lindell, next to Saint Louis University. Students filled the sidewalks and crossed the streets from building to building. Carol and Billy saw the mix of familiar buildings—the Gothic church on the corner, opposite red brick university buildings—and newer, taller glass and multicolored structures that surrounded the campus.

Billy pointed to a stairwell descending from the sidewalk. "We can take the subway to Kingshighway and be at Forest Park in five minutes."

"What's the rush?"

They rode another streetcar west on Lindell past a kaleidoscope of strange new buildings. As soon as Carol got a good look at one, the next came into view. She tried hard to record every image in her mind. At Newstead, they approached the massive stone Cathedral with its green tiled dome that they had seen many times in SD. They had been inside it once for a friend's wedding. "Let's get off here," Carol said.

Tall trees lined both sides of Lindell to the west. Across the street a square was framed by colonnaded buildings and dotted with groups of umbrella-shaded tables. At the far end was a building about the size and shape of the Cathedral, with a confection of rainbow-colored arches.

"I want to see that," Carol said.

They strolled across the square, past waiters bringing trays of food and drinks to diners at the tables. Pigeons fluttered about. "This is what Rome was like," Carol said. She went there one summer with a group of teachers. Billy stayed home and worked, as he tried in vain to keep his stores afloat.

The building at the far end was the Hines Memorial Opera House. Its iridescent brick arches glittered in the midday sun. Banners announced the upcoming productions: *The Magic Flute, Carmen,* and *Treemonisha, Joplin's Early Masterpiece.*

Billy and Carol found one of the last empty tables in front of one of the square's restaurants, a popular spot for lunch. "I wish we had a camera," Carol said.

"The pictures would never make it home," Billy said. "I told you how film spoils and digital photos get erased when we cross back to SD. Meredith and I tried everything we could think of. Buying postcards was the only solution." Carol gave him a thumbs-up. That's what they would do next. The waiter brought pasta and salad, along with the glasses of white wine they ordered to celebrate this momentous day.

After lunch, they browsed the shops beneath the colonnades. One was devoted to opera, with books, posters, and recordings on small brass cylinders—apparently HD's version of CDs. Another shop was crammed with puppets, fanciful costumes, and mechanical birds. Carol loved the store of handmade toys, which featured miniature stage sets, wooden cars (HD style, of course), and painted dolls with tiny necklaces, rings, and bracelets. Billy spotted a newsstand with racks of postcards for Carol to choose from. She selected a handful and also bought a guidebook, *The Intrepid Traveler's St. Louis.* The blurb on the back cover said, *Seen the skyline? Tired of all the street suppers? Discover the hidden wonders of this amazing city.* Carol couldn't wait to read it.

They walked out of the square and turned west on Lindell's broad sidewalks. Latticed metal towers stood every fifty yards. "I saw these on South Grand last year," Billy said. "They pump out cool air." These were a little different—the air they emitted was both cool and perfumed—jasmine with hints of lilac. "This part of town appears to be a cut above," Carol said with a smile.

She was right. The elegant boulevard was lined with upscale stores and apartment buildings, where uniformed doormen tipped their caps to well-dressed patrons. Everything and everyone looked polished and manicured. Like elsewhere in the city, balconies were festooned with living plants, but here, instead of cascades of greenery, they were closely trimmed into intricate, geometric shapes. Billy and Carol studied the window displays of exclusive stores. Faceless female mannequins were draped with long gowns with feathers and floral designs. Male mannequins sported pastel suits with short pants. Gold necklaces over men's suits appeared to be the season's fashion accessory. Jewelry stores showed pendants, armbands, and earrings that overflowed with diamonds, rubies, and other gems.

Two white-haired women, wearing shimmering pantsuits, were walking towards Billy and Carol. Each one had a brocaded pouch slung over her shoulder and strands of pearls woven into her hair. Billy and Carol saw the small white faces of capuchin monkeys poking out of the pouches.

As the women passed, engaged in their conversation and nodding absentmindedly to Billy and Carol, each one gently stroked the head of her pet monkey.

"I think we're seeing how the other half lives," Carol said.

"Other half in more ways than one," Billy joked.

They laughed and held hands as they continued along Lindell.

At the corner of Euclid, they saw the largest store so far, *Mastin's*, which filled an entire block. A string of highly-polished black and silver limousines were parked in front of it. Chauffeurs leaned against the cars and chatted with each other while the owners shopped inside.

Billy and Carol decided to turn right and walk north on Euclid. In SD, this street had a mix of tasteful restaurants, funky shops and early twentieth century homes. Here, it looked pretty much the same. "Diyami told me this was a good area for live music," Billy said. Soon they saw the clubs—*Nile, KitKat, Thrill Club, Terpsichore, Dionysus* and several more. Billy studied the lists of bands scheduled for each club and wished he could hear every last one. The music by Milo Riley and his band at the street supper in HD last year had given him the best night he had had in years.

After a while, they doubled back to see Forest Park. As they walked along its eastern edge on Kingshighway, Billy spotted a sign for *Biggie's Rooftop Restaurant* in front of a ten-story building. "That's perfect!"

They stepped off an elevator onto a large terrace. A waiter led them to a table at the front where they could easily see the entire park. Billy pointed to the Grand Basin, "That's where the fountains come on to form a giant arch each hour. Martin told me his theory that Saarinen came over from SD and was inspired by it to design the Arch there."

Carol studied her guidebook. "It says there is a long lagoon from one end of the park to the other. They use it for crew rowing races." Billy found the lagoon, which ran parallel to Lindell. Two shells with eight oarsmen each moved swiftly along it. They also found the striped tents of the circus which the book said was permanently based in the park. The waiter arrived with the cocktails they had ordered.

Carol's mind raced a mile a minute with questions as she looked out at the sights. Billy was glad to see her so excited and relieved that she was finally experiencing the full wonder of HD. They were turning a page in the glow of the late afternoon light.

"Good god, Billy. This place is so damn beautiful."

"What I can never figure out is, how did we get to be the lucky ones who are here?"

"As I recall," Carol said as she sipped her cocktail, "it began when you chewed out a customer last year."

"Oh yeah, that," Billy chuckled. "But seriously, Carol, shouldn't we do something good with all this? Make the world a better place, like Diyami and Meredith are doing?"

"I'm going to tell the story of HD when I write my 'novel,'" She made air quotes. "I want to make people think."

Billy turned to her. "What about me? What can I do?"

"An opportunity will present itself. You'll see."

"I hope so."

"You can start by giving me a kiss."

Billy caressed her cheek, leaned over, and they kissed. They sat in contented silence as the sun sank toward the horizon and the scattered clouds turned gold and purple.

Hawks and falcons soared and darted in front of them. At the top of the hour, the fountains in the Grand Basin erupted to form a perfect arch hundreds of feet tall.

They took an elevator back down to the busy, rush hour street. When they came out onto the sidewalk, there was a small commotion in front of them. A bright orange police car had pulled over with its lights flashing. Two officers were talking to a distraught woman, who was pleading with them, "I left my identification at home. I'm sorry. I came here to pick up my child at school." The officers grabbed her arms and hustled her into their car. "What about my child?" she howled as the door to the police car shut. The people passing by paid no attention. They kept moving and didn't look at what was happening.

"That's no way to treat people!" Billy yelled at the police. One of them turned to him with an angry look. Carol grabbed Billy's arm and dragged him away into the crowd. "Let it go," she said. "If there's anybody who shouldn't get involved, it's us. You'll just get thrown in jail. This is not the opportunity."

The police car blared its siren and pulled out into traffic. Billy's chest was still heaving with adrenaline. "That wasn't right."

"I guess that's why Leonora and John made sure we have ID."

That night, Billy described the incident to Leonora. "Do things like that happen a lot?"

"Not that much, but more often than they used to. The police are quick to arrest people they think are suspicious. I think they're a little tougher in the Central West End to make sure the rich people feel safe."

"It was weird. No one even turned to look."

"I said you have to be careful."

SEVEN WONDERS

THE NEXT MORNING, Leonora and Carol left early for their excursion to Seven Wonders. Billy stayed behind to see John's homemade computer. Leonora drove to Grand and Olive and parked the car. She took Carol for coffee and pastries at the Metropole, an ornate restaurant with high ceilings, crystal chandeliers, and mirrored walls. "I brought John here the night I met him." She told the story of John's extreme bewilderment at his first time in HD.

"He must have been like a deer in the headlights," Carol said.

"What?"

"It's a figure of speech." Carol mimed the wide-eyed look of surprise.

They both laughed. "I've never heard that one before. I like it."

The pastries were delicious. And the day only got better from there.

They took a streetcar north on Grand. "It's impossible to park in Seven Wonders." Leonora pointed out various sights along the way. Carol, who looked a little bit like a deer in the headlights herself, soaked everything in. They got off the streetcar in front of a tall, white Corinthian column, the Grand Avenue Water Tower. "This is the first of the Seven Wonders, built in the 1870s," Leonora said.

"We have this in SD as well."

The tower was on an island in the middle of Grand. The surrounding streets were lined with old brick buildings painted in a rainbow of bright colors. The sidewalks were packed with vendors at tables hawking all kinds of products—clothing, kitchen wares, toys, watches, and more. "Don't let them engage you," said Leonora. "Most of them are con artists selling fakes."

Leonora pointed out the second Wonder, the Bissell Street Water Tower, a few blocks away— also one that Carol knew from SD.

"How do you get to seven?"

Leonora led Carol to the next corner and pointed south. Carol saw a row of tall monuments and statues stretching over several blocks. Each one appeared to be about 150 or 200 feet tall.

"Five more makes seven. Together, they represent the seven wonders of the ancient world. Let me see if I can remember what they all are. We learned this in school."

Leonora counted on her fingers. The five new wonders were an Egyptian obelisk, covered with hieroglyphics, the statue of Zeus at Olympus, the Tower of Babel, the Colossus of Rhodes, and the Lighthouse of Alexandria.

"That's crazy," said Carol. "How did they get here?"

"Back in the 1930s, an eccentric tycoon, who was a lover of ancient history, thought the wonders of antiquity should be reproduced in St. Louis. He wanted them here, close to the Mississippi, so riverboat passengers would see them. They were covered with a new Hydraulic product, ultrathin NightShine bricks, so the monuments glow in the dark, each one in a different color. They have faded some over the years, but you can still see the effect. The glowing bricks never caught on as a product for Hydraulic, so the Seven Wonders are one of the few places where they were used. The research behind them paid off a few years later when Hydraulic invented Amperic bricks, which generate electricity. It may sound sad, but Amperic bricks are my whole life these days—except for John."

They walked south to see all the monuments. The bookstore Leonora had promised was next to the Lighthouse of Alexandria, the furthest away. All kinds of people were coming and going on the street—Black, white, Asian, and Native American. Carol heard snippets of several languages. They passed a hodgepodge of stores, including art galleries, spice shops, antique dealers and fortune tellers. Middle Eastern music drifted out of dark cafes. The area had a shabby, raffish charm with hints of mystery and danger.

Leonora explained that, as St. Louis rebuilt after the earthquake, this neighborhood attracted freethinkers, poets, artists, and miscellaneous nonconformists from all over the country. The Citizen Shareholder Plan offered a stake and cash dividends to everyone, no matter what they did. So St. Louis became a good place to pursue your dreams and live cheaply. The long-term residents of this old neighborhood accepted the newcomers despite their odd quirks. Better to have a crackpot or two around than a vacant apartment or a shop devoid of customers. The city was growing fast and everyone was making money, so they had more important things to do. Over the course of several years, the area was transformed. Respectable St. Louisans had mixed feelings about Seven Wonders. They were both intrigued by its exotic charms and disturbed by its disregard for rules and conventions.

On the block between the Tower of Babel and the Colossus of Rhodes, Carol noticed several shops with unusual signs: *Numbers for Health and Abundance, Prime Emporium, Mathematical Exchange,* and *Count Your Blessings.*

"What are these places?"

"They sell lucky prime numbers. It's a stupid superstition that too many people believe."

"How do they sell numbers?"

"They claim to be able to identify a prime number that is perfect for each person. They take you through a lot of fancy rigamarole then reveal your special prime number. The longer the number, the more they charge. It's like astrology, only worse."

"Can we go into one?"

"Okay," Leonora sighed. "But don't let them lead you on, or we'll be there all day."

They entered the *Count Your Blessings* store. It was dim and quiet with a faint aroma of incense. A man in a dark business suit came out from behind a curtain. "How may I assist you ladies?" Carol explained that she was from out of town and had never been in a prime number store before. The man began his practiced spiel, speaking in the soft, unctuous tones of a funeral director.

"We offer a range of services, depending on your needs. We firmly believe in tailoring the number to the individual, so that you can achieve your goals. The process begins with a thorough assessment. You fill out a questionnaire, which our team of skilled enumerators will evaluate in order to select your number. If you wish to be more precise, we also offer biometric screening—blood pressure, brain scan, EKG, and retinal measurements—to determine your receptivity to the influence of certain numbers. All of our numbers are, of course, certified primes."

"Do you give customers their number on a piece of paper?"

"With the basic package, your number is inscribed on a parchment scroll. With enhanced options, it can be an attractive book or a leather-bound volume with your name embossed in gold. Of course, longer primes, which offer a more personalized match to your psychic profile, require additional analysis to confirm that they are factor free."

Carol asked the price. The man discreetly slid a price list across the glass counter. The basic package was $999 and the options bumped that up significantly. "Of course, we can provide you with references from our many satisfied customers," he added.

"That's good to know," Carol said.

"Would madame like to make an appointment for an evaluation?"

"Not today, thanks."

Out on the sidewalk, Carol broke out laughing. "That was the weirdest place I've been in a long time." They stopped for lunch at a small Polynesian restaurant, where Leonora told her more about the prime number cult—or "philosophy" as its believers called it.

"People buy prime numbers for wealth, love, or general good luck. They take this very seriously. Nothing kills conversation at a party more than listening to someone drone on about how their prime has changed their life. If you're rich enough, you can purchase one that is selected for you alone. No one else can have it. These primes can be hundreds or thousands of digits long. The longer the prime, the more expensive."

"The idea is that knowing your unique lucky prime gives you a lifetime of advantage. The practice is to print the number divided into six-digit 'words' so it is easier to read. Devotees of prime numbers, called *primists*, study their long primes several words at a time. Many do this as a daily ritual. They believe that they can discover patterns in the prime to guide them in their lives. Mathematicians, of course, dismiss the whole idea of meaningful patterns as complete nonsense, but the belief persists.

"Parents give them as graduation or wedding presents to their children. There's a famous story that every gossip in town repeated endlessly. A wealthy man, Peter Tomlinson, who was leader of the Knights after Hines retired, gave his daughter a prime number over a million digits long as a wedding present. To find his daughter's prime, Tomlinson contracted with an agency soon after her birth, so that the million digit prime could be verified before her wedding day. Signatures, stamps and seals from the agency director and the registered mathematicians involved attest to the supposed rigor of their work.

The traditional wedding gift for primists is a pair of twin primes, one for the bride and one for the groom."

"What are twin primes?"

"Two prime numbers separated by a single even number, like 3 and 5, 29 and 31, 101 and 103, and so on. Peter Tomlinson received whispered criticism for giving his daughter the ostentatious wedding gift of the million-digit prime without a companion twin prime for her husband. It was considered a shocking breach of etiquette. He swatted away the outrage, "Marrying my daughter is all the good luck that young man needs." Here's the best part—the lucky young man was your pal, Giles Monroe. That marriage began his ascent up through the Knights to succeed Tomlinson as the leader."

After lunch, Carol and Leonora continued walking until they reached the Lighthouse of Alexandria. "Here's the bookstore," said Leonora, pointing to a long row of attached houses across the street.

"Which one?"

"All of them."

They entered a door marked "Lighthouse Booksellers" at the center of the row. Inside, walls had been removed to turn several houses into one vast room, filled with aisles of bookshelves. One stairway led to an upper level, another to the basement. A banner above the checkout counter read *A Million Books Under This Roof.* Leonora saw Carol's look of amazement and delight and said, "Take your time. I'll catch up with you later."

Carol wandered the aisles. There was a revelation at every turn. Just to make sure she wasn't dreaming, she looked at Nineteenth Century American Literature. All the familiar authors were there: Poe, Melville, Hawthorne, Twain, Longfellow. Twentieth Century Literature took up several aisles. She didn't recognize any of the titles or authors. As she scanned the titles in the Modern History section, she wished she could do nothing but read them for the rest of her life. It was impossible to choose among the thousands of books in this garden of delights, but she picked up a few that intrigued her, including *General Gandhi and the Defeat of Britain, 1986: The Momentous Year When America Changed Course,* and *Operation Poutine: Canada's Campaign for Dominance.* In the Biography section, she found *Gone Too Soon: The Short, Tragic Life of T.S. Eliot, Prometheus: The Genius of James Whittemore Hines,* and *William Howard Taft: The Man, The Myth, The Timeless Legacy.*

After two hours of exploration, Carol's head was swimming. She found Leonora on a sofa near the checkout counter. As she paid for her books, she spotted one more that she thought Billy would like: *Windows to the World: An Illustrated History of Moviolas 1930-2010.*

Outside, Carol thanked Leonora profusely for taking her to Seven Wonders. Now, if she could only figure out a way to get the entire bookstore back to SD—it would change everything.

"You do know that everything around here runs on bricks. Right?" John asked as he and Billy entered the basement workshop.

"You're kidding."

"No. They invented bricks that generate electricity. These bricks are what made St. Louis such a big deal. I'll show you."

He led Billy to a different part of the basement, where a dusty gray box about the size of a washing machine stood against a wall. A dozen metal tubes snaked down from the ceiling to the back of the box. John removed a basket of laundry that was sitting on the box to reveal a panel with gauges, knobs, and switches.

"The house is covered with Amperic bricks, which are Hydraulic's big product. As the outside temperature changes, each brick expands and contracts very slightly and generates a tiny current. They are wired together in series and feed into this unit. The microvoltages add up to a 48 volt DC current which powers everything in the house." John pointed to the gauges. "This gauge shows the current being generated right now. This other one shows real-time power consumption by lights and appliances. A battery inside the unit stores energy to handle demand surges, like turning on the stove or washing machine."

John pointed out a second box a few feet away next to a large cylinder, about the size of a water heater. "The bricks generate more power than the house needs. Excess power runs this electrolyzer-concentrator, which separates hydrogen and oxygen from water. The hydrogen is stored in this tank. A pipe runs out to the garage where Leonora can fill up her car. Its fuel cell motor runs on hydrogen. The whole system is pretty slick."

Billy was impressed. The previous summer, he had noticed that HD was full of brick buildings of every size and shape. Also he and Meredith had seen an exhibit in the Hydraulic Building about Amperic bricks, but he hadn't put it all together. "So you can get free electricity and fuel from the bricks?"

"Basically, yes. The bricks aren't cheap, but once they're installed, they produce a lot of energy."

"But this house is eighty or a hundred years old. Were they invented that long ago?"

"Today, almost all new buildings are constructed with Amperic bricks. Older ones were retrofitted. Forty or fifty years ago, the owner of this house had the old bricks removed and Amperics installed. It probably took a month or two to do the work. Hydraulic was happy to finance the purchase and installation with a long term loan. Leonora tells me their finance division is very profitable."

"So you pay off your loan and then it's free power forever?"

"Not quite forever. After a few decades, the bricks' performance tapers off. It's a huge problem and Leonora's job is to develop a fix. Many nights she can hardly sleep from worrying about it. That's where you and I come in."

John and Billy walked back to the workshop. John continued. "I needed to build a computer so I can help her."

John's computer sat on the work bench. It was a tangle of cables, exposed circuit boards, and a large, elliptical glass screen. Tools, wires, and electronic components were scattered across the bench. Seeing this jumble of organized chaos brought back Billy's childhood memories of the repair room at his father's store, where John had taught him how to solder simple circuits together and introduced him to the marvels of shortwave radio.

"They don't have real computers over here," John said. "Everything is analog—tubes, coils, prisms, and mechanical parts. It's been a pain to get this thing working."

John explained the issue as he fiddled with the device. "Customers are getting unhappy as they begin to see the performance of their bricks decline. The company is making excuses and trying to keep whole thing hushed up."

He attached alligator clip leads to the main circuit board and flipped a switch below the glass screen. It glowed a pale green and a familiar image swirled up out of the haze—the Windows start screen. "Can you imagine what it would cost to replace all the bricks a large building, much less millions of buildings? Leonora's team is working on treatments to extend the bricks' useful life. But how do you predict which treatment will perform best fifty or sixty years from now? I'm trying to develop a simulation program."

John put on shiny gloves, flicked a switch, and a semitransparent keyboard hovered just above the workbench. He began to type in midair. "They call these 'ghost keys.' It takes a while to get the hang of them, but they're kind of fun." He opened up a spreadsheet that showed a graph of declining brick efficiency. "I made this yesterday. The next step is to load the data modeling program you sent with this historical data and a predictive algorithm that can test the effects of different treatments."

"Sounds like a lot of work."

"Yeah. Getting the computer up and running was pretty straightforward. Don't tell Leonora, but I'm not sure I have the skills to write a good algorithm. I never went to college."

Billy and John talked for hours in the basement workshop. John told him about how he met Leonora over ham radio in 1982, discovered HD, and had a few perfect weeks with her, before she was torn away from him by the Knights in the person of Uncle Martin. The story revealed a side of John—as a thinker and a wounded romantic—that Billy had never suspected. Billy told John about his experiences in HD the previous summer, his encounter with the same Uncle Martin and his threatening boss, Giles Monroe, and how he and Carol rescued Meredith from Monroe and the Knights. They both agreed that the Knights were very dangerous and deserved payback for the misery they had caused. Billy shared the bombshell that Martin had dropped on him—that his father, Big Bill Boustany, the Duke of Discounts, had somehow worked for the Knights for years. "I had no idea," John said. "I saw him almost every day at the store. Not a clue."

In between swapping stories, they dove deeper into the challenges of predictive modeling. John kept coming back to his fear that he didn't know how to design an algorithm that would accurately model performance of the bricks—serious math expertise was needed. Billy could see that disappointing Leonora was the worst thing that John could imagine.

Late in the afternoon, Billy said "There may be someone who could help us."

"Really? Who?"

"Let me talk to Carol first. I want to see what she thinks."

They heard a door open and footsteps above. Leonora and Carol had returned.

Over dinner that evening, Billy said "Carol and I have an idea about where to get help to make the data modeling project go better."

Leonora turned to John. "I thought you were making good progress. Do we need help?"

"The computer is working fine. Writing the best algorithm requires high level math, which is not my strong point."

"What kind of help are you talking about?"

"We know someone in SD," Billy said. "We don't know her well, but she appears to be a brilliant data analyst."

"You want to bring her here?"

"Yeah."

"Does she know about HD?"

"No."

"Do you trust her?"

"Yes," Carol said.

Leonora took a moment to think. She was reassured by Carol's confidence. And the pressure on her from Hydraulic management to fix the brick efficiency problem was enormous—and growing day by day.

"Okay. Let's try it. What's her name?"

"Lisa McDaniel."

SISTERS

WHEN BILLY CROSSED BACK to SD to recruit Lisa to help with the data modeling project, Carol stayed in HD. That both conserved pills and gave her the chance to get started on her stack of books. She very happily spent the day in the sunroom off Leonora's living room, drinking tea as she leafed through her new treasures. Before committing to one of the serious histories or biographies, she was drawn to the guidebook. She blazed through it in little more than an hour. She read about restaurants, neighborhoods, historic sites, day trips, and quirky shops. She checked off places she had already visited, like the Refugees Club, the Mechanical Market, the shops surrounding the Opera House, the Metropole, and Lighthouse Books. She noticed a brief mention of the Knights of the Carnelian: *A philanthropic social organization. You might see plaques around town for charitable projects they have supported.* She got a laugh out of that.

She circled others she wanted to see. Over a glass of wine that evening, Carol asked Leonora for advice.

"I'm not much of a tourist," Leonora said. "My favorite St. Louis attraction is my lab."

Carol went over several activities that piqued her interest:

Hummingbird Cruises. *Glide over the city in a luxury dirigible. Watch the sunset on our champagne tour.*

"Expensive, but I've heard good things," Leonora said.

Joplin Academy of Music. *A world-renowned conservatory built around the historic house where Scott Joplin once lived. Listen to student recitals in its acoustically-perfect concert hall.*

"If you're a fan of serious music, you might like it."

The Earthquake Museum. *Relive the 1931 earthquake that almost destroyed St. Louis.*

"Never been there. I learned about the earthquake in school."

"Here's where I want to go first," Carol said. "Billy and Meredith were there without me last year."

Everything, since 1965. On the alley north of 7ʰ and Pine (below the Mezz). A curiosity shop run by two eccentric sisters. Be sure to sample the taffy, but be prepared for their stories.

Leonora raised her glass for a toast. "Then it's high time for you to catch up."

Carol peeked through the window and saw two white-haired ladies, one busily dusting and another sitting behind the counter holding a cigarette and reading a magazine. The bell above the door tinkled as she entered.

"Welcome to our humble establishment," the dusting lady said in a South African accent. "Look around all you want and let us know if you have questions."

"I'm Carol Boustany. You know my husband Billy and my daughter Meredith."

"How is Mr. Boustany?" said the dusting lady, "We haven't seen him in ages."

"He would be here, but he had to return to California on business."

The lady behind the counter put down her magazine. A thin tube ran under her nose and the cigarette she held was plastic. "Meredith popped in just a week ago," she said. "It was so lovely to see her again." Meredith's visit was news to Carol.

"I have heard so much about you from them," Carol said. "It's such a pleasure to finally meet you. "You must be Churcha," she said to the dusting lady, "and you must be Scienca," to the lady behind the counter. They both smiled. Churcha came up to Carol and gave her a kiss on the cheek.

"We are so pleased that Meredith is still together with that handsome young Cahokian man," Scienca said.

"Young love is so wonderful and exhilarating," Churcha said.

"Billy and I also like him very much."

"We hope you invite us to the wedding. I have already selected a lovely outfit."

"I was a tad concerned when she said they were working together," Scienca said. "It's not wise for husband and wife to do that. Too much togetherness every day can lead to hurt feelings. They never get a break."

"How would you know? "Churcha said. "You've never been married."

"I observe, dear sister."

"At any rate, there isn't much that Carol can do about it." Churcha said. "Young girls rarely listen to their mothers in matters of romance."

"How would you know?" Scienca said. "You've never been a mother."

"I was a young girl once. And I certainly did not listen to our mother's advice regarding the romantic liaison that led us to this city. Neither did you."

"Perhaps Carol needs to hear that story," Scienca said. "It might be beneficial for Meredith."

"We were victims of a most unscrupulous deceit," Churcha said.

"Meredith and Billy shared your story with me. It was shocking. But Meredith's Diyami is very trustworthy." Carol changed the subject. "Please tell me about your lovely shop." Churcha and Scienca were a little disappointed not to be able to tell their story again, but began to point out the items on the walls and shelves. Scienca came out from behind the counter pulling an oxygen tank on wheels that was connected to the tube under her nose.

"We only sell what we like."

"And we have very good taste."

They are just as odd and delightful as Billy and Meredith said, Carol thought. She looked around the shop and saw why it was named "Everything." There was a desktop pencil holder made from a stuffed gopher, dinner place settings decorated with views of St. Louis, African tribal sculptures, prints of old English fox hunting scenes, and much more. And, of course, glass jars with assorted taffy in various colors.

"My husband enjoys antique radios," Carol said. "Do you have any?"

"Of course. Follow me." Scienca headed to the rear of the shop with her oxygen tank trundling behind. The bell tinkled as the door opened and Churcha went to greet the new customer.

"How good to see you, Mr. Monroe," Churcha said. "I have your order ready to go."

Carol peeked behind her. It was Giles Monroe. A chill shot up her spine. She quickly turned so her back was to him. With a panicked look, she whispered to Scienca, "Don't let him know I'm here!" Scienca put her finger to her lips and nodded that she understood. She hurried back to the front of the shop and positioned herself behind Giles. Churcha set the ribbon covered box on the counter.

"Thank you, Churcha. I know I'm a little early."

"We're always ready for you, Mr. Monroe."

"By the way, the last time I was here you mentioned that your young friend Meredith had come in."

Scienca made eye contact with Churcha and signaled her to be quiet.

"Do you happen to know where she is staying?" Giles asked.

Scienca silently mouthed *Don't say anything*!

"Uhh, no, I don't," Churcha said. "But her mothe…" Scienca frantically waved her arms and gestured with her finger across her throat. *Shut up!*

"Her mother, I hear, is a charming person," Churcha said. "Though we have never met her."

"I spent some time with the mother," Giles said. "She's quite a spirited lady."

"Yes, that's what Meredith told us."

"If you see Meredith or her mother again, please let me know. I would love to give them my regards and extend our hospitality to them."

He picked up his box of taffy and turned to leave. Scienca, who was pretending to tidy a shelf, nodded to him. The bell tinkled as the door closed. Carol and Scienca let out sighs of relief. Churcha was puzzled. Without going into much detail, Carol explained the situation. "We had a delicate encounter with Mr. Monroe last year. He's not very fond of our family. It's best not to mention any of us to him. Let sleeping dogs lie."

Carol bought a small, polished wood and brass antique radio. Churcha and Scienca insisted that she also take a large bag of taffy. "It's on the house," Churcha said. They all hugged each other and Carol promised to come back to see them again.

Outside, Carol hurried to 12th Street to board a streetcar to take her back to Flora Place. On the busy sidewalk, she glanced behind her several times to make sure that neither Giles nor his goons were following. When she got to Leonora's, she collapsed onto the living room sofa. Her appetite for exploration had disappeared for now. The glass of wine that Leonora put in her hand was just what she needed.

ADVENTURE OF A LIFETIME

"Ba-de-de-de-deep. Ba-de-de-de-deep. Ba-de-de-de-deep." Billy was assembling patio furniture on the deck of the Pelican building when he heard the unfamiliar sound. *The burner phone!* This was the first time it had rung. Only one person had its number. He rushed into the apartment and fumbled around the kitchen searching for it. *Where did I put that damn thing?* When he returned to SD the previous week, he bought the burner phone—a security precaution he had learned about from watching the TV show *The Wire*—and included its number in the note he mailed to Lisa McDaniel's PO box.

He found the jingling phone underneath the morning newspaper on the table.

"Hello."

"Mr. Boustany? This is Lisa."

"Thank you so much for calling. I have a problem and thought of you." After a little innocuous small talk, he asked "What do you know about algorithms, data modeling, predictive analysis, and stuff like that?"

"That's what my master's degree was about."

"I have some friends who need some help. It's an unusual project. I think you'd like it."

"Okay …" Her voice sounded hesitant.

"It has to do with the reason you contacted me a while ago."

This piece of information piqued her curiosity. "Tell me more."

Billy said the project involved modeling the performance of materials over time. And he reassured her that it had absolutely no connection to national security, nuclear technology, or anything the government would care about.

"Maybe I could work on that on weekends."

"You would have to come to St. Louis. Maybe take a couple weeks of vacation."

"I don't think that's possible."

Billy had to close the sale before he lost her. "I absolutely guarantee you that you won't regret it. You're in for the adventure of a lifetime." He stopped talking. After twenty-three years in sales, Billy had learned the power of silence.

He waited for a long, excruciating minute. Then Lisa spoke, "I don't know why I'm saying this, but yes." Billy pumped his fist in celebration. They agreed that she would come to St. Louis in two days. He suggested that she bring the data modeling software she preferred, as long as it ran on Windows and was available on CD. "Not a download. We're off the internet." He said he would reimburse her for any expense.

After Billy picked Lisa up at the airport, she became apprehensive when he asked her to turn her phone off and remove the SIM card, even though he did the same with both his regular phone and the burner. "We don't want to be tracked and we won't need them." Billy seemed harmless enough, but that's what people always said about serial killers. She didn't want to end up dead in a ditch. When he parked behind the Pelican building, next to the trash can she rooted through several weeks earlier, she glanced around to make sure people were nearby. They walked to the front of the building on Grand and he pointed out the sculpture of the pelicans gliding over the roof, which had been installed since she was last there. He was very proud of it and, again, he acted unthreatening. Billy sensed her fear and realized that going up to the apartment was a bad idea. "Let's walk and talk. Bring your backpack."

They headed north on Grand towards Flora Place. "First, I'm going to tell you what's going on and you won't believe me. Then I'm going to show you, and you'll thank me for the rest of your life." He began with the neutrino analogy....

He was right. His ridiculous story made no sense to her at all. *A parallel world? Yeah, that's rich. What a fool I was to come here!* Then, he said something that was harder to dismiss.

"Those radiation events you detected were probably me and my family crossing to the other world and coming back."

"I'm sorry, Mr. Boustany. There's no way that can be. I'm a scientist. What's your evidence?"

"See for yourself. That will be my evidence. If you're not satisfied, I'll get you a cab back to the airport."

She looked at him and sighed. *This is getting crazier by the minute.* He waved his hand in a broad arc. "Take a good look around. Pay attention to everything—the street, the cars, the buildings."

He led her into an alley between some apartments and a fast food joint. He opened a small box and put two white pills in his hand. "Take one."

"I don't do drugs!"

"These are how we travel. I'm taking one too."

Against her better judgment and everything she had ever learned about personal safety, Lisa took a pill from someone she barely knew. Billy popped one in his mouth, then Lisa did the same. After a few seconds, she experienced the worst headache, nausea and vertigo she had ever felt. Then, just as quickly, it was over.

Billy grinned at her. She looked around. The fast food joint was gone, replaced by a sparkling glass tower wrapped in blue latticework. Weird cars drove up and down Grand Avenue. Music was playing from an outdoor restaurant across the street. *What the fuck!*

Stage One, Deer in the Headlights. Billy thought.

Lisa was a little wobbly on her feet as they walked to Leonora's house. Billy said nothing; he gave her time to adjust. They turned into the alley behind Flora Place. "This way is more discreet. We try to keep a low profile." He spoke slowly and gently to reduce her disorientation. "Carol will be there. She's looking forward to seeing you again. And you can meet our other friends." Lisa nodded dreamily.

Inside, Lisa took a long drink from the glass of ice water that Leonora gave her. "Take it easy," said John. "I'll tell you about the project tomorrow."

"And we'll show you around town," Carol said as she patted Lisa's knee.

Lisa needed to be alone and process what had happened. Leonora showed her to a bedroom where she could lie down. Carol pulled Billy aside. "I had a bizarre experience while you were gone. I went to meet the taffy ladies. It was nice at first. Then, you'll never guess who walked into their shop."

"Who?"

"Giles Monroe. He was picking up an order of taffy. I hid in the back corner, so he didn't see me. But he said something that freaked me out. He knew that Meredith had been in their shop a few days earlier."

Billy grimaced. "What?"

"Did she say anything about it when you were home?"

"No. Just that she and Diyami took Stan to HD Cahokia. His mind was blown."

"I asked Churcha and Scienca never to say anything about our family to Giles. I told them that we'd had a 'delicate situation' with him in the past."

"Did they understand?"

"I think so. They're very sweet, but a little bit in la-la land. Going forward, let's keep our eyes open and be careful."

During breakfast the next morning, Leonora said to Lisa, "The first order of business is to get you identification."

"Bad things can happen around here if you don't have ID," Carol said. "Our daughter learned that the hard way last year."

Lisa had barely slept overnight. She had never been so disoriented in her life. These people were really nice, and they tried to explain the situation as best they could. But it still made absolutely no sense.

They went out to the garage behind Leonora's house and got into her odd three-wheeled car. Lisa studied each detail, from the silver mesh seats, to the swoosh sound the door made as it closed to the vertical tiller for steering. Lisa's face was glued to the window as she watched the city go by on the drive to the Mechanical Market. Billy nudged Carol, who was sitting next to him in the back seat, and held up two fingers. She smiled. *Stage Two.*

Lisa's amazement only grew as they walked through
the Mechanical Market. John pointed out items of interest
in various booths and stalls. At Sergei's shop, they got her
a fake driver's license that listed an address in California.
"If anyone stops you, just say you're visiting St. Louis,"
Leonora said. "That will be easier."

"Name?" Sergei asked.

"Lisa Moon," said Billy. That was the fake name Lisa
had used when she first 'interviewed' him in SD.

On the way back to Leonora's house, they detoured
through Forest Park and midtown, so Lisa could see some
of the city. She didn't know enough about SD St. Louis to
make a real comparison, but she was certain no place like
this existed in her world.

Lisa joined John and Leonora in the basement
workshop for the rest of the day.

Leonora explained the challenge to model future
performance of Amperic bricks—after briefly explaining
what Amperic bricks were. Lisa listened and asked a
whole string of questions. "What historical data exists
on generation efficiency of different brick formulations?
What interventions are under consideration? How are you
collecting data on their impact?" Lisa wanted to construct
an overall model of brick performance over time, then
validate that model against the historical performance of
the existing bricks. That would provide the foundation to
forecast the effects of different interventions. Leonora and
John were impressed with Lisa's quick grasp of the issues
and clear strategy for proceeding. Leonora said she could
get Lisa whatever data she needed.

"The thing that would help me the most would be to
actually see these bricks and the tests you're performing in
your lab. Without that, everything is very abstract to me."

"I don't know if that's possible," Leonora said. "The security is extremely tight."

"Aren't you the boss?"

Leonora was taken aback. Lisa was right—she was the boss. She admired Lisa's brash approach. Many years ago, she too had broken rules when she and her radio reached across to the other world to connect with John. "We'll go on Sunday, when no one will be there."

Billy was always an early riser. He liked to get up before Carol, drink coffee, and read the paper. It was his favorite time of the day. The morning after Lisa's arrival looked beautiful, so he decided to walk the mile or so to the Asian market. He would buy some pastries and be back at Leonora's before anyone else was up.

He went out the back door and through the alley, following the precautions that Leonora had recommended. Very few people were out on Grand Avenue this early. The automatic awnings that extend over the sidewalks were retracted. Birds darted among the shrubs and vines on balconies. *They probably have nests up there,* Billy thought. On the way to the market, he noticed the gray surveillance cameras bolted to lampposts. *That's funny. I didn't see these when Carol and I walked along here week before last.*

He arrived at Gravois and went into the Asian market. He found a bakery stall that had just opened, so he had his pick from their assortment of scones. When he returned to the street, carrying a bag of warm, sweet-smelling scones and a large paper cup of coffee, he saw a maintenance van on the corner with a cherry picker lift. A worker in the lift was working on a surveillance camera mounted high on a post. Another worker on the ground said something to him, then to someone inside the van.

201

Billy, sipping his coffee, walked over and asked "What's going on?"

"We're upgrading the equipment," the man said cheerfully. "Our commitment to keep you safe."

The man returned to his conversation with his colleague in the cherry picker. The back of the van was open and Billy nonchalantly walked around so he could see inside. A third man was working at a laptop. He saw Billy and said sharply, "This is restricted city business, sir. Please move along." He shut the lid of the laptop and Billy saw the logo, *HP*.

As he started back to Leonora's, Billy mulled over what he had seen. *An HP laptop? What is that doing here?*

Not good.

He had only walked a block further when a police car pulled up next to him. An officer hopped out and asked Billy for identification. He fumbled in his pocket and found the fake CSP ID card. The officer looked at it closely and glanced at Billy to make sure the photo matched. He turned the card over and examined the back side. Billy began to worry. The officer handed Billy the ID card. "What's your business here, Mr. Duke?"

"Buying pastries."

"A piece of advice: when you see city work going on, it's wise not to be curious. Enjoy your breakfast."

The scones were a hit with Carol, Leonora, John, and Lisa. Billy told them about the police incident and about what he had seen. "The good news is that my fake ID worked. The bad news is that it looks like we're not the only ones with a computer."

"The Knights' thievery continues," Leonora said.

Over dinner that night, Lisa asked, "How come nobody knows about this place? A parallel world? This is the biggest news in history! It turns all of science upside down."

"Powerful forces over here work very hard to keep it a secret—even from their own people," Billy said. "They don't want anyone from our world coming here."

"What's their problem?"

"It's all very murky," Leonora said. "I think a lot of money is being made off the secret." She told a story of her own experience:

One day, soon after her promotion to Director of Research in 2000, Leonora got an invitation to see the Chairman of the Board of the Hydraulic Brick Corporation, Roger Thornhill, in his office. Though she had met him a few times before, she assumed this was to be a courtesy call to welcome her to her new position.

He was immaculately dressed in a pale lavender suit and sported a carnation in his lapel. He was smooth and soft all over, from his slicked-back hair to rounded cheeks and manicured fingers. He offered her a cup of tea and escorted her across his ornate office on the seventy-third floor of the Hydraulic Building. The Persian rug was so thick that it threatened to swallow up Leonora's shoes. They sat down on the sofa next to large windows that provided a panorama of the busy Mississippi river traffic below. Thornhill congratulated her on her well-deserved promotion and expressed his confidence that she would make even greater contributions to Hydraulic in the future. Leonora accepted his effusive praise, though she didn't enjoy this corporate protocol. She wished she were back in her lab.

After a few minutes of small talk, he changed the subject. "I need your expert opinion on a technical question." He set a wooden box on the coffee table and opened the lid.

"I'm trying to understand the viability of this product." He lifted two small silver cylinders out of the box. "These are a new type of battery, said to be very efficient and rechargeable. Made of lithium." Leonora had never heard of a battery that used lithium.

"Can you take a look at these and give me a report on what you learn." Leonora picked up one of the batteries. The word "Energizer" was printed on it. "I can get you as many samples as you need. This is a high priority—and extremely confidential."

It was an odd request.

Leonora and her research team spent two weeks testing the batteries. They measured the output at various temperatures and discharged and recharged the batteries over and over. The consistent performance was impressive—high energy density, steady current, stability after many charges. They cut a battery open to see its structure and did preliminary chemical analysis on the materials in its cathode and anode.

After the tests, Leonora met with the Chairman again. She reported her findings about the battery's superior qualities. "Does it have commercial potential?" he asked. Leonora said that it could make a good companion to Amperic bricks to store energy produced by the bricks in portable devices.

"Can you manufacture them?"

"No. We don't understand the chemistry in enough detail, so developing a practical manufacturing process would be extremely difficult."

"If I could provide you with formulas and specifications, then could you manufacture them?"

"Yes, but surely this is a patented product. Are you planning to get a license to produce it?"

"No. Hydraulic is going to patent both the battery and the manufacturing technology."

"Who invented it?"

"You did, Miss Matsui. You did."

Leonora began to say something, but Thornhill held up his hand to quiet her. "This is a Knights matter. We won't speak of it again."

Hydraulic Lithio® batteries became a huge success. *It's like having an Amperic® brick in your pocket!* was the slogan. Leonora received many accolades and a ridiculously large bonus. She had never felt so slimy. But years later, she understood what was going on. Those Energizer people—whoever they were—in SD would never know what had happened.

"Wow," Lisa said.

Uncle Martin had told John and Billy that fear of "uncertainty" was the reason for secrecy—but that had nothing to do with it. The Knights were stealing technology from SD.

"I'm reading a biography of Hines," Carol said. "It praises him for his support of innovation and inventions, back in the 1940s and 50s. There's no hint of anything like this."

"They would never let it get into print." Leonora said.

Billy wanted to come along on the visit to the lab, but Leonora firmly said no. "They have a strong policy against visitors, so getting just one person in will be hard enough. I have to keep this as discreet as possible."

"Under the radar," Lisa said.

"What's radar?" Leonora asked.

"Never mind," John said. "I'll explain later."

"But I have the ID John got for me," Billy protested.

"Don't push your luck," Carol said.

Leonora and Lisa drove to the Hydraulic Building downtown, where Leonora's lab filled an entire floor on one of the below-ground levels of the skyscraper. Even on a Sunday morning, downtown St. Louis was busy. Lisa saw the air bridges of the Mezz, which connected buildings from one end of downtown to the other. People waited in line to board the elevators that took them up to stroll in the aerial parks that made the Mezz famous.

When Leonora and Lisa came through the revolving door, the lobby, which hummed with activity on weekdays, was deserted on a Sunday morning. The only person there was a security guard behind a desk. The tinny sound of a radio echoed off the tiled brick work in the lobby of the Hydraulic Building:

This incredible match, deadlocked at ten to ten, comes down to the final point, with each team's top scorers facing off against each other. Wilson of Notre Dame versus Standing Water of Five Hundred N-U. The bowler rolls the stone, Wilson and Standing Bear raise their arms and hurl their sticks down the pitch. Wilson's lands two feet away from the stone and—I can't believe it—Standing Bear plants his stick mere inches from the stone. The hometown crowd erupts and swarms onto the grassy pitch ...

The guard turned off his radio as soon as he saw them.

"Miss Matsui. You rarely grace us with your company on a Sunday morning."

"Hi, Eddie. I need to check on a few things in the lab. And I have a visitor with me."

"Is she a Hydraulic employee?"

"A family friend visiting from out of town."

"Then I'm afraid we'll have to go through the visitor protocol. Won't take long." Eddie laboriously lifted a huge ledger book from a shelf by his desk. He asked Lisa for her identification. He wrote down her name, date of birth, and address. "Ahh, California. I was there a few years ago. I ate avocados every day."

"We're very proud of them."

He continued with more questions about her occupation ("Mathematician."), current and former employers, prior addresses, next of kin, education, professional licenses, citizenship status, languages spoken, hand preference (Lisa didn't understand this one, so Eddie clarified, "Right-handed, left-handed, or ambidextrous?"), and medical history. He entered Lisa's answers into the ledger, then spun it around, so she could sign the bottom of each page before he turned the page and continued. After ten minutes, the questions were completed.

"Last step, Miss Moon, then you can be on your way." He opened up an ink pad and had her press all ten fingers into the pad, then into boxes on the ledger page.

"Who is vouching for Miss Moon as her guarantor?"

"I am," Leonora said. She signed the ledger.

"The protocol requires two guarantors."

Leonora was getting impatient. "Should I contact Mr. Thornhill, so he can be the second guarantor?"

Eddie was flustered. "Of course not, Miss Matsui. Given your position, I can bend protocol today."

Leonora and Lisa walked to the elevator. "I just made my answers up," Lisa whispered. "Will that get you in trouble?"

"Don't worry. I don't think anyone ever looks at that ledger. But it's the way they do things here."

Leonora switched on the lights when they stepped off the elevator. The lab was an enormous room, almost a city block on each side, divided by thick columns that supported the Hydraulic Building above. Small sections of brick walls sat on a hundred rolling carts. Wires protruded from each wall section, hooked up to a mélange of meters and gauges. Leonora led Lisa to one table and picked up a brick which was sliced in half to reveal the interior.

"Let's begin with the basics. Every Amperic brick has horizontal and vertical copper tendons embedded inside. These collect the electric current generated as the brick heats during the day and cools during the night. We wire the bricks in a building into a series so the current is amplified to serve as a practical power source."

"I don't get it. Exactly how does the brick generate a current?"

Leonora picked up a flashlight and turned it on. Its blue beam showed a spidery network of multicolored threads inside the brick. "These filaments are the key. Ultraviolet light makes them easy to see. They're spun from magnetite, phosphorus, and a variety of other alloys. As the temperature changes, the brick expands and contracts very slightly, almost microscopically. The filaments convert that physical stress into direct current. The specific blends of materials in the filaments are Hydraulic's most valuable trade secrets. I've spent most of my career improving filament designs."

"It doesn't seem like a brick could produce enough power to make a difference."

"The current from each brick is tiny, but when we combine the output from the thousands—or even millions—of bricks in a building, it becomes substantial. More than enough to light the building and power all its systems. Most customers use their surplus power to operate electrolysis units, which separate hydrogen and oxygen from water. The compressed hydrogen fuels vehicles. The global economy runs on this power."

"Wow! No fossil fuels."

Leonora went on to describe the problem that threatened everything—the output of Amperic brick power generation declines over time. "Back when the bricks were invented, no one thought about the long term."

"What's the cause?"

"Inside each brick there are hundreds of electrical contact points between the filaments and the tendons. After years of expansion and contraction, microscopic fissures appear, which reduce the efficiency of those contacts."

Leonora then described three methods to restore efficiency that were being tested. The first was spraying bricks with penetrating solutions of minerals and electrolytes to repair the micro fissures at the contact points. The second was lithotripsy, applying high-frequency vibrations to shock the interior structure of the bricks. The third was reversing the polarity of the direct current generated. "This one is deceptively simple. But it requires modifying the fuses on all the electrical panels in the building, so it would be a major undertaking in a large structure."

"Designing these interventions was the easy part. Knowing how well they work over a time scale of decades is the real challenge." Leonora showed Lisa a row of closet-sized rooms along one wall. Each one had a glass door and a cart with a brick wall sample inside. Meters displayed the current produced inside each chamber. "These chambers speed up the heating and cooling cycle so we can see the effects of years of operation. But it still takes time. We can compress ten years of operation into a year."

"That's still a long wait to get results."

"A brick will only expand and contract so fast, no matter what you do."

"When we model the performance data, you'll be able to see a lot further into the future. I promise."

Lisa had analyzed problems far hairier than this one. And, unlike the pompous idiots at NNSA, Leonora actually appreciated her. *This is going to be fun.*

To avoid Eddie's prying eyes as they left, Leonora only took a few of the performance data sheets that she could slip into her pockets. They would give Lisa something to get started on. She planned to bring out a briefcase full each work day.

Back at the house, John had installed the data modeling program Lisa had brought, so they were ready to begin working on the simulation. Lisa was fascinated by the ghost keys. John coached her on how to use the reflective gloves to input data from the paper sheets into the program. It was a tedious process, but Lisa had fun with the weird system. Billy dropped in from time to time, but there wasn't much to see—just Lisa typing with her hands in mid-air. Carol was happily ensconced in the living room reading her new books about the history of HD.

Lisa sensed that John was a patient teacher, so, as she typed, she started asking the million questions that were on her mind.

"How did you find your way from SD to HD?" (She picked up on the terminology the others were using.)

"Under the right conditions a radio signal can get through. There appear to be weak spots in the barrier between the worlds. Leonora and I found one where we could get through. It was a long time ago."

"How does the barrier work?"

"It's some kind of powerful electromagnetic field. Batteries discharge when they pass through—so phones and cameras quit working. Film spoils."

"How did you and Leonora find the weak spot?"

"We tested the strength of the radio signal in different places around the city. I was in SD, she was in HD."

"So you made a map of the barrier?"

"We started. It was crude. Then the big shots put a stop to everything."

"Mr. Boustany gave me a pill. What was that?"

"Another way to cross. The Knights—the people who run everything over here—have them, but it's a deep secret."

"How did you get the pills?"

"Long story."

"Who knows about this?"

"Nobody on our side, as far as we can tell. Over here, the Knights know, but no one else."

"If the barrier is electromagnetic, how does taking a pill enable you to cross?"

"I've thought about that question a lot. My hypothesis is that the pill triggers something like an epileptic seizure—an electrical storm in the brain that momentarily weakens the barrier where the person is so they can slip through."

"Makes sense."

"All we know for sure is that the pills work. When we got them, they didn't come with an instruction manual."

The next morning, Lisa and John worked in the basement on the data modeling project. Billy came down around 11:30 and said that he and Carol were going to walk to a place he knew for lunch about a mile away. Did they want to come? Lisa eagerly said yes, but John preferred to stay behind. He wasn't used to having other people in the house all day, so a little time alone in his workshop appealed to him.

Billy, Carol, and Lisa left through the back door and the alley, then walked up to Grand. "Leonora worries that her nosy neighbors might see too many people coming in and out of her house," said Carol.

As they walked south on Grand, Billy pointed out many things that didn't exist in SD St. Louis—silent streetcars, balconies draped in plants, apartment buildings with walls that opened up, automatic retractable awnings over the sidewalks, groups of scooters zipping along. Lisa loved everything. At the corner of Arsenal, Billy described the street supper he had attended the previous summer. "There were thousands of people, tables set up on the street, and an incredible band. These people know how to party."

"That's the last time you go to one of these without me." Carol said.

At the corner of Gravois, they came to the ten-story Southside National Bank building. "This was the first place where I crossed into HD," Billy said. "It was a complete accident. I thought I was nuts."

"I remember this corner from the satellite data," Lisa said.

"Let's have lunch at my favorite place, Whittemore's Bar. Great food and friendly people. It's just a block down Gravois."

Carol told Lisa that, while Billy had gone to Whittemore's several times last summer, she was only there once, to rescue Meredith from the Knights.

"Well Carol, now you'll have a chance to try their sandwiches," Billy said. He was annoyed and embarrassed that Carol was bringing up his misdeeds from the previous year in front of Lisa. He hoped a good lunch would help them get past those tricky memories. When they arrived at Whittemore's, a heavy chain and padlock blocked the entrance. A sign taped on the door said:

Closed by Order of
The Health Department

"What the hell?" Billy said. He peeked in the window. It was dark inside. A few glasses were sitting on the bar. A barstool was tipped over on the floor. "The place was shut down in a hurry."

Carol pointed to the date written on the Health Department sign—it was three weeks earlier. "I know what happened. Remember that newspaper article about Giles that Leonora showed us? It quoted Mary Jo by name. This is his revenge."

"That bastard!" Billy muttered. He was quiet as they walked back to Grand and Gravois. He saw a surveillance camera pivoting slowly on a lamppost. He looked up and down the street. There were several more cameras than he had seen the last time he was here. Anger at Giles and the Knights stewed inside him.

They entered the Asian Market, which was attached to the Southside National Bank building. Carol and Lisa explored its exotic stalls and ordered lunch while Billy found a table. Lisa chattered nonstop about everything she saw and tasted—the exotic mix of people wearing flowing robes and brightly colored suits, the toy booths, the banners fluttering high above them, and, of course, the incredible sweet buns. Her excitement at experiencing all this for the first time rubbed off on Billy and helped lift his funk.

On the way back to Leonora's house, they stopped to look at a large, round bulletin board on the sidewalk. It was plastered with notices and flyers:

An Evening of Late Joplin Concertos
Tower Grove Music Pavilion

Lost Squirrel Monkey
Answers to the name "Coco"
Generous Reward for Return

Your Prime Number: Key to Love and Happiness
Free Lecture by Dr. J. Ponzi, Licensed
Numerologist

For Sale: Baby Shoes. Never Used

Carol pointed to the largest flyer, which covered up many others:

75TH Annual Seven Wonders Water Festival
August 13 & 14
GET WET!

"I've read that this is quite a party."
I want to go!" Lisa said.

TWICE THE PRICE

THAT EVENING, LISA ASKED, "What's the Water Festival all about?" Leonora told everyone to refill their glasses of wine, then she told the story:

The Seven Wonders neighborhood grew by leaps and bounds in the 1930s, after the establishment of the CSP. A polyglot mix of bohemians, artists, and assorted oddballs poured in from all over. Seven Wonders quickly became known as the place where dreams were born, where rules were meant to be broken, and where revelry and mirth could erupt on a moment's notice.

One of the immigrants attracted to the bohemian enclave was a young writer and theater director who fancied himself to be the second coming of Shakespeare. He was known as "Overflowing" Welles. People in Seven Wonders made a sport of giving people humorous nicknames and Welles got his because he never stopped talking about himself and his grandiose ideas. His real first name was Orson, but no one knew him as that. He wandered the streets of Seven Wonders declaiming soliloquies in a bellowing voice. One day, he found a partner, a handsome young man from a wealthy St. Louis family, who was also obsessed with art and theater. His name was Vincent Price. Because of his moneyed background, the jokesters in the neighborhood dubbed him "Twice the" Price.

"He's in all the scary movies!" Lisa said.

"Orson Welles was kind of a big deal, too." Billy said. Lisa shrugged. She had never heard of him.

Leonora continued.

The two 'theater fiends' were a perfect match. Welles wanted to direct and Price loved to act. They put on impromptu performances on street corners for anybody who would stop and listen.

In those days, before the advances in air cooling design, the nineteenth-century brick homes were stifling on hot summer days and muggy nights. People gathered outdoors on front stoops and sidewalks to gossip, flirt, sing, and dance. So summer was the perfect time for shows by 'Street Corner Shakespeare,' as Welles and Price called themselves.

One evening, a small audience gathered near the Colossus of Rhodes to watch them. Welles had prepared a special dramatic flourish. Price recited the first piece, Coleridge's poem *The Rime of the Ancient Mariner.* When he got to the famous line, "Water, water, every where, nor any drop to drink," Welles turned a wrench on a fire hydrant (he had 'borrowed" one of the special wrenches from a fire station to turn the five-sided valve) and water gushed out onto the street. The audience loved it and soon many were frolicking in the water as Price continued the poem. Others in the neighborhood heard the commotion and joined the fun.

The police and fire departments arrived a little later, shut off the hydrant, and arrested Welles and Price, who by then were acting out passages from *The Tempest*, while standing knee-deep in water.

At the police station, Price's father, a candy manufacturer also named Vincent Price, bailed them out and delivered a stern lecture to his son. It had little impact. The next night, Street Corner Shakespeare gave a repeat performance to a larger audience. Overflowing Welles thrilled them by opening another fire hydrant—adding a new meaning to his nickname in the process. Again, they were arrested, then bailed out by the elder Price. On the third night, the crowd filled the entire block. Stern-faced policemen watched from afar. When Price got to the critical line of the poem, Welles couldn't resist a grand, theatrical gesture. Somehow, he had managed to get another of the special wrenches and he unleashed a torrent of water on the audience. In less than a minute, the police arrested him and Price and dispersed the crowd.

Price's father was exasperated and declined to bail them out. "Let them rot in jail!"

Carol picked up the story, with the history she had read in the J. Whittemore Hines biography:

The elder Price went to his friend, J. Whittemore Hines, managing director of the CSP, to ask for help in dealing with his son, who appeared to be unduly influenced by the rascal Overflowing Welles. As always, Hines had a solution.

The next day, Hines met with the two young theater lovers at police headquarters. He told them that the city would not stand for such foolishness and that they were in serious trouble. He looked in their eyes for signs of remorse, but saw none. So he gave them a choice—using his own flair for the dramatic.

217

"Boys, based on the charges against you, you're looking at about a year in jail if you're convicted, as I am certain you will be. But I'm offering you another option."

He slid two sealed envelopes across the table. "One for each of you. Before you open them, promise me that you will follow my instructions and all charges will be dropped."

Overflowing Welles and Twice the Price looked at each other, nodded their agreement, then opened the envelopes. Welles' envelope contained a train ticket to New York; Price's a ticket to Los Angeles. Hines explained the terms, "Travel to these cities and don't come back to St. Louis until you have built respectable careers in your chosen field of theater."

The two young men left from Union Station the next morning on trains headed in opposite directions. Orson Welles and Vincent Price enjoyed fleeting moments of glory in the bright lights of New York and Los Angeles, then gradually sank into obscurity. They never returned to St. Louis.

But their legend grew in the Seven Wonders neighborhood. A few nights after they left town, some bored teenagers on North Twentieth Street near the statue of Zeus turned on a hose and soaked everyone they could find with streams of cool water. Word spread quickly, and the block became the scene of a riotous party.

Hose parties became a regular occurrence around the neighborhood for the rest of the summer. Adults joined in the fun until no one was left dry. Dignified pedestrians were tempting targets; after getting soaked, they often picked up the hose and sprayed back, much to the delight of the partygoers. Motorists got angry when their freshly-waxed cars were drenched—and were sprayed again when they rolled their windows down to complain. The defenders of public order harrumphed at this hooliganism, but to no avail. Young people from other parts of the city started coming to Seven Wonders to get in on the fun.

The next summer, a mysterious group called the "Liquid Liberators" (which could have been one person or a dozen) followed in the footsteps of Overflowing Welles. The special fire department wrenches were obtained and hydrants gushed once again all over Seven Wonders. Rumors would spread about the location of their next "action" and a crowd usually gathered to cheer when the hydrant was opened and the street was flooded. The police and fire departments played cat and mouse with the Liberators and their many supporters, but were unable to prevent the celebrations.

Leonora opened another bottle of wine and told the rest of the story.

1941 was a brutally hot summer and also the ten-year anniversary of the CSP. J. Whittemore Hines ordered the fire department to open the hydrants of Seven Wonders every Saturday. The newly-sanctioned celebrations took off. Streetcars coming up Grand Avenue were filled with people wearing bathing attire. Impromptu marching bands playing tubas, trumpets, and trombones—all water-resistant instruments—led revelers through the spray.

In subsequent years, the official celebration, now called the Water Festival, was limited to one weekend a summer. In 1945, Hines himself joined in. He rode atop a fire engine, waving and tossing water balloons to the cheering crowd. It was a brilliant political move. His appearance became a tradition, continued by his successors to the present day.

The Water Festival grew larger and more outrageous every year. Labor unions, fraternal orders, sports clubs, and even churches formed "Neptune Committees" to organize their contributions to each year's festivities. One summer, a Cahokian chunkey team showed up in waterproof regalia.

The Water Festival got its biggest boost with the 1958 release of the hit movie, *Meet Me at the Hydraulic*. It was the story of a doomed affair between a demure debutante from an elite family and a dashing young poet who lived in Seven Wonders. The pivotal scene, where the lovers are forced to part forever (they think), was filmed on location at the Water Festival. The dramatic kiss takes place amidst a frenzy of brass bands, ecstatic celebrants, and torrents of water. Audiences around the world were captivated. Before long thousands of visitors descended on Seven Wonders every summer to get a glimpse of the magic and euphoria.

"Awesome!" said Lisa. "It sounds like Mardi Gras on steroids. And it's coming up soon. Count me in!"

Billy and Carol wanted to go. Leonora said, "I've been a few times already. That's enough for me."

John planned to stay home also—he didn't care for crowds.

John and Lisa spent the rest of the week in the basement workshop, entering data and refining the modeling algorithm. Each evening, they asked Leonora for more data about brick performance going back decades. The next day, she would bring a pile of files, which were invariably on paper and a pain to work with. Lisa, who was a very fast typist, did the data entry—she had played piano as a child and had agile fingers. She was having a blast as her hands danced through the air on the ghost keys. They made gradual progress and generated preliminary outlines on the effectiveness of the spray solutions, lithotripsy, and polarity reversal. Despite her repeated requests, John would not share them with Leonora. "We can't draw any conclusions until the modeling process is complete."

During the long periods when they had to let the program crunch numbers, Lisa continued asking John questions about HD and especially about his theory of the barrier between the two worlds.

"What do you know about how the barrier actually functions?"

"Not much. Just that it is weaker and easier to cross in some places. And those places move around in some kind of precession dynamic. The odd thing is that the barrier is permeable at all. You would think that, in general, there should be no communication or movement possible between the two worlds."

"It would be cool to have a better map of the barrier."

"Sure, but that would be a lot of work."

"Maybe not that much. I think we could map the barrier in the general St. Louis area in a week or two."

John was intrigued.

Lisa explained that her idea would involve two people with portable shortwave radios, one in SD and one in HD. They would go to the same locations at the same times, on a predetermined grid, and attempt to transmit to each other. Signal strength meters would give them an accurate measure of barrier permeability at each point on the grid. It would only take a minute at each spot, then on to the next.

"It's something to think about," John said.

The next day, John and Lisa had the first modeling results that they were ready to present to Leonora. They walked her through the models in detail. She had many questions. She was surprised that lithotripsy, which she had been optimistic about, didn't model well. John intentionally saved the most effective treatment for last.

"Polarity reversal appears to significantly counteract efficiency decay. It causes a gradual increase in efficiency at about the same rate as the original decay. By reversing the polarity of a building's system every ten or fifteen years, its life as a strong, stable power generator could be extended indefinitely."

"If our algorithm is correct," Lisa cautioned.

"Is it?" Leonora asked.

"Where I come from," Lisa said, "we never say that anything is certain. The best we can hope for is to have 'high confidence' that we're right."

"Do you have high confidence?"

'Yes, we do," John said.

Leonora beamed. She hugged John, then Lisa. "Thank you for everything. Tonight we celebrate."

Leonora ordered a catered meal and a case of expensive champagne from the Azalea Tea Palace. It was way too much for five people, but she didn't care. A solution was in sight.

The caterers piled the dining room table high with sumptuous dishes and an iced bucket of champagne. The aromas alone were enough to put a smile on everyone's face. Leonora raised her glass in a toast. "To all of you, my best friends and the saviors of the Hydraulic Brick Corporation. Your work will get the executives off my back."

"How will you explain it to them?" Carol asked.

"I'll say we did a lot of calculations and I have 'high confidence' in the predictions. They won't ask how the calculations were done, and I won't tell."

"To the brilliant work of John and Lisa," toasted Carol.

"To a team effort," toasted Billy.

"To the most amazing opportunity I've ever had," toasted Lisa.

"To Leonora, for rescuing me," toasted John with a quavering voice and tearful gratitude in his eyes.

They ate and talked for quite a while. Everyone was savoring the triumph of the moment. Leonora asked John to play the Chuck Berry CD. He inserted it into his jury-rigged CD player and *Johnny B. Goode* blasted through the house. Billy and Carol knew the words by heart and sang loudly as they danced up a storm. Lisa got sucked in by the music and bopped with abandon. Leonora pulled John out of his chair and cajoled him to dance with her. He shook his head *no*, but she insisted until he gave in. He moved awkwardly—he was a jazz and classical guy, a listener not a dancer. It was the first time he had danced since his mother and father twirled around with him when he was six years old.

The music could be heard across the street, where a teenager on a scooter was watching the house.

After a few songs, John turned down the music and Leonora opened another bottle of champagne. A cloud that no one wanted to acknowledge hung over them. For Billy, Carol, and Lisa, the time in HD was coming to an end.

"I have to get home soon, before the people at my job wonder where I am," Lisa said. "But I want to come back. I've hardly seen anything here. That water festival sounds like a hoot. I'm not missing that!"

The others were quiet.

"You may not be able to come back," said Leonora.

"Why not?"

"It's dangerous. We've told you about the Knights."

"But we just saved their bacon! Isn't that worth something?"

"They won't see it that way."

"They're not the most generous people in the world," Billy said.

"There's another problem," Leonora said. "It takes pills to travel back and forth. We have enough to get you, Billy and Carol back to SD, but then we're running low."

"Can't you get more?"

"No. The Knights don't just hand them out."

"Billy, you told me this would be the adventure of a lifetime. All I have done is work in the basement. I'm not settling for a one-way ticket home now!"

"There may not be any other choice," Carol said.

"John told me how he and Leonora found weak spots in the barrier where they could cross."

"That was a long time ago," Leonora said. "We were lucky."

"Actually, we might be able to do it again," John said. "Lisa has a pretty interesting idea." He explained her plan for systematically mapping the barrier with modern equipment to locate weak spots.

"Why do this now?" asked Billy.

"First, because the permeable barrier is an amazing phenomenon that no one understands," Lisa said. "So we would be advancing science."

"Second, if we can find places where the barrier is weak enough, we could cross over without help from a pill," John said.

"Like I did last year?" Billy asked.

"Yes. Crossing unaided may work in an especially weak spot. Leonora and I located spots like that long ago, but they move around. You probably found a few by luck."

"But my ability to cross disappeared last year, like Martin told me it would."

"Maybe or maybe not. That could just be the Knights' cover story. The actual determining factor could be the slow drift of weak spots in the barrier because of precession. You may have learned to cross in places that were weak at the time. Once the weak spot moved somewhere else, you couldn't cross in those places any longer and would think your ability had disappeared. The bottom line is if we can map the barrier systematically, we might not need their pills any more."

Billy liked the idea of sticking it to the Knights. "I'm in. When do we start?"

They cleared the remains of the lavish dinner off the dining room table and spread out a large map of HD St. Louis. Lisa recommended a square grid sixty miles on a side, centered at the downtown riverfront, the site of the Arch in SD. "We set measurement points every two miles on the grid, for a total of nine hundred points. We drive around with shortwave radios, one in SD and one in HD to transmit from the same place at the same time to measure the strength of the signal coming through. If we make ten measurements an hour, we finish in a little over a week."

"Will a measurement every two miles give us enough detail?" Carol asked.

"Let's start with the big picture. We can do more granular measurements in any area which looks promising."

Lisa, Leonora, and Billy went over the map to identify routes that would allow for quick driving from one grid point to another. The routes made sense in the older parts of the city, where the streets were the same in both HD and SD. But in newer areas, Billy didn't recognize the major streets, so he couldn't tell if there were corresponding streets in SD. A century's worth of independent development patterns in each world had led to divergence. Billy, who knew SD geography well—he had spent years identifying high-traffic suburban locations for his stores—couldn't say for sure if it would be possible to reach the grid points in SD as easily as could be done in HD. And the mapping plan depended on having the radios transmit from the exact same places at the same times in both worlds.

"We need to overlay a map of SD St. Louis on top of this one," Lisa said.

Obviously, SD maps didn't exist in HD. They were stumped.

"I could go home and bring one back," Billy said. "But that would use up two pills."

They were all acutely aware of the dwindling number of pills. It was a tough choice. Each pill used was gone forever, but mapping the barrier was the only hope of finding a sustainable way to travel between the worlds. If it didn't work, the Knights would remain in total control of crossing.

Leonora had the pill supply, so she made the final decision for Billy to go. Lisa wrote a resignation letter for him to mail to her boss at NNSA. "If I have to choose between the job and HD, it's no contest!" Billy slipped across the next morning and returned twenty-four hours later with a map, a limp, and a story.

The crossing into SD was uneventful. Billy was still getting used to how easily the pills made it happen. At the apartment, everything looked fine even though he had been gone for two weeks. He called Meredith, then drove over to the trailer at Cahokia to see her and Diyami. There he met the kid, Jamal, who was now working for them.

Billy was impressed that Diyami's plan was beginning to make headway. He, Meredith and Diyami took a walk in the woods behind the trailer. "Jamal doesn't know about HD," Meredith explained.

Billy briefed them about the mapping project and how it might help them find places where they could cross without pills. Diyami shared his plan to talk with his father by radio in Cahokian—so no one could listen in. Billy said he would have Leonora send the frequency to Diyami's father.

Diyami's phone rang and he stepped away to take the call. Billy spoke quietly to Meredith.

"Did you visit the taffy ladies recently?"

Meredith grinned. "Yes! I figured you and mom would go there. Did they tell you?"

"No, but they told Giles and now he's looking for us."

"Giles?" Her face sank. "Why did they do that?"

"Honey, they don't understand our problems with the Knights. And you had no way of knowing they would talk to him."

"I'm sorry dad. I just had to see them."

"I know. Let's all be especially careful."

On his way back to St. Louis, Billy picked up a detailed street map at a gas station, then went to Pho Grand for carryout. He ate dinner in front of the TV in his apartment as he watched a Cardinals game and a History Channel documentary—this one was about the CIA. He relished these familiar comforts of home in SD.

Early the next morning, he was straightening up the apartment before leaving and took a look outside the window. A car was parked across the street that hadn't been there when he went to bed. Two men were sitting in the front seat; one was looking at Billy's building with binoculars. Billy ducked away from the window as fast as he could. He couldn't tell if the man had seen him or not. *Shit!* Going outside didn't seem like a wise move, so he sat on the floor.

A few minutes later there was pounding on the front door downstairs. A voice yelled, 'Mr. and Mrs. Boustany. We need to speak with you."

More pounding. "We know you're in there. We can wait all day if we have to."

Billy thought about calling 911, but what could they do? A stranger knocking on your door isn't much of an emergency.

"We just want to talk. Nothing else. It will be easier on all of us if you just open the door."

Billy reached up onto the table and grabbed the street map. He took the return pill out of his pocket. *Here goes nothing.* Right after he popped the pill, he remembered— the Refugees Club didn't have a second floor. It was one big, three-story room. The next thing he knew, he crashed onto a table in the middle of a backgammon game. Pieces flew everywhere and the players were shocked out of their minds by the man appearing out of nowhere. Billy apologized to everyone in sight, then hustled out of there as fast as he could. He hobbled up the sidewalk toward Flora Place. HD looked better than ever.

"Who were they?" Carol asked.

"I didn't ask for business cards, but who do you think? The goddamn Knights."

"When did this happen?"

"About ten minutes ago."

"Are you okay?"

"Just bruises, but some aspirin would be nice."

In a few hours, John and Lisa identified efficient routes in both HD and SD. They made a spreadsheet with locations, times, and driving directions for both worlds. The plan was ready to go. Leonora would do the driving in HD and John or Lisa would do the transmitting. Billy would go back to SD to do the driving there, with help from Meredith and Diyami for transmitting. He planned to rent a car and stay at a motel—he wasn't going anywhere near the Pelican building. Diyami could transmit results in Cahokian to his father in HD every night, using the radio link they had established. Herbert would then call John to report the signal strengths from SD. To conserve pills, Carol would stay in HD. Her original plan was to visit some of the places in her guidebook, but, after Billy's run-in with the Knights, she wasn't about to risk it. The tourist attractions would have to wait. This was fine with her. She still had a few books to go and could then get started on the ones in Leonora's library.

The plan was set. The mapping could begin in two days, as soon as Billy had his equipment ready in SD. Leonora broke out another bottle of Argentinian champagne to celebrate. Billy felt like a real spy now.

"We spotted Boustany on the other side, but we couldn't catch him."

Two large, heavily-muscled men, Josh and James, who barely fit into their tailored suits, stood in Giles Monroe's plush office. Bringing bad news to him was always an uncomfortable experience.

"What about his wife, the one with the baseball bat?"

Both of the men winced at Giles' mention of Carol. Less than a year earlier, she had whacked all three of them on the knees in a single day.

"We didn't see her, but we think she was there. They have been together every other time we have watched."

"You let them get away? What do I pay you for?"

"We're sorry, Mr. Monroe. We scouted the place and there were only two exits, which we had covered. They must have climbed out a second story window on the far side of the building. It won't happen again."

"You're damn right it won't! Next time, I'll go over there myself if that's what it takes to get results."

Giles waved his hand to dismiss the two men and watched them slink out of his office. *I'm surrounded by idiots!* Everywhere he looked, someone was screwing up. First, one of the most promising young Knights had returned from a long expedition to the other side with a worthless prize, the ridiculous iPhone or ePhone or whatever it was called. Now, his best spotters had failed to carry out a simple kidnapping.

Maybe I'm the idiot. My prime is giving me the answer, but I can't decipher it. For the past few weeks, Giles had been ruminating over a repeating six-digit phrase buried in his prime number—637404. He found it on three different pages of his well-thumbed compendium. He had contemplated it by candlelight, hummed it forward and backward, and written it out longhand a hundred times— all practices recommended by his numerologist—without success. Now, in a moment of peak frustration, as he gazed at the river traffic far below his seventy-fifth floor office, the words inside the prime became crystal clear to him. *Friends from afar, enemies up close.* Why did it take him so long to see the obvious?

He buzzed his secretary to summon the two spotters back into his office. They came in anxiously, fearing the further abuse he was about to heap on them.

"I'm going to give you another chance. I think that Boustany is here. Maybe his wife too. I want you to look day and night until you find them. Start with their friend, Leonora Matsui. She's a shifty one. Report back to me when you have something. Don't let them see you."

TEDIUM

ACCORDING TO THE SCHEDULE, Billy had six minutes to drive from one grid point about two miles to the next. Then he would stop for a minute so Meredith or Diyami could turn on the radio and transmit on the agreed-upon frequency—the same one that John and Leonora had stumbled upon in 1982, which allowed some transmission between the worlds. Meredith or Diyami would say, "CQ, CQ. This is SD." When John or Lisa replied from HD, "HD here," they recorded the reading from the signal strength meter and switched off. If they needed more time to get a good reading, they would take turns counting aloud from one to ten. Then on to the next grid point to repeat the process. A hundred measurements a day. They worked from six a.m. to seven p.m. Leonora did all the driving on the HD side, even though it meant working late into the night to keep up with her Hydraulic duties. "I'm happy to lose sleep if we can make a useful map."

Carol rode along with Leonora and John one day. It was a good way to see more of HD. She missed Billy and Meredith and enjoyed hearing their voices, even if they were garbled by the barrier's interference.

Billy enjoyed the time in the car with Diyami and Meredith, who brought him up to date on the progress they were making with SD Cahokia. Sometimes it was difficult to get to the next grid point on time if they ran into traffic or road construction. Lisa had said, "If you're late and miss the transmission, then go on to the next grid point. We can double back and fill in the missing points later." At the end of each day, from the trailer in Cahokia, Diyami would call his father in HD to give him the readings from each grid point covered that day. These longer transmissions had a greater risk of eavesdropping, so Diyami and Herbert took the precaution of speaking in Cahokian. No one in SD could possibly understand it and the Knights were not likely to have Cahokian allies.

The third morning, both Diyami and Meredith had conflicts with prior appointments, so Jamal went with Billy. Jamal drove and Billy operated the radio. Billy had to hide the real purpose of what they were doing, so he said he was helping a friend test radio equipment. That didn't make much sense to Jamal, but then plenty of what he had seen since starting to work in the trailer didn't make sense. He was excited to spend time with Billy, a real entrepreneur, and he peppered him with questions about his years in the electronics business, like "What was your secret for success?"

"Listen to the customers and work my butt off."

"What's the best way I can make money in electronics?"

"Buy Amazon stock."

"Which is better, PlayStation or Xbox?"

"I don't have a clue. I sold people whatever they wanted."

This surprised Jamal. He assumed that a big shot in electronics would know everything about video games, which had been one of his obsessions since middle school. Over burgers at the Steak 'n Shake on Hampton Avenue, Jamal told Billy about his current favorite game, *Total War: Shogun 2*. "It's in old-time Japan, with ninjas, geishas, and shit. You gotta build up your armies, make alliances, and get weapons before you can fight battles with the other clans. It is seriously deep." Billy had never given a second's thought to video games, which seemed like mindless addiction to him, but Jamal made this game sound pretty cool. He agreed to take Jamal up on his offer to show him how to play. "I'm not sure when I'll be able to do it, but we will." Billy liked this kid.

The elevator door opened into a large, windowless room with rows of long tables. Moviolas were a few feet apart on the tables and a person sat staring at each one. The chief of police explained the operation to Giles Monroe, "Each moviola is attached to a camera that watches a street corner. This system is very effective when we see a crime in progress. But searching for a person in a crowd is like looking for a needle in a haystack."

"Have they seen the people I warned you about?"

"Not yet. We're doing everything humanly possible, Mr. Monroe. It's very slow work. When the streets are full, my people have to check each face against the books of photos. By the time they identify someone, that person has usually left the area."

"Then put more people on the job. Our city has been infiltrated."

"I have no one left. This is stretching our resources beyond the breaking point."

"You are failing at critical city business and should be ashamed of yourself. A new team of experts will be here soon to review this operation. They will tell me how effective your system is. I expect better."

The chief wanted to say more, but Giles turned away as two men, his spotters Josh and James, approached.

"Good news, sir. We think we've found them," Josh said.

"You were right," James said. "There are several people staying inside Leonora Matsui's house."

"It's not me who's right," Giles said. "My prime is right. Study your prime every day. That's my advice to you."

Josh and James described what they had discovered. From across the street, they had seen a number of men and women inside Leonora's house, though the only one who came outside was an old man who walked dogs every day.

"He's one from the other side who I allowed to stay last year as a concession to Ms. Matsui and her uncle." Giles said. "He's harmless, practically a recluse."

"We suspect that Boustany, his wife, and his daughter are there. We saw a younger woman, but the curtains make it difficult to get clear identifications."

"We spoke to a policeman who covers the area. He remembers stopping a man who resembled the photo of Boustany, but he had valid identification—a current CSP card. So that may have been a coincidence."

"There's more," James said. "Last week, one of our freelancers got a tip that caterers from a nearby restaurant delivered food to Miss Matsui's for a fancy party. She watched the house the rest of the day and night to see who would attend, but no party guests showed up."

"Why the hell did it take her so long to tell you about this? What do we pay these freelancers for?"

"Sir, she couldn't reach us," Josh said. "We were on the other side looking for Boustany."

"What do we do now?" James asked.

"We're going to pay a visit to Miss Matsui's home. Get your people ready."

"Tonight?"

"No. Tomorrow night. I want to go with you. Until then, I have important meetings preparing for the Water Festival. Keep watching them."

Giles' secretary hesitated before knocking on his office door. He had twice ignored her calls on the intercom and he hated interruptions. But this situation was urgent, and would become an emergency when Roger Thornhill, chairman of Hydraulic Brick Corporation, arrived in the next few minutes. She worked up her courage and knocked. Giles opened the door a few inches.

"What do you want?" he hissed.

"Mr. Thornhill needs to speak with you. His assistant says it's extremely important."

"Put him in the next open slot on my calendar."

"Apparently it can't wait. He's on his way now."

Giles closed the door for a moment, then opened it wide. He was all smiles as he spoke to the man he escorted out of the office. "I need a few minutes to take care of a small piece of business. We can resume shortly."

To his secretary he said, "Show our guest up to the cupola so he can enjoy the view. And get him some refreshments."

The secretary led the stranger away just as Roger Thornhill stepped off the elevator. He and Giles went into the office and Thornhill closed the door.

"To what do I owe the pleasure?" Giles asked the elegant, silver-haired man.

"I have been told that you're planning to raid Leonora Matsui's home."

Giles was taken aback that Thornhill knew about this plan. "We have good reason to believe that she is harboring dangerous intruders."

"So what?"

"We can't allow such a situation to continue. It could lead to uncertainty and jeopardize everything."

"Have you lost your mind? Don't give me your 'uncertainty' nonsense. The real risk, as you surely know, is the collapse of Hydraulic stock value. If the market finds out about the decay of Amperic bricks, we will all be in deep trouble."

"What does that have to do with eliminating Miss Matsui's intruders?"

"Her research is our only hope of fixing the problem. She tells me she is close to a solution, so I don't want anything—and I mean even the tiniest thing—to upset her. When is your raid supposed to happen?"

"Tomorrow."

"I strenuously object. Take this matter to the Knights' Inner Council before you make a move."

"As Supreme Protector, I have the authority."

"Your authority will vanish if Hydraulic goes bankrupt and the city falls into chaos. May I remind you that our precious CSP is a major stockholder. What will the public say if you have to cut or stop the dividend checks?"

Giles knew he was cornered. "Perhaps we can postpone our action for a little while."

"Miss Matsui has asked to update the board on her solution at the next meeting, in two weeks. Call off your spies and don't go anywhere near her. I don't want her to have one whiff of suspicion that she's being watched. We can revisit your concerns after the meeting."

Giles nodded and held out his hand to seal the agreement. Thornhill shook his hand, squeezed hard, and held on. "I mean it, Giles. If you damage Hydraulic, you're finished."

Thornhill left and Giles needed a moment to regain his composure. *I'll leave Miss Matsui alone, but Boustany won't get off the hook so easily.*

After several days of mapping, Billy was getting bored. The work was both tedious and nerve-wracking. Each day began at a predetermined point, like the Old Courthouse in downtown St. Louis or a bridge over the Mississippi south of the city. They drove west, making measurements every two miles, then they drove south to the next line of the grid and doubled back east, again making more measurements. Most of the time, the readings were within a narrow range, between -42dB and -30dB, which corresponded to signal strengths of S2 to S4—weak signals that indicated a relatively strong barrier. Then, on the fifth day, they transmitted from Chesterfield Mall, about twenty miles west of the Arch. There was no response from John in HD. "He must have missed the rendezvous," Billy said. He and Meredith drove to the next grid point, two miles further west. Again, no response. The same thing happened at the next two grid points as they drove west. That night, when Diyami reported the measurements to his father, Herbert told him that John had transmitted from the far west rendezvous points on time, but had heard nothing back.

For the next two days, the signal strengths were back in the S2 to S4 range as they crisscrossed the Illinois side of the river. Then on the eighth day, on a country road east of Edwardsville, they measured a signal of -6dB, a signal strength of S8. John's voice came through loud and clear and Billy could hear his excitement during the brief transmission. They had found a weak spot in the barrier! The measurements at the next few grid points were back to -42dB. A few miles further east, at Highland, Illinois, the signal disappeared completely, just like it had at Chesterfield Mall.

Billy stood next to Diyami as he made the call to his father that night. After he reported the day's results, Billy told him to say that the mapping could stop because they had found a weak spot. Diyami translated Billy's words into Cahokian, then listened to the reply from Herbert. He turned to Billy, "John and Lisa say we need more data and should continue with the plan."

"That makes no sense! We found what we're looking for," Billy said. Diyami translated that statement, then listened to a long transmission. "They insist we keep going and my father agrees with them. We're dealing with scientists. They don't like to stop experiments before all the data has been collected. We can complete the grid in two more days. After that, we can go back and measure the weak spot in more detail." Billy didn't like it, but he agreed to finish the original plan.

They mapped for two more days, but didn't find another weak spot. On the call that night, Herbert relayed instructions from John and Lisa for more detailed mapping east of Edwardsville. They would measure signal strength in all directions a quarter mile and half mile from the original location to determine the contours of the weak spot. Then Billy could try crossing without a pill.

"What if my ability to cross has disappeared, like the Knights said it would?" Billy asked.

Diyami asked the question in Cahokian, then translated Herbert's reply, "There's only one way to answer that question."

Herbert continued for a few minutes in Cahokian. Diyami listened, then closed his eyes. He appeared to be deeply affected.

"What did he say?" Billy asked.

"Lisa analyzed the data from all our measurements and was able to extrapolate an overall map of the barrier. All the places where a signal, strong or weak, got through lie inside a perfect circle, about twenty-five miles in diameter—like a bubble. Outside that circle, the barrier is completely impenetrable."

"So we—and the Knights—have been able to cross because there's a bubble in the barrier over St. Louis?"

"Yes. But it's not over St. Louis. The center of the circle is the Grand Plaza of Cahokia."

Billy felt exposed. He was standing in a field of waist-high corn a hundred yards from the dirt road where Meredith stood next to her pickup. A morning of detailed mapping of the weak spot suggested that the barrier was thinnest here. Would it allow him to cross into HD? *Time to give it a shot.* He waved to Meredith and she waved back. It had been many months since he last tried this—and that attempt had failed badly. He stood still, closed his eyes, and directed his attention deep down to the core of his being to search for the feeling that signaled the onset of a crossing. Could he summon it once more? He heard a faint buzz. *Is this the beginning?* He opened one eye to see an airplane slowly circling in the bright midday sky. *Don't be paranoid! There's no way they can see me.* He took long, deep breaths and surrendered to the faint threads of sensation that began to swirl behind his eyes. He shuddered, then felt a sharp headache and a familiar twinge of vertigo. The buzz got louder. He peeked again. *Shit! It's coming this way.* He lifted his foot and struggled to take a step forward. The vertigo rose up in full force and he sank to his knees. The buzz stopped. He reached out with his hand to steady himself. Instead of cornstalks, he felt soft leaves. He was in a field of soybeans. Meredith's pickup wasn't there. He looked around and saw a blue shape in the distance—Leonora's car! Three people got out of the car as he ran toward it. He high-fived Lisa, who had a huge grin, and Leonora, who was puzzled by the unfamiliar gesture. Carol gave him a big hug.

"It worked! We don't need no stinkin' pills!" Billy said.

"Are you OK?" Carol asked.

"I'm fine. Lisa, you're a goddamn genius." He high-fived her again.

"Do you think the Knights have discovered this weak spot?" Carol asked.

"Why would they bother?" Leonora said. "They've got the pills."

Billy told them about the airplane that seemed to be approaching him as he left SD. Carol laughed. "C'mon, Billy. You've watched *North by Northwest* too many times."

GET WET

A RADIO PLAYED in Leonora's kitchen as Lisa waited for the coffee to brew:

Good morning, St. Louis! And what a spectacular morning it is! Today's high will be ninety-nine degrees, with seventy-eight percent humidity, bright sun and no wind. It's going to be perfect!

You call that perfect? It sounds miserable.

Have you been living under a rock? It's Water Festival Day. Ninety-nine degrees means all soak and no chills for all the revelers heading to Seven Wonders.

Yes, the big parade starts at noon and I hear that people are already packing the subways and streetcars.

We're having another fantastic celebration of our friend, good old H_2O. And we'll be there broadcasting live, so you won't miss a dribble or a drop.

Get wet, everybody!

We have some special Water Festival music for you this morning, from St. Louis' favorite son—the one, the only Milo Riley!

Milo is a tradition at the Water Festival, but this year he's on his big tour of Asia.

We'll miss him, but that's Milo—always the ambassador taking St. Louis to fans around the world.

Did you hear him at the Sons of Rest street supper last year? That was a performance for the ages.

There's no one like Milo! He asked us to play a song for everyone going to the Water Festival this morning—here it is, "Keeper of the Flame."

The long, looping melody of a Middle Eastern flute filled the air. Lisa, the first person up in the house, poured herself a cup of coffee. This was the day she had been waiting for. The Water Festival! The adventure of a lifetime that Billy had promised her.

She peeled a banana as the drums and a guitar or sitar or something she couldn't put her finger on joined in (it was an oud). Then the vocals, in a heartbreakingly beautiful tenor.

"We flicker through the night,
Embracing all our light,
You are my forest sprite,
And I'm the keeper of the flame."

Lisa danced around the kitchen. She was a Beyoncé and Lady Gaga fan, but this guy was actually pretty good. No, he was awesome! She wished Dawn could hear this. Maybe she could take her a CD, if they had CDs here—she would have to ask John to make one. She wanted to tell Dawn everything about this HD place. Better yet, she would bring Dawn here someday. It will blow her mind. And now, she didn't need the pills anymore. *Thanks to who? Thanks to me!*

Carol entered the kitchen and watched Lisa gyrating madly to the music. Lisa saw her and stopped, embarrassed. "This guy is fantastic. Milo somebody."

"Milo Riley," Carol said as she poured herself some coffee. "Billy saw him perform last year at the street supper he told you about. He keeps saying it was the best night of his life."

"We should leave soon. The radio says that zillions of people are already heading to the Water Festival."

Carol nodded. She was just as excited to see the big spectacle as Lisa was.

Leonora made sure that Billy, Carol, and Lisa had plastic bags for their money and IDs. "You will be soaked. There's no way to avoid it. And watch out for pickpockets." Out on Grand, they were the last people who were able to squeeze into a jammed streetcar. As they headed north, the sidewalks were filling up with people on their way to Seven Wonders on foot. Someone in the streetcar tossed a water balloon in the air. It landed on a woman's broad floppy hat and splashed everyone standing next to her. "Hey! Save it until we're outside." The passengers laughed. The craziness had begun.

As the streetcar trundled north, the conductor announced, "Next stop, Grand and Dodier. Sportsman's Park." Billy leaned past other passengers to get a look out of the window. Sportsman's Park was the old baseball stadium, from before he was born. He didn't want to miss it. When the streetcar stopped, Billy saw a new Sportsman's Park, a gossamer, flattened sphere, white like an immense baseball. The outlines of the stands inside were visible. Red brickwork traced the outer surface in a pattern of baseball stitching. Two pylons shaped like baseball bats towered above. Support wires splayed down from the tops of the pylons to the edges of the sphere below. A ghostly, translucent, animated hologram of a batter floated above the stadium. Every time he swung, the words *Be a Brown Believer* appeared in a swoosh behind his bat. Billy wished he could go to a game here. *Maybe someday.* The streetcar started moving again.

The next stop was at the Grand Avenue Water Tower. Billy, Carol, Lisa, and the other passengers got out to join the boisterous crowd that spilled from the sidewalks into the street. Some people wore raincoats, others were in loose, brightly-colored clothing, and still others sported skimpy bathing suits. A group of tuba players tooted a jaunty melody. Vendors peddled souvenirs and snacks. A long banner hung down the Water Tower. In large red letters, it said *GET WET!* Lisa spotted a vendor selling T-shirts with the same slogan. She quickly bought three of them and held them up for Billy and Carol. "You've told me we need to blend in. These will be perfect!" Billy noticed that surveillance cameras hung from many lampposts and stone-faced policemen stood on every corner. Blending in was a good idea.

They wandered down Twentieth Street along with thousands of other festival goers. Carol pointed out other Seven Wonders monuments visible in the distance—the statue of Zeus, the Tower of Babel, and the Colossus of Rhodes. Hoses on rooftops showered everyone with gentle, cooling spray. Children dashed through the crowd, pelting each other with water balloons. One balloon hit Lisa's shoulder and exploded. She yelled in mock outrage, then took a balloon offered by another kid and hurled it at the perpetrator. She soon became an enthusiastic participant in the free-for-all balloon battle. She was unwinding from all the hours spent doing high-level math in John's workshop. Carol watched the colorful crowd and wished she had a camera to capture the chaos and mischief.

A side street that sloped downhill toward the Mississippi was covered with plastic sheets for two blocks. Spouting fire hydrants filled it with water and people of all shapes and sizes took turns spinning their way down the hill. Lisa yelled, "The world's longest slip 'n slide!" She tugged Billy's and Carol's hands and pulled them onto the plastic with her. They slid and twirled, holding hands and laughing, the entire two blocks, then ended lying in a pool of water at the bottom. Lisa was eager to do it again, but once was enough for Carol and Billy.

Back at the top of the slide, they tried to shake out their drenched clothing and hair, but decided it was a losing battle and continued walking along Twentieth Street. Billy bought everyone some grilled chicken on skewers from a booth advertising *Authentic Malayan Lok-Lok*—he was always ready to try new street food.

As they approached the statue of Zeus, Carol was the first to hear a slender, ethereal sound. She poked Billy and Lisa in the ribs, "Listen! It sounds like angels singing." They stopped and cocked their heads this way and that to try to locate the music. Notes were building on top of notes, higher and higher. "It seems to be coming from everywhere at once," Billy said. A man nearby noticed their bewilderment and pointed to a tent across the street. Its sign said *St. Louis Armonica Society*. "If this is your first time, don't miss it," he said, then dashed to join others dancing in the spray of a fire hydrant.

They crossed the street and stepped inside the large tent. The music resonated from every direction. About twenty people stood with their eyes closed, swaying dreamily. At the far end, three musicians were playing odd instruments on tables. Each instrument consisted of a series of glass bowls on their sides, nested inside each other, all turning on a horizontal shaft. The musicians dipped their fingers in pans of water, then touched them to the edges of the spinning bowls. Each finger produced a note and they could spread their hands to play chords, like on an organ. Carol recognized the piece they were playing, Pachelbel's *Canon*. Soon, she, Billy, and Lisa were as enchanted as everyone else in the tent. After a few minutes, the music ended and the spell was broken. The audience clapped politely. One of the musicians thanked everyone, then explained the instruments.

"The glass armonica was invented in the 1760s by Benjamin Franklin. He was inspired by seeing a musician play a tune by rubbing his fingers on wine glasses filled with different amounts of water. Franklin looked for ways to improve everything, so he hired a glass blower to build perfectly tuned bowls and mount them nested on a shaft. This allows us to play multiple notes at the same time. Franklin took his armonica with him everywhere he went for the rest of his life. Now, here's a piece from a different tradition."

The musicians wetted their hands and began the spiritual, *Swing Low, Sweet Chariot*. The low notes vibrated inside each listener's chest. It was remarkable.

Back out on the street, people were lining up on the sidewalks. The big parade was about to begin. Billy, Carol, and Lisa worked their way to a good spot. They saw the first marching band in the distance. Cheers erupted as it approached. Tubas, trombones, and trumpets belted out *The Battle Hymn of the Republic*. Drum majors held banners high that said *75ᵗʰ Annual Water Festival—Get Wet!* Next came a group of synchronized umbrella twirlers, followed by fifty children playing piccolos. The parade went on for about twenty minutes. There were bands of all sizes and descriptions, jugglers, stilt walkers, a huge inflatable catfish, live elephants that squirted water from their trunks, and a giant bathtub on wheels, overflowing with bubbles. People inside it mimed scrubbing motions and tossed water balloons into the crowd.

Two fire trucks parked at the nearby intersection turned on hoses pointed into the air. The plumes formed an arch of water over the street and made glittering rainbows in the sun. Spray rained down where Billy, Carol, and Lisa were standing. Loudspeakers boomed with an announcer's voice.

"Give a warm, wet St. Louis welcome to the sponsor of this year's Water Festival, the Citizen Shareholder Plan and its managing director, Gi-i-i-les Monroe!"

The largest float of the parade passed under the watery arch. It had a replica of the St. Louis skyline and a slogan in large script, *Prosperity and Progress for All.* An enthusiastic chant erupted in the crowd, "C-S-P, C-S-P, C-S-P!" On a platform at the top of the float, a man stood and waved to the adoring crowd. Billy pointed him out to Lisa, "There he is. Giles Monroe, king of the assholes!"

Lisa nodded. She had heard Billy, Carol, and Leonora talk about how much they hated this guy. Then she noticed another man standing next to him. He leaned over and said something into Monroe's ear. Giles chuckled and the man smiled. Lisa saw his face. It couldn't be, but it was— Ralph Pellegrini. *No! No! No!* She couldn't take her eyes off him.

Carol happened to glance over at Lisa and saw that the color had drained out of her face and she was shivering uncontrollably. "Billy! Billy! Something's wrong." Carol and Billy led her through the crowd to find a quieter place. Lisa was in a daze. Billy bought coffee from a vendor and offered it to her. She cupped it in her hands to feel its warmth. Her shivering eased. Carol rubbed her shoulders.

"What happened? You look like you've seen a ghost."

"Worse."

"Remember when I told you how my superiors ordered me to stop investigating your radiation events?" Lisa said in Leonora's living room that evening. "The person who made that decision was on the float with Giles Monroe today."

"You've got to be kidding," Carol said.

"No. His name is Ralph Pellegrini. He's a deputy director of the CIA."

"What's the CIA?" Leonora asked.

"The Central Intelligence Agency. It's the U.S. government's main spy organization."

"There's more than one?"

"In SD, the U.S. government is much bigger and more powerful than it is here," Billy said. "Several huge organizations are devoted to collecting intelligence."

"And making trouble," John said. "The CIA has a long history of propping up dictators and starting wars, among other things."

"What do they want here?" asked Leonora.

"They deal in secrets and HD is the biggest secret ever." Lisa said.

"Whatever they're trying to do, I don't see how it leads to anything good," Billy said.

Leonora slumped down in her chair. "What's with you people? Wars, the giant bombs, and now the CIA. And I thought Giles Monroe was our biggest problem."

For the rest of the evening, they all mulled over what to do now. Was there any way out of this mess? Should they tell Uncle Martin? Should Billy, Carol and Lisa go home to SD where they would be safer? Should Leonora and John leave town? There were no good options.

The next morning, Billy remembered the men he saw working on the security cameras next to the Asian market. The ones who had an HP laptop. *Were they connected to the CIA? What if I tracked them down again to learn more about what they're doing?* They could be anywhere, so it would take too long to find them on foot. He thought about asking Leonora to drive him around to look for them, but knew that Carol would shoot that plan down in a heartbeat. After yesterday, she was afraid. Then he remembered that Leonora had a scooter in the garage. He could figure out how to drive it. How hard could it be?

Billy slipped out the back door before the others got up. Leonora hadn't driven the scooter in a long time ("Those things are a menace and I'm too old."). It had a full tank of hydrogen. Billy opened the garage door and got on. He touched the throttle button, immediately lost control, and drove it into a trash can. *Crap! The kids around here make it look so easy.* He took a deep breath, then tried again. He rode back and forth in the alley, slowly and carefully, until he got the hang of it. *OK, let's go.* He took it out onto Grand into the traffic. Other scooters zipped past him and he got a few dirty looks from people who thought he was going too slow. No one was working on the cameras at Grand and Gravois, so Billy turned west on Gravois and kept looking. No luck. He turned back and went east on Gravois. He found the van with the cherry picker at the intersection with Arsenal. He pulled over on the far side of the street and watched. Two men worked for a while, then lowered the lift and drove away. Billy followed discreetly. *I'm undercover! This is so cool!* They headed east on Arsenal to Jefferson, then south to Cherokee, then east on Cherokee.

After a few blocks, they approached a large complex of brick buildings. White letters on a tower said *LEMP*. Billy recognized it as the long-abandoned Lemp Brewery. It appeared to be a thriving business in HD. Several trucks were parked outside and men loaded barrels of beer onto them.

The van turned into a brewery gate and a security guard waved it through. It went down a ramp that led to a lower level. The guard firmly told a pair of onlookers to move away from the gate. Then he harshly gestured to a delivery truck to go somewhere else. Billy wondered how he was going to get past this guy. His father's words came to him, "When you're dealt a losing hand, bullshit is your only friend."

Billy got off his scooter and sauntered up to the gate.

"This is a closed area. No admittance," the guard said.

"I'm the new guy."

"From Langley?"

"Yeah. I just crossed over this morning."

"They told me to expect you. I have a question. How are the redskins doing?"

Billy froze. Was this guy asking about the Cahokians? Then he realized the guard was talking about the Washington Redskins football team in SD.

"They got beat again on Sunday."

"Damn!"

"No way they can keep up with Manning and the Giants."

"It's going to be a long season."

"You ain't kidding."

"That's what I hate about this place. You can't get any sports scores."

"Do you need to see my ID?"

251

"No. That's just for the locals." The security guard pointed to a door. "The stairs will take you down to the place."

"Thanks. Can you watch my scooter?"

"Sure."

Billy walked past the guard, entered the building, and breathed a sigh of relief. His bluff worked! He started down a spiral staircase. At the bottom, there was a space with heavy vaulted ceilings supported by thick stone columns. It was the cave under the building where barrels of beer used to be aged in the nineteenth century. Billy heard voices up ahead. He peeked around a corner. There was a brightly-lit room with computer screens on tables. Three men were talking. Billy inched closer so he could hear them while staying out of sight in the shadows.

"How did the camera feed come through this morning?"

"Looks good. Speaking of feed, did you bring me lunch?"

"Of course, my friend. Your favorite—curried chicken with fried pickles."

"Shit! I would kill for a Big Mac with fries."

"When in Rome, eat like the Romans."

"Fuck you."

They all laughed.

"How is the facial database coming?"

"It's a royal pain. I have to scan all these photos one at a time." He pointed to a scanner and thick binders with photos. "I'll be doing this for weeks."

The third man noticed something, then said to the others, "Look sharp. Here comes Darth Vader."

From the far end of the room, Giles Monroe and Ralph Pellegrini approached. A young woman with a limp was at Giles' side. Billy crouched down further behind a barrel to make sure they couldn't see him. He overheard their conversation as they walked past him.

"When you understand the patterns inside your number, it gives you a real advantage," Giles said. "I used to be a skeptic, but I wouldn't be where I am today without my number. I consult it before I make any decision."

"That's quite remarkable," Ralph said.

"I can get you an appointment with my numerologist. She'll change your life."

"Thanks. I'll consider that for the future. Right now we have a lot on our plates. Let's see how the team is doing."

Pellegrini, Giles, and the young woman approached the technicians at the computer monitors.

"Good afternoon, gentlemen," Giles said. "Are you making progress with the face matching project?"

"They call it facial recognition, sir," the young woman said.

"Yes, facial recognition. How far along are you?"

"It's going quite slowly, sir. There are more than a million photographs to scan."

"We need this badly. You must find a way to speed things up."

"We could do so if we had more equipment, especially better scanners," the technician said. "But we need to go back to our place to get them."

"My people would have to assist you, but I can't free them up right now."

"There's another way," Pellegrini said. "If you could provide us the means of travel, we could procure the needed equipment without inconveniencing your team."

Giles held up his hand to silence Pellegrini. "Ralph, you know that's impossible. We have already discussed this."

"But you want us to activate the system as soon as possible. It won't work properly until the database of photographs is complete."

"I don't need the entire system to work right now. The immediate priority is to locate specific intruders."

"Of course," Pellegrini said.

"Have you put the photographs of those three people in your system? What did you call them, Ralph?"

"High value targets."

"May I see the high value targets, please?"

Pellegrini nodded to the technician to pull the photos up on the monitors.

"I am almost certain that these intruders are in my city now," Giles said. "Use your system to find them. Let me know the minute you do."

"Of course, Mr. Monroe," the technician said. Giles, Pellegrini, and the limping young woman left.

Billy peeked out from behind the barrel. On the monitor, he saw photos of himself, Carol, and Meredith—taken when they had been kidnapped by the Knights the previous year. He ducked back behind the barrel as the technicians talked.

"Lord Vader isn't about to give up his magic pills. They're his leverage."

"Pellegrini will get them sooner or later. He's patient—and very persistent."

"All he needs is one pill. Then Langley will analyze it and figure out how to make them."

"Then we won't have to kiss Darth Vader's ass any more."

"It's almost funny. He still thinks he's in charge."

They continued to talk about technical issues with the camera system. Billy crept around the corner and climbed the spiral staircase as quietly as he could. At the top, he walked out into the daylight and waved to the security guard, "Thanks for watching my scooter."

"No problem. Go 'Skins!"

"Go 'Skins!"

"If you hear about next week's game, let me know."

Billy gave him a thumbs up, hopped on the scooter, and sped away. To avoid cameras, he took back streets and alleys all the way to Leonora's house.

Carol was steaming mad when Billy walked in. "Where the hell have you been?"

"I did a little reconnaissance."

"Talk to me before you do anything. I was worried to death. No more surprises!"

Billy told the others what he had found. "Giles is getting help from the CIA to tighten his surveillance of the city. They're building a facial recognition system."

"What's facial recognition?" Leonora asked.

Lisa explained. "You build a database of photographs—everyone in the city—and computers can compare those photos to people in security camera images. You can instantly identify a person walking down the street."

"I saw some of their photos on a screen—me, Carol, and Meredith. Giles called us 'high value targets.'"

"He knows we're here?" Carol asked.

"Yeah, and they're looking for us. Also, the CIA guys made fun of Giles after he left—they aren't that enamored of him. They're trying to get hold of the pills for themselves so they can do whatever it is they want."

"So we're in deep shit," Carol said.

"Actually, I think all of HD is in deep shit."

Leonora stood up and paced back and forth as she tried to come up with a plan. "We've got to get you to someplace safe."

"Back to SD?" Carol asked.

"The CIA might be looking for us over there too," Billy said. "Remember the *North by Northwest* plane I saw that you thought was so funny?"

"How about Cahokia?" John said. "You've always said that the Knights don't go over there."

No one had a better idea. John called Herbert, Diyami's father, to let him know they were coming. Within ten minutes, they all squeezed into Leonora's car. With their suitcases and backpacks, including Carol's books about HD, it was a tight fit. Leonora brought a small suitcase, which she stuffed into the trunk.

"What's that?" Billy asked.

"Something I don't want to leave here."

Billy, Carol, and Lisa hid on the floor of the car as they drove out of Flora Place. Leonora saw two men standing on the corner watching them. She waved to them with a smile and they waved back. "One thing to be thankful for," Leonora said. "The Knights can be idiots when you most need them to." She watched for police or other cars following them, but she didn't see anything. They all let out sighs of relief when they crossed the bridge into Illinois, where the Knights had no power.

PINPRICK

THE RED HAWKS' LIVING ROOM was crowded with five unexpected visitors and their assorted bags and backpacks. Herbert and Juliet were a bit flustered by the sudden influx, but they were glad to see Billy, Carol and the others. After hugs were exchanged and Juliet brought out a tray with ice water, Billy explained why they had to leave St. Louis in such a hurry. "The Knights have teamed up with a secretive government organization from our world and they are looking for us."

"It's bad," Carol said. "We didn't know where else to go."

"You came to the right place," Juliet said. "We will find a path forward."

"Diyami and Meredith may be in danger too."

"In the other world?"

"This organization is very powerful. Who knows what they will do?"

"Our people learned a long time ago that the U.S. government can't be trusted," Herbert said. "I have a radio transmission with Diyami scheduled for tonight."

"They need to come over here. It will be safer."

"Tell them to use pills if they still have them," Leonora said. "There's no time to find the weak spot again."

There was nothing to do until the radio transmission, so everyone was able to unwind. Billy had been to Cahokia twice before; each time he had expected never to see it again. But here he was, once more in this serene and beautiful city with Herbert and Juliet, two of the calmest people he had ever known. Their presence gave him confidence that, whatever happened next, all would be well.

Herbert showed them an empty apartment down the hall, which was reserved for faculty visiting the university. With it, there would be room for everyone, even after Diyami and Meredith arrived. Billy, Carol, and Leonora helped Juliet make dinner. Lisa, like every first-time visitor to Cahokia, went out onto the patio to gaze at the Grand Plaza. The glass pyramid of the Temple of the Children sparkled in the afternoon sun. Groups of people strolled across the plaza. Groundskeepers had etched large designs in its groomed, packed earth—a catfish, a flock of birds, and a human figure with wing-like arms and a hawk-billed nose. John saw her and joined her.

"What do you think?"

"It's crazy. Ridiculous. Spectacular. Who built this?"

"Indians. Diyami is trying to do the same thing in our world."

"How the hell is he going to pull that off?"

"I don't know. They did it here, so maybe he can do it there."

"That would be pretty cool."

"There's something I want to talk to you about."

"What?"

"Bubbles."

John and Lisa stayed on the patio for almost an hour, engaged in deep conversation. As the sun sank low in the west, the others came out. Dinner was almost ready. Juliet lit a bundle of sage and gathered them in a circle. She chanted a prayer to the Great Mystery and gave thanks to the four directions. They sat around the firepit and ate. The setting sun cast a soft glow, first pink, then orange, on the white buildings of Cahokia.

Herbert called Diyami on the radio at the appointed time. They spoke in Cahokian for a few minutes, then signed off. "I told Diyami to come here right away. He has a few pills. Their associate, Stan, is with them. They thought it best to bring him also."

Meredith rushed to embrace her parents as soon as she saw them. They introduced her and Diyami to Lisa, whom they knew about, but had never met. Stan hung back by the door. He wasn't sure what was going on, but was happy to be back in HD, even if under strange circumstances. *Maybe all circumstances are strange when HD is involved.*

"Why did you need us to come so quickly?" Diyami asked.

"This is not the day any of us expected when we woke up this morning." Herbert said. "We wanted to make sure you were safe."

Juliet said there would be no more talk until the morning. "We're all exhausted. We will need clear heads."

The table was piled with corn cakes, gooseberry syrup, and bacon when the group gathered in the Red Hawks' apartment the next morning. Herbert poured coffee for all who wanted it.

"It's time to bring everyone up to speed," Billy said. "Things have gotten a little more complicated."

"Please wait, Billy," Leonora said. "I have asked one more person to join us. He needs to hear this."

"Who?"

"Uncle Martin. I called him a little while ago and his driver is bringing him here now."

"He's in the Knights. Can we trust him?" Meredith said.

"Of course. He got you and your parents away from Giles last year and he gave me the pills we've all been using."

"I don't like it," Meredith said. Diyami nudged her to be quiet.

Uncle Martin arrived a few minutes later. He walked slowly, with a cane, and shook hands with everyone. Leonora introduced him to Lisa and Stan. He shook Lisa's hand warmly, "I am honored to meet the genius who saved Hydraulic." He winked to Stan, "An attorney? I'll be on my guard not to say anything incriminating." Martin happily accepted a plate of corn cakes and bacon. "Your usual excellence, Mrs. Red Hawk."

Billy looked around the room. Little more than a year earlier, he had not yet met or even heard of most of these people. He had been preoccupied with his failing business and was going through the motions of family life with Carol and Meredith. John was a distant figure from his past who he rarely thought about. Now they had the awesome responsibility to deal with an earth-shattering reality— together. A line of a song from his childhood came back to him, *What a long, strange trip it's been.*

"We're all here because of an accident that happened to me just last year."

Leonora interrupted. "Actually, it began when John and I found each other many years ago."

"And I was the villain then," Martin said cheerfully, in between bites of the corn cakes.

"Whenever it began," Billy continued, "The chain of events led to many wonderful things, but also to some frightening things. Today we have to decide what we can and should do about the frightening things." He looked directly at Martin. "All of this relates to your organization, the Knights of the Carnelian. Before we go any further, I need to know that you won't divulge what we talk about today to anyone outside this room."

Martin closed his eyes for a moment. "You have my word."

Meredith stood up. She was angry. "Really, Martin? Really? You didn't come galloping to the rescue when the Knights kidnapped me."

"You're right, Miss Boustany. I didn't help you then because I didn't know about your situation until after you escaped, with the help of your mother and her baseball bat. That's when I realized that Giles Monroe was hiding information from me. In all of my many years with the Knights, that had never happened before. The Knights have done great work for a very long time to protect our city and help it prosper and grow. But I fear they have become corrupted, drunk on their own power. I want to stop that just as much as you do. So I have no qualms about keeping your confidence today." He turned to Billy. "Again, Mr. Boustany. You have my word."

"Is everyone okay with Martin's assurance?" Billy looked at Meredith. She frowned, but nodded yes. "We've learned some extremely disturbing information in the last few days. That's why we got out of St. Louis as fast as we could. First, you need to know the background." He asked Lisa to explain that she worked for the government in SD and how she first came to meet him and Carol a few months ago. She also described how her investigation into the St. Louis events was stopped by her superiors. Then Billy told how he and Carol had brought Lisa over to help with computer simulation to solve the problem of Amperic brick decay. "We took a chance on her and she came through," Carol said.

"I thank you and John for your service to our most important industry," Martin said.

"That's not all they did," Billy said. "John and Lisa developed a plan to map the barrier between the two worlds to see if we could find weak spots where it was possible to cross without the pills."

"Similar to your discoveries from long ago, John?" Martin said.

"Yes, but far more thorough and accurate."

"Very impressive."

"Everyone in this room helped with that, Martin." Billy said. "And we succeeded. Just last week, I was able to cross without a pill."

Martin was surprised. This was big news. A person's ability to cross unaided always disappeared after a few months. Billy had lost his last year.

"Then, day before yesterday, Carol, Lisa, and I went to the Water Festival in Seven Wonders. We wanted to celebrate and see the sights. We got more than we bargained for."

Lisa told the story of watching the parade and seeing two people atop the CSP float, waving to the crowd—Giles Monroe and Ralph Pellegrini, the high-level CIA official who had shut down her investigation.

Diyami and Martin had never heard of the CIA. Lisa explained what it was and Stan chimed in. "It's a massive spy agency that does shady stuff. I have never dealt with them and hope I never will. Legally, they're not supposed to operate within the United States. Whether or not they obey that could be another story."

"HD is geographically inside the United States," Carol said. "But a parallel universe may count as a foreign country."

That got a laugh from the group.

"They are definitely up to something in HD," Billy said. He told of his experience from yesterday of following workers who were putting up surveillance cameras to an underground room. They were CIA people from SD. Giles Monroe and Pellegrini were there and Billy listened in on the conversation.

"Good lord, dad," Meredith interjected. "That's dangerous!" She had long thought of Billy as kind of a wimp. He was pleased that he had finally impressed her. He went on to describe the facial recognition system, including the photos of the "high-value targets"—himself, Carol, and Meredith. He glanced over at Meredith and enjoyed the look of shock on her face. Then he described Pellegrini's attempt to talk Giles out of some pills, no doubt so the CIA could copy them and be able to cross between SD and HD whenever they wanted. "When Giles was out of the room, the CIA people made it very clear they think he's a fool."

"What do you know about this, Uncle Martin?" Leonora asked.

"Nothing," he sighed. "Giles has dropped a few vague hints about a new approach, but that's it. Billy's information confirms what I have feared—I have been cut off and put out to pasture."

263

"Are there others in the Knights you could tell about this? Perhaps they could stop it."

"I doubt it. Giles has them all in his thrall. I don't know why. He has little to offer besides his appeal to fear and greed. But that may be enough, with human nature as fallible as it is."

"Then _we_ have to do something!" Meredith said. "You can't just let the bad guys win."

"Like what?" said Billy. "How are we going to fight both the CIA and the Knights?"

John spoke for the first time all morning. "Actually, there may be a way to disrupt their plans. It's a long shot and you may not like the consequences."

Everyone looked at him.

"When we mapped the barrier to look for weak spots, we saw that the only places where any communication between the worlds was possible lay within a circle, a perfect circle, about fifty miles in diameter."

"Fifty-two-point-four miles, by my calculations. Give or take." Lisa said.

"Outside the circle, there was absolutely zero communication. The radio signals didn't penetrate at all."

"The circle is a region where the barrier is weaker. It's like a bubble," Lisa said. "with the center right here, at Cahokia. Give me a moment and I'll demonstrate." She went into the kitchen and returned with a tray, which she set on the table. The others gathered around. On the tray were a bowl of water, a small bottle, a straw, and a toothpick.

"Imagine that the barrier between the worlds is the surface of this water." She poured a few drops of liquid from the bottle into the water. "I'll use this soap to make bubbles." She put one end of the straw into the water, then blew a puff of air. Large bubbles appeared on the water. "At some point, a bubble formed." She jiggled the bowl and the bubbles shook. "Bubbles can be stable for a long time."

"The bubble in the barrier over Cahokia and St. Louis has been here for more than a hundred years, as far as we know." John said.

"But it doesn't take much to pop a bubble." Lisa took the toothpick and gently touched it to the largest bubble. It disappeared instantly. "A little pinprick will do the trick."

"Are you saying you can pop the bubble in the barrier?" Diyami asked.

"Maybe," John said.

"What happens then?"

"It becomes like everywhere else. No bubble means no communication, no travel. Complete separation of the two worlds."

"Wow," Billy said.

"The CIA's plans would be finished. As far as they were concerned, HD would have disappeared."

"You can't do that!" said Meredith. "It would disappear for us too."

"Yes," John said. "That's the consequence you might not like."

"What right do we have to rip the two worlds apart?" Carol said.

"As much right as Giles and the CIA have to do whatever it is they're doing," Leonora said. "Almost everyone in both HD and SD is completely unaware of the other world. So nothing changes for them. They go on and live their lives. The only people who would be affected would be us in this room, the Knights, and the CIA. No one else would miss a thing."

"But we would miss it," Meredith said. She looked at Lisa. "This is all your fault. You gave them the hint about HD."

"I had no idea what I was looking at," Lisa said. "There's no way I could have anticipated this."

Billy came to Lisa's defense. "If we could see the future, we all would have done things differently. I know I would have."

Chaos erupted as several people started to talk at once. They were alarmed by the enormity of John and Lisa's idea. Martin stood up, whistled, and waved his cane back and forth to quiet everyone down.

"I was crossing between the worlds before most of you were born," Martin said. "It's been quite an experience. Magical, you might say. We are all fortunate to have been part of it. But one thing is clear from what Billy has told us. The way things have been can't endure. Something is going to change. Either we let Giles and the CIA people change it, or we change it."

Billy's head was spinning. Ending communication between HD and SD is not what he thought they would be talking about. "Can we take a break? I need some time." No one objected. They all felt overwhelmed.

Billy and Carol refilled their coffee cups, then walked over to a corner of the room.

"What the hell are we going to do?" Billy asked.

"Maybe John's idea is too much. But how else can we stop the CIA?"

"Those bastards. Our tax dollars at work. You know what pisses me off the most? They've made me afraid to go to HD St. Louis, the most beautiful place I've ever been."

"Cahokia is pretty nice too."

"Yeah, but it's not our city."

Diyami led Meredith, who was visibly upset, out to the patio. They were soon joined by his parents and Stan. Billy watched them from the living room. They were deep in conversation. Diyami was comforting Meredith. Billy wished he could hear what they were saying. One thing was sure, they were the ones Meredith now turned to for support. His little girl was moving on. *That's life. You can't hold on to the past.*

"Are we in danger?" Herbert asked. "I fear this bubble will bring invaders to us."

"The Knights know better than to interfere in Cahokia," Juliet said.

"But what about the CIA?" asked Meredith. "They could care less." She turned to Stan, "You said that they're not allowed to do work inside the United States."

"Yes, that's true over there, but no law from SD will protect HD. Mrs. Boustany was right about that."

"Without the bubble, they can't touch us," Diyami said.

"That young woman said that Cahokia is the center of the bubble," Juliet said. "I can't stop thinking about that. Is it a gift from the spirits?"

"When I was on the river," Diyami said, "the spirit told me to let the ancient places be our teachers."

"If the bubble is popped, it may be over for them," Juliet pointed to the people in the living room. "But it doesn't have to be over for us. Let us seek guidance." Juliet closed her eyes and began to chant. The others stood in a circle around her.

When the group gathered again in the living room, Billy looked around at everyone. *We're an unlikely bunch to have the fate of a world—or two—in our hands.* He was the first to speak. "As Martin said, we have to do something. Whatever the CIA and Giles have in mind, it won't be good for HD, and who knows what it might mean for SD. We need a plan— and we all have to agree on it. John and Lisa have made a suggestion. Does anyone have an alternative?"

"No," Meredith said. "I'd like to hear more about popping the bubble." Billy was surprised that her attitude had changed. He nodded to John to begin.

"The barrier is an electromagnetic phenomenon," John said. "It exists everywhere to keep the two worlds separate. The bubble appears to be an unusual region in the barrier that allows signals, and people, to pass through under the right circumstances. So we need an electromagnetic pinprick."

"We think that an intense burst of electric energy that travels through the barrier can pop it," Lisa said.

"How intense?" Billy asked.

"A million volts, more or less" John said. "For a fraction of a second."

"How the hell are you going to do that?"

"With a resonant transformer, also known as a Tesla coil. It generates high voltage, high frequency alternating current that can transmit energy through the air. We would place the transformer in HD and a tuned receiving circuit at the same geographical location in SD. Flip the switch, power flows through the barrier, and the bubble should pop."

"I don't like the sound of 'should,'" Billy said. "How certain are you that it will work?"

"I haven't tried it before."

"But our theory is sound," Lisa said.

"How long would it take to build the transformer?"

John smiled. "I saw a good-sized Tesla coil not too long ago—and it's for sale. I can modify it in a couple of days. Building the receiving circuit in SD should be no problem."

Damn! thought Billy. *Do I really want to do this?* He turned to Martin, "What do you think?"

"I don't understand the technical details, but I have faith in Mr. Little and Ms. McDaniel. Your CIA could send over thousands of people and we couldn't prevent them. This plan could protect our way of life. As an added benefit, it would knock Giles off his high horse, something many would welcome."

"What about you, Diyami?"

"Ending travel and communication between the worlds will put us back where we thought we were last year. Meredith and I will pursue our work in SD." She nodded and hugged Diyami's shoulder.

"I support the motion on the floor," Stan said.

"Leonora?"

"I'm with Uncle Martin."

"Carol?"

"I haven't seen enough of HD to say goodbye without regrets. But then a lifetime of HD wouldn't be enough for me. So we must protect it."

"Herbert? Juliet?"

"The spirits spoke to me," Juliet said. "They gave Diyami a mission. We want him to succeed."

Herbert gave a thumbs up.

"What do you want, Billy?" Carol said.

"Last year, I hated it when Giles told me that the existence of the two worlds needed to be kept secret. All his bullshit that people couldn't handle that knowledge. Now I'm not so sure. Maybe we are better off with each world on its own. This silly little bubble thing has been a hell of a ride, but it's too dangerous in the wrong hands. You give people something wonderful and they'll find a way to screw it up. Let's pop the bubble."

No one said anything. The weight of the moment was heavy on all of them. Billy had an urge for a group hug, a kumbaya closure.

"We'll get started right away," John said.

The die was cast.

Juliet stood up. "May the choices of this council bring peace and serve to protect all beings," followed by something in Cahokian.

Billy wanted to say "amen," but he wasn't sure if that was appropriate.

A few minutes later, while everyone was still processing what they had decided, Leonora and John approached Diyami. "May we speak with you and your attorney?"

"Yes. Why?"

"We have something for you. A gift. To balance the accounts."

BOOM

"WHAT THE HELL are you going to do with this thing, John?" The vendor couldn't quite believe that John Little, one of his best customers, actually wanted the ungainly object collecting dust at the rear of his booth in a far corner of the Mechanical Market. He had sold John everything from broken moviolas to scroll readers and pneumatic power supplies, but always small items, some of which rose only a notch or two above the level of useless junk. He recognized John as a fellow bottom feeder and tinkerer, who loved nothing more than taking things apart and putting the pieces together in new combinations. Over the past year, he had helped John learn his way through many quirks of HD technology.

"I don't know. Maybe see if I can electrocute myself."

"That's about all it's good for. I'll let you have it for the scrap value of the copper. That way, once you get tired of it, you can break even."

"Deal."

The object was an industrial-strength Tesla coil— a slender, seven-foot tall cylinder that rose up from a flat circular base and was topped by a doughnut-shaped aluminum ring. John squatted down and found a half-corroded plaque on the base that said it was rated to produce nine hundred thousand volts at a frequency of five hundred kilohertz. *Close enough. I can make it work,* John thought.

"How are you going to get it out of here?"

"We have a truck."

The vendor looked at the two tattooed Cahokians with John. This was definitely his weirdest sale in quite a while. Diyami and his friend Anak wrestled the two-hundred pound coil onto a motorized cart, then walked it out to the parking lot, where they loaded it into the back of a Kahok Beer truck.

John explained how the coil works to the group assembled in an empty room next to the loading dock of the Kahok Brewery. "It functions as a resonant, or oscillating transformer. We supply a current to the primary coil." He pointed to the base with its spiral rings of copper tubing. "It acts as a capacitor that builds up a charge, which then transfers to the secondary coil on the vertical section, which is tightly wound by thin copper wire. Energy oscillates between the two coils and can build up a high voltage in the secondary coil—this one goes to nine hundred thousand volts."

"What's the doughnut at the top?" Carol asked.

"That's the high-voltage terminal. When the voltage reaches its peak, it discharges energy through the air to grounded objects nearby. I'll show you." John walked over to the wall and pushed down the lever on a switch. Blue lightning bolts of electricity streamed out from the top of the coil. Everyone dove to the floor to protect themselves. John pulled the lever up to turn the coil off. "Relax. It's harmless," he said with a smile.

"Jesus! Are you trying to pop the bubble right now?" Billy said.

"I can turn this on and off all day long with no effect on the barrier. The voltage dissipates to grounded objects in all directions. What we have to do is focus this high voltage through the barrier. Think of this coil as a transmitter of energy. We'll make a receiver in SD that is tuned to its specific frequency. That will pull the energy from the coil through the barrier and create our pinprick."

"John and I have worked out the design of the receiver," Lisa said. "I can go to SD, get the materials, and build it quickly. The trick will be to place the receiver at a location in SD that precisely matches the location of the transmitter in HD."

"My father and I are working out the coordinates for a location here that matches the property we own at the trailer park in SD," Diyami said.

"After we turn the device on, how long will it take to pop the barrier?" Leonora asked.

"The coil will generate a hundred high-voltage pulses a second. One pulse may do it, or it might take a hundred or a thousand. We'll get a result pretty fast," John said. "If it disrupts the barrier, a lot of additional energy may be released, so the equipment will probably get fried."

"Is that dangerous?" Meredith asked.

"I don't recommend standing nearby when we do it."

The group spent the rest of the day working out the details of the plan. The "event" was targeted to take place at noon five days later. To verify if the bubble had popped or not, they agreed on timed radio transmissions between HD and SD every five minutes for an hour after the event, once an hour for the next six hours, then once a day for ten days. No contact would mean success. Diyami, Meredith,

273

Stan, and Lisa went back to SD that evening to begin work on the receiver. Billy and Carol, who weren't needed for this work, wanted to stay at Cahokia in HD until the day of the event.

That evening, they sat on the Red Hawks' patio having a glass of wine and watching the sun set over the Grand Plaza. "I guess we're really doing this," Billy said.

"Yeah," said Carol.

"Do you still think it's a good idea?"

"What other choice do we have?"

Billy shrugged as he sipped his wine. He wasn't so sure.

Herbert and Juliet joined them on the patio with dinner.

It was that kind of day for Jamal. Everything was happening at once. Stan had closed the deal on the site of the new freight terminal, an abandoned Venture store a couple miles west of the trailer where there was room to park lots of trucks. Jamal was supposed to make sure the drivers knew where to go and ferry them to the motel if they were staying overnight. The printer was out of paper and toner, so he needed to make a run to Office Depot. Three students from Sitting Bull College in North Dakota had arrived to begin their four-week internships. Meredith asked Jamal to be their supervisor, answer their questions, and give them something useful to do.

In the midst of this chaos, Jamal sensed that something was up with Diyami and Meredith. Diyami sat at his desk in the back of the trailer, sometimes working and sometimes staring off into space. Meredith was more manic than usual, talking fast on the phone while glancing over at Diyami with a worried look on her face. Then there was the new girl, Lisa somebody, who had shown up out of nowhere. She had a long, whispered conversation with

Diyami and Meredith, then they all left for several hours. When they returned, they avoided talking to Jamal.

This ain't right.

The next morning, Jamal was the first to arrive at the trailer. Diyami and Meredith came in a little later, with muffins and Starbuck's coffee to share. Diyami was in an upbeat mood, enthusiastic about the new cinnamon latte flavor he had discovered. Meredith smiled peacefully. As they finished up, Diyami said to Jamal, "Let's take a walk outside."

"Stan wants me to make some calls right away."

"Stan can wait."

The three of them walked into the woods behind the trailer park. Dappled sunlight filtered through the trees. Yellow wildflowers were in bloom. Jamal was apprehensive.

"Jamal, you have been so important to our work here," Meredith said.

Uh-oh. Is this when I get fired? Do they want an Indian to have my job?

"It's time for you to know the big picture," Diyami said. "Cahokia is about a lot more than the freight business."

"I know that."

"You do and you don't."

"I remember that time up on the mound when you were telling the drivers about the canals and the university."

"You said it sounded 'almost real.'"

Diyami opened his hand to reveal two white pills. "One for you and one for me."

"Oh, shit. My momma was right. You're dealing dope! Is that what this whole Cahokia business is about?"

Diyami laughed. "This isn't a drug. It's a door—with the promised land on the other side. And the door is about to close."

"You deserve to see it," Meredith said.

"You want me to take that pill? And then what?"

"That which is 'almost real' becomes completely real."

Jamal thought long and hard. Diyami and Meredith were the first people outside his family who ever took a chance on him. Could he take a chance on them? He picked a pill from Diyami's hand and popped it into his mouth. *Is this the stupidest move I've ever made?*

Meredith handed him a floppy, broad-brimmed hat. "I almost forgot. You'll need this."

Diyami swallowed his pill, then held Jamal's hand. They both doubled over with headache and vertigo and collapsed into the wildflowers. Meredith watched them disappear with a faint shimmer. It was the first time she had seen someone else cross over.

Four hours later, they still hadn't returned. Meredith began to worry. She could imagine what Jamal was going through, but how much of Cahokia did he need to see? After another hour, her phone rang. An unknown number from St. Louis.

"Meredith, it's me."

"Where are you?"

"North St. Louis. After Cahokia, Jamal wanted to see his neighborhood. We took the speedboat to downtown, then the subway to Seven Wonders. We've been all over, even to the street he lives on."

"How is he doing?"

"He's worn out, but happy. Can you pick us up? We're at the MV Market, 4300 North Twentieth Street."

Diyami and Jamal were sitting on the sidewalk as Meredith drove up. Jamal looked dazed and had a loose grin. When she got out of the car, he gave her a long, tight hug. "Thank you, thank you, thank you," he whispered.

"All six stages in a few hours," Diyami said. "That's a new record."

Less than a day to go. Billy was helping John with preparation of the Tesla coil. John was unusually quiet—even for him. Billy sensed that he was nervous that some last-minute hitch could derail everything. John checked and rechecked the connections on the coil, which was mounted on a flatbed cart. When he needed a tool, he held out his hand towards Billy without making eye contact and issued single word commands, like a surgeon in an operating room. "Wire stripper...needle-nose...tape." John's plan was to roll the cart out to the agreed-upon spot in HD at the last minute and then connect a high-voltage power cable. The location was in the Kahok Brewery parking lot, where people came and went, and he didn't want to attract attention. Anak had put up a temporary fence around the section of the parking lot John needed to use, under the pretext of pavement repairs.

The radio transmissions from Diyami said that he and Lisa had the receiver ready to go. Because rain was in the forecast, they were going to set it up it inside a tent at the corresponding spot in SD, about a hundred yards south of the trailer that was the office of the ABSOM Cahokia Native Development Corporation. The receiver didn't need a lot of power, so Diyami planned to run an extension cord out to it.

A gloomy sadness washed over Billy as he watched John work. They were about to close the book on the best part of his life. The plan called for Carol and him to cross back to SD first thing in the morning, for the last time.

That evening, he and Carol strolled around Cahokia. The pink and purple sky was reflected in the glass walls of the Temple of the Children. They watched children laughing and shouting in a playground, then stopped at a café. Billy ordered his final Kahok beer.

"This place is so beautiful," he said.

Carol knew how sad he was. No one could read his emotions like she could. She held his hand. "It will still be beautiful when we're not here. We'll always have the memory. And we will get to help Diyami and Meredith build something like it."

Billy sipped his beer in silence. He looked even more morose. Then Carol had an idea. "Let's go to St. Louis. Tonight."

"You know that's too dangerous. They're looking for us."

"We'll go to that Leveetown place on the riverfront. My guidebook says it's packed every night. No one will notice us. The hydrofoils run back and forth from Cahokia until two in the morning. C'mon!" She had an unmistakable glint of mischief in her eyes. "It's now or never. I don't want our last memory of HD St. Louis to be hiding on the floor of Leonora's car."

Billy was tempted by Carol's enthusiasm, even though the idea sounded foolish, "We can't let anything screw up tomorrow."

"We'll be back in plenty of time—before anyone knows we're gone. No more 'coulda, woulda, shoulda.' We'll wear our big, floppy hats so the cameras won't recognize us."

It would actually be fun, Billy thought. *One last chance.*

The wind rippled Carol's hair as the hydrofoil zoomed down the canal. Stars filled the sky above and the St. Louis skyline glittered up ahead. She and Billy stood at the front of the boat so they could soak up every last detail of the world passing by. The hydrofoil entered the Mississippi, then carved a graceful turn as the pilot cut power and the hull dropped into the water. It pulled up to the floating dock next to the Illinois end of the Eads Bridge. Billy and Carol disembarked with the other passengers, then rode the elevator up to the main level of the bridge. St. Louis was a sparkling vision spread out in front of them. A sign pointed to the "Leveetown Gondola" about a quarter mile to the south. "I read about this in my guidebook too," Carol said. "Let's do it!"

Black water of the river swirled below as the gondola, suspended from a thin cable, made its way toward the Missouri side. Looking down brought back a nightmare Billy had the previous year, in which he was crossing the river on a tightrope, then stumbled and plunged into the murky depths. The memory gave him a shudder.

Music from Leveetown could be heard several minutes before the gondola reached shore. The place was jumping. They descended from the gondola terminal into the teeming streets. Groups of people edged past each other. Animated signs flashed on every building to advertise restaurants, nightclubs, and curio shops. Some were elegant and others cheap and tawdry. Barkers handed out flyers and cajoled pedestrians to come into their establishments. Strings of lights zigzagged above the streets as far as the eye could see. It was hard for Billy and Carol to fully believe that this was the place where, in SD, the Arch stood in silent grace and glory.

Billy's qualms about this escapade had lifted. Now he wanted to see everything. He led the way as they explored up one street and down the next. They listened to a trio of bagpipers on one corner and watched a troupe of acrobats on another. Carol held his hand—this was no time to get separated—and felt his elation. They were here together for a final, wonderful night. From time to time, Billy glanced around for surveillance cameras. He noticed a few, mounted on lampposts up near the twinkling lights. *We're safe in the crowd as long as we keep moving.* Just in case, he pulled his hat down to better hide his face.

They came to a building unlike the others in the neighborhood. It was four stories tall, with walls of glowing brick. A sign near the roof said *Milky Way* in twelve-foot tall letters. Music from inside pumped out a thumping beat. A long line of people stood on the sidewalk, waiting to go in. Billy approached a young woman who was with a group of friends. "What's Milky Way?" he asked.

She broke in to a wide smile. Her lips, like those of her friends, were outlined in lime green lipstick. "It's the ace place of all ace places. Don't you dare miss it." Billy was intrigued, even though he normally disliked waiting in line for anything. "What do you think?" he asked Carol.

"I hear it's very ace," she joked. "Why not?" She was in the flow of this beautiful evening.

After fifteen minutes, they were let inside. The music was deafening. Dancers gyrated on multi-level dance floors. A long bar on one side served drinks. On the other side, people sat at a row of shiny devices sprouting flexible tubes. They inhaled deeply from masks connected to the tubes. Each person inhaled for a minute or so, then got up and staggered away as another person took their seat. Far above, the vaulted ceiling was covered with thousands of tiny lights. Billy pointed them out to Carol. "I guess that's why it's called Milky Way," he shouted over the music.

Billy and Carol stood and watched the people dancing, drinking, and inhaling. They began to groove to the music, which reminded Billy of Milo Riley's band at the street supper last year. He thought the sound system was extremely clear too. From his years in the stereo business, he appreciated such things. After a few minutes, he began to feel underwhelmed. *It's a disco, a very cool disco, but not that different from the discos back home.*

Then the music faded out and the flashing lights stopped. A bell chimed a single, echoing note. Everyone stood still. Carol and Billy wondered what was going on. From somewhere, a woman began to sing in a sweet soprano. A tenor voice joined her. After a minute or so, the room was filled by a hundred voices singing a tender melody. Another group of voices started singing a second melody in counterpoint to the first. Waves of sound waxed and waned, reverberating in Billy and Carol's ears. They looked at each other with goofy grins. She leaned toward him and whispered in his ear, "Stage six." He nodded in agreement. The words of an old song popped into his head. *This ain't no disco, this ain't no fooling around.*

People in the room turned their faces up to the ceiling as they sang. The tiny lights were moving. Carol poked Billy to get him to look up. The pinpoints of light were drifting downward, like snowflakes. It was as if they were moving to the song. People lifted their hands to catch the first ones that came within reach. They weren't just points of light, but luminous letters encased in transparent globes. *A, G, X, O, M* and all the rest of the alphabet. Billy grabbed a T, then an E. Carol got a V and more letters lodged in her hair. The little globes were squishy and about the size of ping-pong balls. Billy saw a man push three of the globes together. They merged into one, which now contained a word. A woman made a long string of words and flung it around her neck like a feather boa. Others were covered in globes that stuck to their clothes. People batted the globes to their friends. All the while, the singing continued. Carol closed her eyes, raised her arms, and twirled around in a blissful trance.

BLA-A-A-P! BLA-A-A-P! BLA-A-A-P! A klaxon horn sounded. The houselights came up and all the globes fell to the floor. The singing stopped. People looked around in confusion and shock. A voice spoke over a loudspeaker, "All patrons should walk quietly to the front exit. There is no emergency, there is no danger. Repeat: there is no danger. Do not panic. The authorities have detected intruders in the vicinity and must take necessary precautions to ensure your safety. Milky Way will resume operation shortly."

Billy and Carol looked at each other with sudden fear. Each knew what the other was thinking. *Have they found us?* The crowd was slowly shuffling toward the door to the sidewalk. People murmured to each other. Some were agitated. Others urged their friends to stay calm. Billy and Carol had no choice but to be pulled along with the crowd.

"What are we going to do?" she whispered.

"Hope our fake IDs work," he replied. Thank God they had remembered to bring them.

Several minutes later, they were close enough to the door to see what was happening outside. Two policemen stood on the sidewalk. As each person approached, one policeman looked at their identification card and the other looked at their face, then down to a clipboard, then back to the face. After a few seconds, they waved one person to move on, then started with the next. The two policemen were young, no more than twenty-five years old, and appeared to be nervous and uncomfortable as they worked. Billy and Carol were almost to the door. Only a few people were in front of them. Carol whispered, "Here goes nothing." Billy made sure his hat concealed as much of his face as possible. She winked to him and gave a discreet thumbs-up. Just as the person in front of them was waved on and the policeman held out his hand for Billy's ID, Carol made a horrible sound, "Ga-ga-ga." She lurched forward into the other policeman, knocked the clipboard out of his hand, and crumpled to the ground. Her entire body convulsed again and again. The two policemen stood there in open-mouthed panic. They had no idea what to do.

Billy knelt down beside her as she shook. Her eyes rolled back in her head. Drool and spittle dribbled out of her mouth. People crowded around to see what was happening. He shouted, "Back off! Give her air! She's having a seizure!" He pried her mouth open and stuck his fingers inside to prevent her from swallowing her tongue. He looked up at the policemen. "She needs a doctor! Find a doctor." They stood there, paralyzed and dumbstruck. "She could die," Billy shouted. He gave them the nastiest look he could muster. "If you don't go get an ambulance RIGHT NOW, you're going to be in so fucking much trouble you won't be able to see straight!" The two policemen looked at each other, then they both turned and ran off for an ambulance. Carol kept shaking. Her eyes were now closed. Someone gave Billy a coat to drape over her. After a few seconds, the shaking subsided somewhat. She opened one eye and looked at Billy. He nodded. They jumped up, elbowed through the crowd, and dashed away. Billy stepped on the policeman's clipboard, leaving a footprint on a sheet of paper with three photographs—himself, Carol, and Meredith.

They ran as fast as they could toward the Eads Bridge, pushing through groups of startled pedestrians. They heard sirens blaring behind them as they got onto the bridge. Fortunately, the bridge was a pedestrian park, so heavy concrete bollards prevented vehicles from driving onto it. Adrenaline surged as they kept running to the other end of the bridge, almost a mile away. They hopped on the elevator down to the dock, where the hydrofoil *Corn Mother* was about to leave for Cahokia. They got on board in the nick of time. The boat headed upriver, accelerated to rise up on its foils, and turned into the canal. Billy and Carol were still breathing heavily as the lights of St. Louis receded behind him. It was more running than either of them had done in a long time.

"I had no idea you knew how to do that seizure thing. You almost had me convinced."

"There's a lot about me you don't know, Mr. Boustany."

He put his arm around her and she lay her head on his shoulder.

Small talk was hard to come by during breakfast in Herbert and Juliet's apartment. Everyone was tense. John was going to flip the switch in a few hours and, most likely, sever the two worlds forever. Billy and Carol decided that it was best not to mention their brush with disaster in St. Louis the previous night. Herbert and Juliet were bravely contemplating the prospect that they would never see Diyami again. They had already made peace with that the year before when they blessed his mission in SD. But the pills which brought him back had given them a reprieve. Now they faced the loss of their son a second time. Somehow, it was harder than the first.

Leonora said that she had spoken with Uncle Martin by phone. "He still thinks our plan is the right one, even though it will be sad for us. He sends his best wishes to all of us."

Billy and Carol gathered their things, including the bag of HD books that Carol was determined to take with her. Herbert gave her a few more, including a history of modern Cahokia, *A Gathering of Arrows*. Carol asked him what the title meant.

"One arrow can be easily snapped, but when you hold a bundle of arrows in your hands, no force can break them. Native peoples learned the hard way that, as individual tribes, they couldn't stand up to the power of the United States. By coming together at Cahokia, we gained the strength to build our own future."

John and Leonora accompanied Billy and Carol to the lower level of the building, where they would cross back into SD. Leonora gave them four pills for the crossing.

"The extras are just in case—if the bubble popping fails."

John surprised Billy and Carol by hugging them. As he wrapped his long arms around them, he said, "One of two things is going to happen. Either we never see each other again, or we'll be talking on the radio tonight."

Billy and Carol each swallowed a pill and, a minute later, were walking through the weeds toward the ABSOM Cahokia Native Development Corporation's trailer. Diyami, Meredith, Stan and Lisa were inside. Diyami had given Jamal they day off. He was still reeling from his visit to HD and couldn't handle any more astonishment. Meredith embraced her parents. She was fighting back tears.

"It's okay, honey," Carol said. "We're making the right decision. You'll see."

Meredith nodded her head and tried to smile. "I know."

Billy saw Leonora's suitcase in the corner.

"What's that doing here?" Billy asked.

"I'll explain later," Meredith said.

Diyami and Lisa led Billy out to the tent in the woods, following the path of an orange extension cord in the grass. Lisa lifted the tent flap. There was a vertical diamond-shaped structure about three feet tall mounted on a plywood base. Wires were strung between the vertical and horizontal axes every half inch. It looked like a net or a kite.

"That's it?" Billy asked. The antenna appeared flimsy and insubstantial.

"It doesn't need to do much," Lisa said. "Just generate a weak field that will draw the energy from John's coil through the barrier." She pointed to the power supply on the plywood. "Diyami will plug it in right before noon."

Back in the trailer, Lisa made an announcement. "I'm going back to HD before we pop. Diyami gave me a spare pill."

"Why?" Billy asked.

"I'm not done with that place. John, Leonora, and I work really well together. I want to see what we can do next."

"What about your job and your family?"

"If the people I work for ever find out what I've been doing, I'll be screwed for the rest of my life. And I don't have much family. I've written them letters, which Meredith will mail after today."

It was almost noon. They went outside. Lisa patted a small backpack she was holding. "Computer parts and CDs for John." She went around hugging everyone goodbye. When she came to Billy, she said "It's the adventure of a lifetime, just like you said."

She swallowed the pill, convulsed, and disappeared.

At 11:55, Diyami called his father on the radio, as planned, to confirm that everything was ready to go. They spoke briefly in Cahokian, Diyami gave a thumbs-up, and signed off. Meredith saw that he was upset and put her hand on his shoulder to comfort him.

Diyami plugged in the orange extension cord. Stan gave binoculars to everyone and they went outside. "Lisa said to stand away from the metal trailers." With the binoculars, they could see the tent through the trees.

"11:59," Diyami said. "12:00."

They saw a reddish glow through the fabric of the tent. The ground began to shake and, a second later, a tremendous, thundering boom erupted all around them. Windows on the trailer shattered. The alarm on Stan's rental car went off. As the echo of the boom trailed off, they looked at each other. No one was hurt.

"That's some weird shit." Billy said.

At 12:05, Diyami attempted to contact HD on the radio. There was no response. As agreed, he tried again every five minutes for the rest of the hour. Silence every time. "I think it worked," he said. The reality sank in.

Stan drove Billy and Carol home to St. Louis. The radio news was frantic with reports of broken windows and malfunctioning traffic lights from all across the St. Louis area. A few water mains had cracked, but there appeared to be no injuries or major damage. Seismologists at Saint Louis University were still analyzing their data, but preliminary results did not indicate that an earthquake had occurred.

Stan stopped the car on the side street next to the Pelican building. "You don't have to get out," Billy said. "We'll talk in a few days." As Stan drove away, Billy looked up at the building. "Home sweet home." He noticed that a window on the second floor was broken. "Damn! That was a new window."

A voice spoke from behind him. "Mr. and Mrs. Boustany." Billy and Carol turned around. It was Giles Monroe and the two burly guys, Josh and James.

"What the hell are you doing here, Giles?"

"I've been waiting for you. I knew you would show up sooner or later."

"How long have you been here?" Carol asked.

"We came first thing this morning. When you eluded my people last night, did you think that was the end of your dealings with me?"

She did her best to suppress a laugh.

Giles gestured for Josh and James to grab Billy and Carol. He spoke first to his two goons. "My friends, I told you that my number would lead us to them. Always study and trust your prime."

"Yes sir, Mr. Monroe."

Billy started to laugh. He tried to speak, but he couldn't stop laughing. Giles was puzzled. After a moment, Billy pulled himself together. "I knew today was going to be weird, but I didn't expect it to be this weird."

"Once again, you are going to avail yourselves of the Knights' guest services. No one will let you off the hook this time." Giles took a small silver case out of his pocket. As the men held Billy's and Carol's mouths open, he pushed white pills down their throats. Then he gave the men pills and took one himself.

"I don't think you're going to like how this ends," Carol said. They all began to convulse and then slump to the ground. When Giles and his men came to, they saw that they were still outside the Pelican building in SD. They looked around, bewildered.

"What have you done?" Giles said.

"Exactly what you've always wanted," Billy said. "We made it so no one from this world would bother your world again."

Giles opened the silver case once more and popped three pills into his mouth. Josh and James watched in horror as he went into violent convulsions. Billy and Carol were standing over him when he woke up.

"One minute, you think you're on top of the world and the next minute the world is on top of you." Carol said. "I'm sure that you will find life over here satisfying."

"But your friend Pellegrini may not be so friendly anymore." Billy said.

Statement from the National Aeronautics and Space Administration

Yesterday at 12:00 PM Central Daylight Time, a classified military satellite made an unplanned re-entry into the earth's atmosphere, resulting in a sonic disturbance over the St. Louis, Missouri metropolitan area. No large fragments reached the ground. NASA regrets any inconvenience. If you have property damage caused by this event, please contact the Federal Emergency Management Agency (FEMA) for assistance.

Six Months Later...

Two NEWS ANCHORS, Neil and Cindy, wearing matching yellow blazers, sat behind a desk with "Sunrise St. Louis" over a photo of the Arch behind them.

"And for our next story, Tracy Jamieson is here to tell us about a mystery that was solved last night."

"Thanks, Neil. Almost a year ago, a strange sight appeared in South St. Louis. Two large metal pelicans floated above the roof of a building on South Grand at Shenandoah. The sculptures were controversial in the neighborhood and the owner, William Boustany, formerly the owner of the Duke's Digital stores, would not explain his plans for the building. Last night, Boustany unveiled a new event space, The Misfits Club, at the location. It's part restaurant, part neighborhood gathering place, and part whatever-you-want."

Cut to Billy on camera in front of the building, underneath a sign with the Misfits Club logo—a square peg and a round hole. "The world is full of people who don't quite fit in, who have something to offer, but no one to offer it to. The Misfits Club is a place for them and for everyone who wants to broaden their horizons."

Cut to Billy inside the building, standing next to a sign with the club's philosophy. Behind him was a framed T-shirt that read *GET WET.* "We believe in possibilities, in second chances, in crazy ideas. When you walk in the front door and see these questions, you'll know if the Misfits Club is right for you."

Close up of the questions.

Are you alone?

Are you far from home?

Do you have regrets?

When the crowd goes one way, do you go another?

You are welcome here.

Tracy narrated, "The Misfits Club held its grand opening last night. The main event was the book launch of a science fiction novel, *Dispatches from an Imaginary World*, by Boustany's wife, Carol."

Cut to Carol at a podium with listeners in chairs. "This is the story of a world that doesn't exist, but maybe once did. A world where the barrier between reality and imagination is thin and permeable. Where you can wake up on one side of that barrier and fall asleep on the other."

Cut to shots of a band playing and people dancing, including a woman who held a giggling toddler on her shoulders as she danced in front of the stage. "Also, there was a big surprise, live blues by Chris Cox, one of the most exciting young musicians in St. Louis. Cox disappeared from the music scene for almost two years. But tonight it was like he hadn't missed a beat. His fans were thrilled to see him again."

Cut to Tracy back on the studio set with co-anchors Neil and Cindy.

"At first, I wondered if the Misfits Club was something that St. Louis needed. But the longer I was there last night, the more I could see that it has real potential. Stay tuned."

"You said it was a restaurant. What kind of food do they serve?"

"A very eclectic mix of sandwiches and unusual snacks. One item, in particular, should not be missed. Right on the premises, they make a special taffy that is the most delicious thing I've ever put in my mouth."

"Taffy?"

"Yes. I brought pieces for you and Cindy. In my opinion, it's worth going to the Misfits Club just for the taffy."

Cindy took the piece of taffy that Tracy offered.

"Thanks, Tracy. I can't wait to try it after the broadcast."

Cindy turned to the camera.

"Well, today is a day for mysteries solved. For months, rumors have been circulating about a new manufacturing company called Morning Star Brick Enterprises, with headquarters in Cahokia. Very little is known about it and its website says almost nothing. That may change this afternoon, when Morning Star Brick Enterprises holds its first press conference, at the Chase Hotel. They promise major announcements about both their product and significant investments in the St. Louis area. Sources have told Sunrise St. Louis that they will reveal a revolutionary technology for sustainable power generation."

"Bricks and sustainable power generation? How do those go together?"

"Good question, Neil. We'll find out at the press conference."

"How many are out there?" Diyami asked.

"A couple hundred," Meredith said. "The PR people really did their job."

Diyami paced back and forth, studying his notes. He was nervous and his gray business suit was uncomfortable. His first idea had been to wear something more Native looking, but Meredith and Stan had convinced him to go in a more conservative direction.

"Your face gives you all the Indian cred you'll ever need."

"We're still courting investors, so we want to emphasize confidence and high-tech innovation."

Diyami cut a striking figure—six foot three, geometric tattoos across his cheeks, nose, and forehead, black hair down to the middle of his back, and the tailored suit with a bright blue tie. He said absentmindedly. "Sure." He was afraid of falling flat with the audience, like he had done so painfully in his first talks on Indian reservations the year before. Meredith put her hands on his shoulders.

"Today, we're selling a product. That's a lot easier than trying to convince people to change their whole lives. You're going to do great." She looked him straight in the eyes. "Okay?"

"Okay."

Stan went over the agenda for the fifth or sixth time. "I will welcome everybody, tease them with our concept, give a brief overview of the company, and mention the patents. Next, we play the video, then you come on to talk about the technology. You're the main attraction. Don't forget the manufacturing plan—they will love that here.

Meredith will go over the pilot projects and moderate the Q and A. Finally, we pose for photos, and then it's over."

"And tonight we party," Meredith said.

Diyami asked to be alone for the final minutes before the press conference began. It was too late to back out now, but he still wondered if he had made the right decision. The dilemma had troubled him since the day after the bubble was popped, when he, Meredith, and Stan opened Leonora's suitcase and fully understood what it contained. Diyami's first reaction was "This is wrong! We can't accept this. We can't build Cahokia on a lie!" Stan, in his lawyerly way, presented an analogy.

"What if you found a hundred dollar bill on the street?"

"I'd give it back."

"What if the rightful owner was nowhere to be seen?"

"I don't know."

"Let's say you're following a righteous path."

"I would do something good with the money."

"Yes. But this isn't a hundred dollar bill. It's a billion dollar bill that can give us the resources to build Cahokia."

Meredith and Stan brought Billy and Carol into the conversation. To them, the choice was obvious. Billy explained that the Knights had copied inventions from SD for years. His own father had probably been part of it. No one over here ever knew the difference. "Face it. We're all tainted. The worst thing we could do would be to keep this from the world."

Diyami remembered words that he had heard so often from his mother, "Prophecy is always true. How it manifests depends on us." He embraced the brick business.

In the bare room behind the stage, he bowed to the four directions, put his hand over the arrowhead necklace under his shirt, and quietly chanted a prayer of thanks to the Great Mystery. He saw his mother and father standing next to him in a circle of light. He also sent a blessing to the benefactors from the other world, his world, who gave him the secrets to bring a new Cahokia to life. "May the warm winds of Heaven blow softly upon your house, Leonora Matsui and John Little."

"Ladies and gentlemen, welcome to the future. I'm Stanley Huffman, general counsel of Morning Star Brick Enterprises." He held up a brick in one hand. "Today, we're going to show you how this brick is, literally, the building block of a green energy future for the world. This amazing technology is the brainchild of a brilliant engineer, Mr. Diyami Red Hawk, president of Morning Star Brick Enterprises."

Cameras flashed as Stan spoke. A slide with the Morning Star brick logo filled the screen behind him—a hawk with outstretched wings and human legs. Billy and Carol watched from the back of the room, bursting with pride. Though they had never intended it, they too had helped make Morning Star Brick a reality.

Stan continued and explained that Morning Star Brick had patents pending in the United States and all major jurisdictions in the world on both the products and the proprietary manufacturing process. "No other company has anything that comes close to what we are presenting to you today. It's a game changer."

Stan played a promotional video which had soaring music, swooping shots of urban landscapes and gorgeous sunsets. Smooth animations led the viewer from the inner workings of a brick to the humming symphony of a city of electric buildings. A soothing female voice spun the dream.

Imagine a power source with no moving parts. Imagine a stream of clean energy that flows all the time—when the sun shines and when the rain falls, when the wind blows and when the air is still. Imagine buildings that silently power an entire city. Imagine that your house produces the fuel for your car. That's the promise of Morning Star Brick.

The lights came back up after the video ended. Stan said. "Please give a warm welcome to the genius who is bringing this brilliant future to life, Diyami Red Hawk." Diyami strode onto the stage to a round of applause. Stan handed him the microphone. As he was about to speak, a voice shouted from the audience.

"This man hasn't invented one damn thing. He's a fraud and a thief! I know because he stole the bricks from me!"

Heads turned to see who was making the fuss. A disheveled, middle-aged Black man at the side of the room angrily waved his fist. Stan took back the microphone from the flustered Diyami.

"Mr. Monroe, you have been abusing and harassing us for weeks. You know that you don't have one shred of evidence to back up your outlandish complaint." He gestured for security to remove Giles Monroe, who kicked and screamed all the way to the door.

"Ladies and gentlemen, we apologize for the disturbance. This poor man suffers from a delusion. If you have any further questions about him, please direct them to the St. Louis Police Department."

Stan handed the microphone back to Diyami, who looked across the sea of expectant faces in front of him. *How am I going to get this back on course?* In a far corner, he spotted a man with long, stringy hair wearing a shapeless hat. The man raised his arms and ragged pieces of his sleeves dangled down. Diyami blinked, and the man was gone. He lifted the microphone and spoke.

"As you can see, I am of Native American heritage. Something that is true for my people is also true for Morning Star Brick. We were here first."

The audience chuckled, then applauded. Diyami had cleared the air. From the side of the stage, Meredith beamed.

Diyami described in broad terms the concept behind generating power from bricks. He listed some of the additives mixed into each brick, including phosphorus, magnetite, and copper. "Because our patents are still pending, I can't go into the technical details." He showed slides with examples of a single-family home, a three-story apartment building, and a twenty-story office tower to illustrate how tiny currents generated within each brick multiplied up to scale. Graphs outlined payback periods of fifteen to twenty years for the initial investment. He also stressed the reliability of brick power. "We have done both rapid-cycle testing and computer simulations which project steady power generation for seventy-five years or longer."

On the business side, Diyami said that the headquarters would be next to the Cahokia Mounds State Historic Site. "We want to honor the ancestors who built the largest city north of Mexico." He then said they were in negotiations to locate a manufacturing facility in the economically-deprived, northern part of the city of St. Louis. "I want to acknowledge the invaluable help of Jamal Henderson, my Cahokian brother. Jamal has done so much, including introducing us to his wonderful mother, Danielle, and his uncle, Alderman Alonzo Henderson." He pointed to Jamal, his mother, and his uncle seated in the front row. They stood up and waved to the audience. "Alderman

Henderson's support for the St. Louis manufacturing facility has been instrumental in moving it forward."

Diyami went on to explain that a north St. Louis manufacturing site not only had excellent access to road, rail, and river transportation, but also was in an area that was once an important population center of the Cahokian civilization. "Large Native mounds were destroyed in the nineteenth century. They are the reason one of St. Louis' nicknames is 'Mound City.'"

Diyami's deliberate, precise way of speaking enhanced his credibility. He had the audience, including some hard-nosed journalists, in the palm of his hand.

Diyami introduced Meredith as the Vice-President of Marketing. She described the pilot projects already under construction in the area and invited reporters to sign up for tours. They had established a speakers' bureau so Diyami and other Morning Star representatives could be scheduled for conferences and interviews. Interns, including Native American college students and Jamal's friends, Wesley and Jasmine, walked the aisles handing out media kits with contact information. When Meredith opened the floor for questions, almost every hand in the room shot up. The first question was for Diyami, "Why did you name it Morning Star?"

"In the tradition that began at Cahokia, Morning Star was a great warrior, the son of the Earth and the Sun, who defeated giants and brought life to the people."

An hour later, Stan had to call the questions to a close. Photographers mobbed the stage.

The party that night at the Misfits Club was the best South St. Louis had seen in years. Neighbors called the police to complain about the noise and loud music. When the police got there, they quickly saw that the place was filled with politicians, business leaders, and other luminaries, so the officers stayed out on the sidewalk, helped partygoers to their cars, and mollified the neighbors as best they could. The evening spawned a legend—over the following years, far more people insisted to Billy that they had been there than could have possibly squeezed into the club.

On a clear, spring morning Meredith and Diyami were driving south from Memphis on Highway 61, toward Clarksdale, Mississippi. They had left St. Louis the day before and had spent the night in Memphis to break up the trip. Diyami got his first taste of real Memphis barbecue, which was every bit as good as Meredith had told him.

This was a terrible time for them to be traveling. Since the press conference a week earlier, they had been overwhelmed with phone calls and emails. The media clamored for interviews. Architects and builders wanted demonstrations of the bricks, potential investors needed deal sheets. They had to decide whether to accept invitations to speak at conferences in Las Vegas, Berlin, and Sao Paulo. The little trailer at Cahokia was jammed with people. The new headquarters building was under construction. Jamal's phone buzzed nonstop. Stan was losing his mind.

Still, this commitment could not be broken.

Diyami loved driving with the window down. He was at the wheel of their pickup. He had passed his driver's test right before the press conference and was now a full-fledged citizen of SD. Stan had worked patiently to make him legal—first going through the painstaking process to get him accepted as an enrolled member of the Osage Nation, then haggling with the Social Security Administration to get his number, and finally helping him obtain the driver license from the Illinois DMV.

"Want to listen to some music?" Meredith asked.

"Sure."

She opened a CD case and inserted a CD into the player. "My dad made this for us. He said it would be perfect for this trip."

A driving beat filled the truck, then a strong, baritone voice sang.

Goin' down to Louisiana, gonna get me a mojo hand.

"What's mojo?" Diyami asked.

"Magic. I think."

"That's what we're looking for."

Got my mojo working, but it just don't work on you."

"Who's the singer?"

"Muddy Waters."

"With a name like that, does he sing about the river?"

"I don't know. You'll have to ask my dad."

Diyami tapped his fingers on the steering wheel to the beat. Meredith checked the GPS. Their destination was about three hours away—Poverty Point, Louisiana. In previous months, they had visited Moundville in Alabama, Etowah in Georgia, Spiro in Oklahoma, Angel Mounds in Indiana, and Aztalan in Wisconsin—all to no avail.

They crossed the Mississippi into Arkansas, then continued south to Louisiana. Shortly after lunch, they drove into the parking lot of the Poverty Point World Heritage Site. A cheerful ranger greeted them in the small museum and said that there was a marked trail around the site, as well as a guided tour that would begin shortly. Diyami and Meredith thought the guided tour would be a good idea.

The guide first emphasized that no strenuous climbing was required for the one-hour tour and that water bottles were recommended. The other six people on the tour, all experienced historic site visitors, held up their water bottles to show they understood. As they walked out into the central plaza, the guide began her practiced spiel.

"Poverty Point is the oldest Native American ceremonial center we know of in the United States. The first construction dates from 1800 BCE—almost four thousand years ago—and the site was continuously occupied until 1100 BCE. To put it in historical perspective, Poverty Point was thriving when Stonehenge was built and when Pharoah Akhenaten and Queen Nefertiti ruled Egypt. Its layout is unique in the ancient world. The central plaza, where we're standing, is surrounded by six concentric, C-shaped ridges. The outermost ridge has a diameter of three-fourths of a mile. Archaeologists believe that houses stood on the ridges and that Poverty Point was home to hundreds of people, or more."

Diyami looked at the closest low ridge and remembered the spirit's story of the curve of hills that spoke to a lost, hungry young man. He stood still and closed his eyes to listen for that voice. *A whisper? Maybe. Maybe not.* He and Meredith had to walk quickly to catch up with the group as the guide led it through the ridges to the large mound on the other side. "This is called Mound A. It is the second-largest earthen mound in eastern North America. Only Monk's Mound, at Cahokia in Illinois, is larger. However, this mound was built more than 2,000 years before Cahokia." The guide said that going to the top of the mound was optional. Meredith and Diyami were the only ones who wanted to. From the top of the mound, the geometric layout of the concentric ridges was clearly visible. Meredith joined Diyami in silently soaking up the majesty of this place.

The tour circled around the back of the ridges, past two more mounds, to the museum. As the group dispersed, the guide spoke to Diyami. "We don't get many Native Americans here. Where are you from?"

"Cahokia."

Her eyes widened. She was impressed. She shook hands with Diyami and Meredith and asked them to find her if they had any more questions. "Look around all you want. The site closes at five o'clock." They wandered for an hour, looking at mounds and reading informational plaques. They saw a couple alligators in the bayou next to the central plaza. When they got back into their truck, Meredith asked, "What time do we need to be back?"

"Nine."

They found a motel in Delhi, a sleepy northern Louisiana town about seventeen miles away. After eating fried chicken in one of the town's few restaurants, they drove back to Poverty Point as the last glimmers of light faded in the western sky. Diyami parked the truck behind some trees on the side of the road a half mile before the gate. He grabbed his knapsack out of the back and they walked in the dark toward the site. Though there probably weren't security guards at such a remote place, he and Meredith didn't want to take a chance. They skirted the dark museum building and proceeded to a spot near the middle of the central plaza. They sat down in the grass. Diyami checked his watch. *8:47.*

There was just enough moonlight that Diyami didn't need to turn on the flashlight. They were miles from the nearest town, so a profusion of stars filled the sky. He took the battery-powered radio out of the knapsack. He stretched out the telescoping antenna and attached it to the radio. He connected the microphone, then turned the radio on and dialed it to the correct frequency. A couple of minutes still to go. Meredith held his hand and gave it a hopeful squeeze.

There was nothing to say.

Precisely at nine, he picked up the microphone and spoke in Cahokian, "This is SD calling HD. SD calling HD." He waited, but there was no response. After a minute, he tried again. Still, nothing but silence. After his third call, he heard a whistling sound, then a wheezy voice speaking Cahokian, "This is HD. Are you there, SD?"

Diyami replied in English, "Yes, father, I'm here!"

"Meredith, too?"

"Yes!" Meredith said as she hugged Diyami's shoulder.

"Are you at Poverty Point?" Diyami asked.

"We are," Juliet said.

"We found the second bubble," Diyami said.

"Yes, oh yes," Juliet said.

Diyami took a small container out of his pocket, opened it, and handed Meredith a little white pill.

Within moments, Diyami and Meredith were kneeling in a different field. Herbert and Juliet ran to them, then helped them to their feet.

"Just as the spirits prophesied, the ancient places sustain us," Juliet said. She pointed upward. "The Path of Souls." The Milky Way with its infinite sprinkle of stars stretched across the sky from east to west.

"We can only stay a short while this time," Diyami said. "But we have much to talk about."

At the top of the tallest tree on the edge of the field, a hawk watched them in the starlight. He was satisfied by all he saw.

Acknowledgments

Special thanks to:

The audiobook team, Andy Coco and Jean Ponzi. They have spent more time in HD than anybody, except me.

Mac Mayfield, my technical guru, who helped make the technologies of HD sound semi-plausible. He's the guy to talk to if you have any questions about Amperic bricks, scrolls, or ghost keys.

Thanks to:

Everyone who read early drafts of this book and gave me feedback to make it better: Mario Borunda, Andrea Bruce, Jim Findlay, Stan Huffman, John Hurley, Linda Wetzel Hurley, Mac Mayfield, Steve Pick, Jean Ponzi, Sarah von Pollaro, Camille von Schrader, Will von Schrader, and Patty Wirth.

ABOUT THE AUTHOR

Eric von Schrader has made documentary films, produced television shows, and written countless business and educational programs.

He was born and raised in St. Louis, Missouri, where he spent years exploring the city and imagining what might have been.

He lives in Carpinteria, California.

Visit Eric's website at www.ericvonschrader.com for photos, background information, and other fun stuff about the *Intersecting Worlds* books. On the website, you can also join his email list.

For updates about the books, follow on Facebook: https://www.facebook.com/auniverselesstraveled

A Note

If you enjoyed this book, please take a moment to help others discover it. Consider writing a brief review on your favorite website for books. Just a few sentences will do.

Thanks.

Made in the USA
Coppell, TX
30 October 2023

23599901R00180